11/18

THE BROKEN LAKE

Shelena Shorts

Lands Atlantic
Publishing

The Broken Lake
Published through Lands Atlantic Publishing
www.landsatlantic.com

This is a work of fiction. Names, characters, places, and incidents are the product of the author's imagination or are used fictitiously. Any resemblance to actual persons, living or dead, events, or locales is entirely coincidental.

ISBN: 978-0982500514

THE BROKEN LAKE

Chapter 1
HOME

Having already died twice, one would think I'd know what it feels like. But apparently not. That wonderful weightless feeling of floating was me being cradled in the arms of perfection, a perfection I absolutely confirmed on the day he carried me away from death.

For eighteen hours, I had been missing. Abducted. Holed up in a dark basement, waiting for Andy to kill me. Every second, I prayed that Wes would find me, hoping he'd picked up on the one clue my captor so arrogantly and inadvertently left. And somehow, even through the darkest hour, I knew everything would be okay.

It's easy for me to say that with such confidence now, but the truth is, I was terrified. I had just convinced Wes to relax and not be so worried that our history would repeat itself. Just because I'd prematurely died on him in two previous lives didn't mean it was going to happen again. I believed that with assurance. And he was starting to as well, until I ended up on death's doorstep. Lifeless.

But the good news is that I'm here. The bad news is, I was sure Wes was freaking out about my future. I just didn't know how much. My mom made it impossible for me to talk to him while I was in the hospital.

From the way she was acting when I first woke up, I thought she knew about Wes' secret or my previous lives, but she didn't. She only knew what Wes told the police, which was how he had overheard Andy demanding some information when he took me. The connection was enough to turn my mother into a lioness protecting her cub.

Up until then, she'd only known Wes' uncle had founded medical research labs. Not that Wes is running them now, or that they're working on an experimental medical breakthrough using serums derived from gator blood. And she certainly didn't expect some crazy man to cause me to spend two days in the hospital for blood loss and a mangled hand.

And then, when I was finally heading home, all I wanted was to see Wes, and all she wanted was to hover. She talked to me the entire way, but I was somewhere in Westonland. I tried to hang in there while she talked about my upcoming finals, but zoned out once she started talking beyond graduation.

I was eighteen now and she had no idea that if the past repeated itself, I wouldn't even have a future beyond nineteen. I briefly thought about whether or not I should warn her in case something did happen, but then I be-came distracted with plotting on how I could see Wes *alone*.

As soon as we pulled up to our house, she ran around to my side of the car to help me out.

"Mom, I'm fine. My legs aren't broken."

"You need to be careful, Sophie, if you ever want to write again."

I'm not sure it was that serious. Andy did break my hand in seven places, but I was pretty sure I'd be okay. "I'm fine."

"Just let me help you."

I let her guide me out of the car and lead me into the house. Once inside the foyer, I reached for my bag with my left hand and she scowled at me. This was not going to be easy. I was about to protest when the phone rang. Still clutching my bag, she went to answer it.

"Hello? I told you, she isn't up for any questioning. Well, I think it can wait. Fine." She rolled her eyes and hung up the phone.

"Who was that?"

She started up the steps with my bags. "The police."

Practically on her heels now, I prodded for answers. "What do they want?"

"They want to talk to you about Andy's death."

There wasn't much to talk about in my opinion. He was sick, injected himself with serum stolen from Wes' lab, and it killed him. Not sure what there was to discuss.

"Why?" We were in my room by then, and she was avoiding eye contact with me. "Why, Mom?"

"They just want to make sure he wasn't murdered."

I almost laughed at the ridiculous insinuation. "They already know that. He had a heart attack from the injection he gave himself."

She turned around and let out a stressful sigh. "Yes, Sophie. He died from the injection. Except he couldn't

3

have given it to himself with his hand broken in a zillion places."

My eyes narrowed as I watched her busily straightening up my already clean room. "But he did. I know he did, and his hand was fine."

"Well, it wasn't fine when the police arrived."

The information registered. "Wes broke his hand?" I sat on the bed, half pleased and half worried.

She looked at me. "And he was alive when it happened."

I pieced together the rest. "And they think Wes injected him afterward." She nodded. "Well, that's simply not true," I said, shaking off the accusation.

"Well, you can tell them that when they arrive. They're on their way."

"What's the big deal anyway? He almost killed me." I had a hard time sympathizing with the dead man.

"I know. But in the grand scheme of things, even the victims can't just take the law into their own hands and kill someone."

"So...What? Do they want to arrest him or something? That's ridiculous."

"I don't know. They just want your account of what happened."

My head was starting to spin and it wasn't from blood loss this time. I pushed her out of my room with the excuse that I needed to prep for a shower. In two seconds, I was dialing Wes' number. Each ring dragged out in slow motion.

Finally, smooth and gentle, with an edge of eagerness, he answered. "Hello?"

"Wes!" A feeling of warmth radiated right out of my chest.

"Sophie."

"Oh, my gosh, I'm dying here, Wes." I sometimes have a wrong way with words, and as soon as they were out, I realized those were *not* the best choice. "I mean, I miss you. Please, please come and get me."

He chuckled. "I'm on my way."

"Wait. My mom says the cops are coming over here to ask me questions about what happened."

I wasn't too worried about the idea of them coming. In a way, I couldn't wait to tell them that Andy got what he deserved, but somewhere deep inside I was worried about what sort of other questions they might ask. Like about Wes' past, or my past, for that matter? How long could Wes go without anyone else picking up on his true identity? We couldn't very well explain away the fact that he was given a cold-blood transfusion in 1915, and now he's nearly immortal.

Now I started to get nervous about the police dipping into his background. I needed Wes to tell me what to say and what not to say. "What should I tell them?" I asked.

Without even a pause, he answered, "Tell them the truth."

"Huh? I can't tell them that. Then they'd know about you. You don't mean…"

Certainly he didn't want me to explain the real reason Andy took me—so he could obtain the secret to Wes' near immortality. There was no way Dr. Thomas and Wes had spent almost a century keeping secret the fact that Wes was a one-of-a-kind medical prodigy, only to have it revealed like this. All of their work would be for nothing. And what would people do with him if they found out? I envisioned horrible scientific experiments and needle pricking. I cringed but he snapped me out of my approaching panic.

"No, Sophie. Not *that* truth. Just the truth about what Andy did. You don't have anything to hide."

"But what about Andy's hand? They think *you* injected the serum."

Soothing me with his calmness, he answered, "They can think what they want. I didn't kill him."

I sighed with a sense of trust and assurance that this whole nightmare would be over soon. After we hung up, I took a shower to get the hospital smell off of me. Aside from having to keep my hand dry, and the soreness from the needle marks in my arm, I felt good. I got out of the shower and took a good look in the mirror. I hardly had any swelling left in my cheeks. There were a couple of small bruises that could be covered up with a little makeup. The only other noticeable damage was a little cut mark in the corner of my mouth. Considering what I had been through, I didn't look so bad.

I applied a little foundation to cover the bruises, and then blow-dried my hair. It was difficult to do basic things, but I was so ecstatic to be alive I practically bounced around my room getting ready.

The doorbell rang around 4:00. I went downstairs, and my mom had already opened the door. Two uniformed officers stood broad-chested in our hall, with their feet shoulder-width apart. She escorted them into the living room where I entered into an interrogation about the events surrounding my miserable and cruel captor's death. Only now, it wasn't about Andy trying to kill me, but about someone perhaps murdering him, a false victim. I tried not to glare as the first officer broke out his notepad.

"We're sorry about what happened to you, Ms. Slone, but we have to ask you some questions. Standard ones, of course."

I gave him no indication as to my willingness, or unwillingness, to answer his "questions," and my mother, still standing with her arms crossed, and watching, shifted her weight to one side.

The second officer chimed in. He was a little more rounded than the younger officer and his oval face and balding head somehow made him appear more sympathetic.

"Ms. Slone, we understand that you've been through a lot and have suffered a great deal. We don't mean to disrupt your recovery, but this is our job."

I raised my eyebrows, hoping he'd get to the point.

He continued. "We know Mr. Walters tried to harm you."

That was the first time I had heard Andy's last name spoken out loud, and hearing it mentioned so formally seemed to give him a level of undeserving respect.

"Officer, Andy didn't try to harm me. He tried to kill me."

They looked at each other. "Right," replied the first officer. "Can you tell us what happened?"

"Yes, I can. Andy pulled me over, pretending to be one of you guys." I hoped the mention of his impersonation would irritate them a little. "And then he chloroformed me and took me to some basement and tried to kill me."

"Right. We know that much. What we don't know is exactly what happened in that room. Can you share it with us?"

I took a deep breath. It wasn't something I wanted to relive. But, it seemed like the only way for them to get the picture and leave me and Wes alone. I told them how Andy thought the cold-blood antibodies were the key to some revolutionary cure, and then I started deviating from the truth. I told them that Andy believed medical labs were purposely hiding a prevention for death. I said that once he found out Wes was the late Dr. Thomas' great-nephew, he wanted to cash in on the research. He was crazy, I told them. Then I explained how I convinced him the cold-blood serum mixed with human blood would make him live longer.

They looked like they wanted to laugh and I wasn't sure if it was due to my account or Andy's stupidity, so I continued. "Andy's elevator obviously didn't go all the way to the top floor. So he injected himself, and for a while he thought it was working. That's when he decided to drain me of all my blood so he could sell it." I shook my head and shuddered.

"Why did he want to sell it?" the rounder officer asked.

"Because he was insane. He actually thought he could mix some potion and sell it to dying people for millions of dollars."

The first officer spoke again. "So where does Mr. Wilson come in?"

A lump started to build in my throat, but I kept it under control while trying to remember the secondhand account my mom told me. "Well, I was talking to Wes on the phone when Andy pulled me over, and Wes overheard him threatening to hurt me."

That was partly true. I was on the phone with Wes all right, but he overheard Andy call me Lenny—a name that Wes would associate with me from one of my past lives. But they didn't need to know that part.

"So, Ms. Slone, at what point did Mr. Wilson arrive?"

This is where the story gets blurry for me, because I don't really remember. I thought I was dead and floating to heaven, for Pete's sake. I had no idea what the heck was happening around me, but I do remember Andy screaming in pain. The cold-blood must have reached his heart right about the time Wes arrived. Even if that wasn't what happened, it sounded good to me.

"I was about to pass out from blood loss." Somehow that didn't sound strong enough, so I restated it. "I was about to pass out from that maniac draining my blood, when I heard him fall to the floor. I opened my eyes to see him clawing at himself. Then he started shouting and freaking out. That's when Wes arrived. He didn't know why Andy was flipping out, so he grabbed his hand and they struggled. That's all I remember."

They each nodded and raised their eyebrows at each other. Then the round one spoke.

"Thank you, Ms. Slone. That's all we need." They both stood up. "Again, we're sorry about what happened. We're glad you're all right."

"Yeah, me too."

The officers made their way to the door. My mother and I followed and watched as they approached their police cruiser. I felt uneasy about the whole encounter, even more so when Wes' familiar black car pulled up. My heart skipped a beat when he got out. Part of me wanted to run across the yard, but my wits told me to stay put and let him casually come to me, *after* he walked right past the two officers who had just inquired about his possible guilt for murder.

It was no surprise that Wes handled the situation with his usual coolness. The officers were sitting in their cruiser by the time Wes began his walk up my driveway. Giving a respectful gesture, Wes glanced into the car window and nodded at both of the officers as he passed. I couldn't hold back my smile as he drew near.

"Hello, Wes. Please come in." My mom greeted him, taking control of our encounter.

"Thank you, Ms. Slone."

"Wes," I said, pressing myself against his chest, careful not to bump my hand. I felt him inhale the scent of my hair as he gently squeezed me. "I missed you," I whispered.

"I missed you too." He pulled away and gave me a look-over. He ran his thumb over my cheek, and I could see his disappointment when he noticed my covered bruises.

"I'm fine, Wes. Thanks to you."

My mother cleared her throat. "Why don't you guys have a seat? I'll make you something to drink."

I took his hand and pulled him toward the living room sofa. He hadn't taken his eyes off of me since he walked through the door, and I couldn't tell if he was staring at me or my bruises.

"It's really not that bad," I told him.

"I'm so sorry this happened to you." He put his head down and I sensed his withdrawal.

"Wes, it's not your fault."

"I would have killed him if—"

"But you didn't," I said quickly. It didn't seem to make him feel any better, so I added another fact. "I would've killed him too, you know?"

He smiled. My mom brought us two glasses of lemonade and then she looked skeptically at Wes. "Thanks, Mom." I motioned with my eyes for her to leave and she hesitantly took the cue.

"Do you mind if we go somewhere to talk?" Wes asked.

"I'd love to."

We got up and went to the closet to pull out my coat when my mother reappeared.

"Sophie, where are you going?"

"We're just going for a little drive. I'll be right back."

"Are you sure that's such a good idea? You just got home."

I leaned in to give her a kiss on the cheek. "Yes, Mom, I'm sure."

"Be careful. Please take care of her, Wes."

He nodded in agreement. We got in the car, and I still felt a sense of distance.

"Your mom is worried," he said.

"I know. She doesn't handle stress very well. She'll be fine."

"What if she's not?"

"Oh, she will be. She just needs some time to settle down."

"I don't want to come between you two."

"Wes, you won't. She likes you and she's completely grateful for you saving me. She just needs a few cappuccinos to settle her nerves."

He laughed softly, but it sounded distant and unfamiliar. I started getting nervous. He placed his hand on my thigh which relaxed me a little.

"Are you hungry?" he asked.

"Yes," I answered casually. I wanted normalcy again, and I was starving.

"Anywhere in particular?"

"No, you pick."

He squeezed my leg and I put my hand on top of his. He chose the little sandwich shop where we had eaten many times. This time, I ordered a grilled chicken sandwich and bowl of chicken noodle soup. It was what my grandmother called make-you-feel-better food. What I hadn't factored in was trying to eat it left-handed. Struggling to balance a spoonful of hot soup with my uncoordinated left hand only highlighted my injury. Noticing him frown, I pushed the bowl to the side and dug into my sandwich.

"Aren't you going to eat?" I asked.

"I'm not hungry."

"Then why did you order?"

He thought about it for a second. "I thought I was hungry, but not so much anymore."

"What's wrong?"

He sidestepped my question. "Can you tell me what happened in that basement?"

"Wes, I don't really want to think about that too much."

He leaned forward. "Sophie, I need to know what you went through. When I saw you strapped to that chair, I..." His eyes started to glaze over.

"Stop. Please. It wasn't that bad," I lied. "He was just some crazy, washed-up guy who wanted to be like you."

"How did he know what I was like?"

I started reeling off what I could remember of what Andy had said, and Wes stopped me at the part about the military operation.

"Whoa. Slow down. What study?" he asked.

"Oh. Sorry. I don't know, really. He said they were experimenting with making soldiers stronger or something. I think he said it was extracts from the blood. He said it worked, but only temporarily. He said the government halted the project and sent the soldiers to rehab and then home. That was the end of it, until he saw me on campus. Then when he saw me with you, he figured out who you are, and he thought I was Lenny. He wanted to have everlasting life, like he thought we did."

Wes was shaking his head.

"So, anyway, I convinced him that he could be like you if he injected himself with cold-blood."

"Why was he extracting *your* blood?" His face was hard and I knew he was seeing an image of me passed out in the chair. I wanted to replace that with a more positive image, so I hurried the story along.

"I convinced him that my blood was the missing ingredient to the serum, and he believed me."

"Sophie, why would you do that? He almost killed you."

"I didn't think it through. I just thought that if he tried it, he'd kill himself and then I'd be okay." I was finished eating and pushed my plate away. "So what did you do to him?" I asked, not even sure I wanted to know.

"When I came in and saw him leaning over you, I grabbed him by the back of his neck and threw him up against the wall. You were completely out of it and beyond pale. I took the needle out of your arm and that's when I saw your hand." His jaw tightened and he stared off at what I was sure was some unpleasant visual. He took a deep breath before continuing. "I was untying your ropes when he came at me. That's when I paid more attention to him. He looked like he was on some sort of high. I had my hands around his neck when he screamed from a pain I hadn't caused yet.

"You mumbled that he had the blood in him, and then I realized what was happening. He started convulsing and grabbing at his chest so I dropped him on the floor. He was looking up at me with a revolting plea in his eyes and that's when I leaned over and gave his hand a much-deserved squeeze." He paused. "And then he died." I leaned forward because he was speaking so softly by then. "I would've killed him."

I reached my good hand across the table and placed it over his. "But you didn't."

He exhaled an unconvincing sigh of relief. "Because of you."

I felt he was giving me way too much credit, but I took it and ran with it. "That's what I'm here for," I said, smiling. "To make sure you're all right."

"I would've been just fine if I had...killed him." He was unremorseful in his admission, and I wasn't surprised, nor did I really blame him.

"Me too," I also admitted. "But the cops might not have been fine with it. They're already all over you about the hand. You could've left his hand alone, you know. He was dying anyway."

"No, I couldn't have."

"Okay, maybe you're right. He deserved the hand, *again*." I smiled.

He returned the gesture. "You ready?"

I thought of telling him about the dream I had when I was there and then decided not to. I figured it could wait until I actually remembered what was on the pages. It didn't make sense to tell him I *almost* saw the formula Dr. Thomas had used to transfuse him. Besides, I didn't really care about it then. I was sure it would come up sometime in the future, but for now, I was only concerned with the two of us. So I answered yes, and together we walked out to his car with his arm comfortably around my shoulder.

As we crossed the parking lot, we were both captivated by the view over the mountain. There was a huge mural of bold red and orange hues stretching across the sky. It made me feel so calm and alive. After Wes opened the car door for me, he put his cool palms on both sides of my face and leaned down to press his perfect, gentle lips to mine. It was then that I knew he wasn't going anywhere, and there wasn't any feeling better than that.

Chapter 2
MELTDOWN

We were about a mile from my house when I realized our alone time was about to end, so I asked him if he would stay with me that night.

He placed his hand comfortably on my thigh, while driving, and answered, "Of course. You don't have to ask me."

The perfect corners of his mouth turned into a full-blown smile, and then he winked. My stomach instantly got all tickly. I didn't know what was wrong with me. It was as if it was our first date again. Almost like starting over, and I suppose it was.

I mean, I did almost die, thinking I would never see him again. Yet here we were, together. I felt so happy, so complete, and *so* scared. *Why am I still scared?* Almost like when I thought I was dying. I could almost see him slipping away right before my eyes. No, not him slipping away from me...*I* was slipping away. Maybe not at that exact moment, but I was. It was only a matter of time. I felt it. Feared it. It made me almost sick to my stomach.

He squeezed my leg to snap me out of my reverie. "Sophie, what's wrong?"

I looked at him, and he was more desirable to me at that moment than he'd ever been, and I didn't think that was possible. I wanted him with me every second, forever, yet something in me was gnawing at my insides, almost taunting me. Telling me, *You don't have much time. It can't last forever. You will die. It will come for you.* I felt a jolt.

"Sophie! What is it?" The car slowed as he pulled over, and I melted into a basket case as the tears started spilling over. "Is it your hand?"

Are you kidding me? My hand? I wish. That was nothing compared to the knots and turns going on in my stomach.

"Sophie, what's wrong? Tell me, please."

I couldn't stop, and I actually don't think I wanted to. I had held in so many emotions over the last few days, that all of it was bound to come out sometime. Only now the relief of escaping death was coupled with the haunting knowledge that it was coming anyway. It was too much.

"I'm sorry, Wes. I'm an idiot."

He started frantically searching his console for a tissue. When he didn't find one, he used his thumbs to wipe away the dripping river.

I moved his hands. "I'm okay, really."

A big, unintentional sniffle sent his car door flying open and him rounding the front end of his hood to get to me. A couple of blinks later and he pulled me out of the car like a toddler.

"Shh," he whispered. "It's all right. It's okay."

I buried my face in his chest and squeezed him with all the strength I had.

"Come on, Sophie. Stop it. Tell me what it is."

I couldn't speak again.

"Now, now. You're fine," he assured. He rested his cheek on the top of my hair and gently rocked me back and forth long enough for me to calm down.

"I just want you to stay with me," I murmured.

Sparing me the pullback to view my face, he kept his face in my hair and whispered, "I will. I told you I will. You know I will."

"Okay," I answered, hoping it could be dropped and forgotten. I knew better.

"What is this all about?" he prodded.

I very unattractively wiped my nose with my hand and shook my head. "It's stupid."

"No, it's not. You're upset. Now what is it?"

"It's nothing." I tried to slide myself back into the car, and he wasn't having it.

"No you don't. You can't drop this now. What did I do?"

Wiping my nose again in defeat, I mumbled, "You didn't do anything. It's me. I just had a moment, that's all."

Still not letting me escape into the car, he grabbed hold of my face, and I felt my cheeks squish my lips together. It was a lovely sight, I'm sure.

"Sophie, what kind of moment?" he pressed.

My gaze touched every part of his face until I had no choice but to settle on his deep brown eyes, and that only confirmed why I was avoiding them to begin with. I could never refuse them. They were the perfect shade of dark chocolate, with depth that went on for miles. They made it impossible for me to pull away.

"I'm not staying with you tonight if you don't tell me."

My mouth fell open at his threat and my eyebrows scrunched together.

"Okay, so I will stay with you, but I won't like it."

I pressed my lips together firmly until he corrected himself.

"Okay, I will like it, but I'll go crazy."

I caved. "Okay, fine. I was just worried you wouldn't want us to be together after what happened, and then when I figured out that you did, I was so happy. Then I realized I was *too* happy, and then I got all scared that it would go away again. I don't want to die." There, I said it.

He took a deep breath and lowered himself, so that he was eye level with me. He was about to say something but decided against it. Instead, he kissed my salty lips until even I began to like the taste. Placing my palms on the sides of his cool face, I pulled him closer to me. If my body hadn't been so overwhelmed with electricity shooting through my limbs, I might have wanted to cry again.

"Sophie," he said, pulling back just enough so his forehead still touched mine, "you are not going to die, and I am not leaving you, and you're not leaving me."

"But..."

He cut me off with another kiss that pushed me back against his car with more assertiveness than I was used to. He was emitting a fire with the intention of burning everything in his path, including my brain, my voice, my fears, my doubts. It was me and him, and no one else on the planet.

It didn't matter that we were on the side of the highway. It didn't matter that he was a human mutation. It didn't matter that I was the walking dead. It didn't matter that it could all be gone in the blink of an eye. Nothing else mattered but me and him, and one question that I couldn't help but ask.

I broke for air. "Does this mean you've worked on your clarity?"

With Wes, clarity was time, and time was of the essence. When the cold-blood transfusion was administered to save him from bleeding to death, it transformed his cells. Not only did it make it impossible for him to regulate his body temperature, it changed the way he ages. It changed the way he thinks. It changed his concept of time. It changed everything.

It had taken him years to concentrate well enough to keep his mind on pace with what was going on around him. His biggest fear was that 365 of my days would only feel like an instant to him. He had mastered it well enough, except, he told me, when I made him lose concentration.

He chuckled. "I'm working on it now."

"Really?"

"Really." He kissed me again.

"So does that…"

"No, Sophie. Don't push it. I just want you to know how I feel about you." He kissed me again, gently. "I love you."

"You loved me before," I noted. "What's different now?"

"What's different is that I thought I'd lost you again and realized I don't want to waste time not showing you how much you truly mean to me. I love you more than anything, and I want you to know."

I smiled. "But I do know."

"No you don't. Not really. I have loved you forever, and love you now—more than air. It's that simple. I would give it up for you in a heartbeat." He grabbed my face again and gave me a light shake to let me know he seriously wanted my attention. "I love you, and I'll never leave you again. I promise."

Something in me wanted to weep again, but then the old Sophie came back, and I got a grip and simply, but honestly, stated, "I love you too."

He took me home, and although I still felt a nagging worry deep inside, the fighter in me was coming back. I didn't have to give in to fear, and I wasn't going to. But I was going to spend as much time with Wes as the seconds would allow.

As we pulled up to my house, my mom was peeping out between the front curtains. "You promise you'll be back. Right?"

He ignored the question and walked with me up my steps.

"Wes?"

"Sophie, don't ask me silly questions." I was about to demand a confirmation when Mom opened the door, prompting us to step inside.

"Did you guys have a good time?"

"Of course we did," I answered, smiling artificially.

She noticed and gave me a wide stare. "Good. Now you need to get some rest."

"No, I don't. I'm fine," I replied with equally wide eyes. Wes was standing there, uncomfortably in the middle of our stare war, when my mom turned, thanked him for returning me safely home, and practically shoved him out the door.

I yelled after him, "Talk to you later, Wes. I'm going to get my mom a cappuccino!" I turned to face her. "That was not necessary, Mom. He could've stayed awhile."

"I know, but I really want you to get some rest."

"No you don't, you just didn't want him here."

"That's not true, Sophie."

"You're not fooling anyone, and it was downright rude."

She dropped her shoulders in admission. "I'm sorry. You're right and that was not called for. I don't mean to be rude. I'm just worried that you're growing up too fast. He's way..." I thought she was going to say out of my league, and I was *really* going to put her on mute. "He's way too old."

I thought about a few responses then decided not to argue, so I started up the stairs.

"Sophie, stop." I turned. "Honey, I'm sorry. Give me a break. I almost lost you. I just want you to be a kid and graduate high school and do what normal kids do. Not be into high-technology, medical-breakthrough, secret-lab stuff that can get you kidnapped."

"Two things wrong with that. One, it was not Wes' fault. And two, I'm not a kid anymore. I'm sorry, Mom. I love you, but you have to relax. Wes saved my life and you owe him more than a shove out the door."

"Okay, you're right—again. I'm sorry."

I finally made it to my room. I had accepted her apology, but it wasn't owed to me. It really bothered me to see her shove him out like that. Being an outcast is all he has ever known. Before his transfusion, his hemophilia prevented him from interacting with other kids, or even having a normal life. Since his transfusion, he hasn't been able to truly make friends and let them in enough to trust them.

Wes was an exceptional, kind, giving, and selfless person who deserved more love and acceptance than I could give. And thinking about how my mom shoved him out made me want to go back downstairs and...

"Sophie?"

Oh, my gosh. She knocked on my door and walked right in.

"Mom."

"Hi."

Hi? This can not continue. In the last year, I could count on one hand how many times she had come into my room. Now, at a time when I valued my privacy the most, she was popping in.

"What is it, Mom?"

She tiptoed across my room, to my bed, and sat at the foot. "I just wanted to see if you needed anything."

"I don't need anything, but you already know that. Why are you really here?"

"All right. I just want to spend some time with you."

Yikes.

I sat down beside her. "Mom, please stop this. You're going to drive me crazy. I just want things to get back to normal, and it can't with you hovering like this."

She stared at me like she'd lost her favorite puppy. I didn't mean to hurt her feelings, but that was how I felt. Yes, I did want my privacy back, so I could spend it with Wes, but her hovering was making me remember my near-death experience even more.

"I just want to see you more. I feel like I don't have much time left with you."

"Is that what this is about? It doesn't have anything to do with what happened?"

She flinched at the question. "I would be lying if I said it didn't. I was scared to death while you were gone. Now I have you back and I know you'll be safe, but it made me realize that I don't have much time to take care of you before you're gone."

A golf ball-size lump built in my throat at the mention of time left and gone, all within one minute. I shook the thought, but knew I couldn't argue with her concerns. It wasn't fair to push her away.

"Okay. I get it. I will spend more time hanging out downstairs, but you can't act weird. I just want things to be normal."

She stretched out her hand and, like we were making a secret pact, we shook hands and both whispered, "Deal."

"Are you sure you're okay?" she asked.

"I'm good, Mom. Really."

"There isn't anything you want to talk about?"

I shook my head. "No. Really. I'm fine. I promise."

She gave me a hug. "All right, but I'm here. Any time. You hear me?"

I nodded. "Yeah, I do. Thanks." Then I guided her to my door, watched her walk downstairs—and quietly locked my door behind her. A few deep breaths later, I put on my cutest pajamas and unlocked my second-floor terrace door and waited for Wes.

Normalcy was all I kept saying to myself, but the truth was, it didn't feel normal at all. I wanted him with me like I had wanted my childhood blankey. I felt alone without him. I briefly wondered if I was being unreasonable, but then decided I wasn't. I almost died—almost didn't have a chance to feel him near me again. Now that we were given more time, that is exactly what I wanted. I needed it like…what was it he said? Air.

Air, which was getting thinner and thinner as the minutes passed until his arrival. It was past twelve by the time he climbed the deck steps and showed up.

"What took you so long?" I whispered sternly.

He bent over to give me a kiss and then murmured. "I was giving your mom a chance to settle in with her cappuccino."

I laughed and pulled him down onto my bed, pressing every single inch of me against his cool, perfectly sculpted physique. I even pressed my toes against his shins. I made sure every part of me was soaking up his presence then buried my face in his sweet, fresh scent, and closed my eyes. The air that filled my lungs took the place of the soft blanket on my bed. It wrapped itself around my nerves and bones, keeping warm a heart that was beating for an undetermined amount of time. I pressed myself even closer to shake the thoughts of how many beats remained.

"I love you," I whispered into his chest.

He kissed my cheek, whispered it back to me, and began stroking my hair. And I knew that, for the moment, my normalcy was back.

Chapter 3
WORK

M r. Healey told me I could have as much time off as needed from the bookstore, but I wanted to work. It brought things back to normal faster, and I couldn't imagine Ms. Mary working every afternoon in my place. She was on the verge of retirement and the few afternoons she worked opposite me were more than enough for her.

Going back was good for me, and so was inhaling the musty vanilla scent that I used to shower off as soon as I got home. Now, since nearly losing all the senses I had, I grew to appreciate everything, including the scent of Healey's Used Books. I breathed it in, just happy to be back.

But the actual working part ended up being quite a challenge. I couldn't ring people up with a cast on my hand and my fingers still sore. Even if I could fumble my way through the register, bagging was impossible. I ended up shelving most of the time and even that took me twice as long, but Mr. Healey was nice about it. I guess some help at the store was better than no help at all, and I was more than willing to do it. So much that I shelved each book with a small smile.

As usual, Dawn Healey arrived at work after me and she sprinted to where I was. "You're nuts," she announced.

I laughed. "What?"

"You're nuts. How am I ever supposed to get my dad off my back about my laziness when you're practically working in your hospital gown?"

I chuckled. "I'm not in a gown."

"Might as well be. But, seriously, you don't have to be here yet. The store could certainly manage without you for a while."

"Yeah, I've been told that a thousand times. I *want* to work. It makes me feel normal again."

She pressed her mouth together and drew it up on one side. "Fine, but if I almost died and my boyfriend rescued me on a white horse, we'd be riding off into the sunset right about now, saying good-bye to this place. That's for sure." She turned around to go put her stuff in the back. After a few perky strides, she turned. "I'm glad you're here, though."

Glad I was here? *Me too, and that's an understatement.* As I shelved some more books, I started wondering. Riding off with Wes wasn't such a bad idea. In fact, I could see visions of it dancing around in my head. I even paused for a minute to give the images the attention they deserved, but my thoughts were interrupted before I could get too carried away.

"Hey, you."

I smiled a large grin. "Danny."

"Sophie. You're a soldier." He came up and gave me a strong one-arm hug. "You actually came."

"What? You didn't think I would? You guys act like you haven't seen me. You *did* come every day I was in the hospital. I told you I was fine."

"Yeah, but you were doped up." He laughed. "Dawn bet me whether or not you'd come to work today."

"And?"

"And," he said, heading back toward the front, "I won twenty bucks."

At least someone around here knew me. I wasn't a quitter, that's for sure, and Danny knew me well enough to pick up on that. He had come to be like the big brother I never had. I really liked him, and Dawn too. They were great friends, but Dawn was like the younger sister. One that needed to be kept out of trouble. Even still, she was my closest friend here.

My other best friend was in Virginia. Kerry and I were still really close, but I hadn't seen her since I visited last summer, so it was nice to have Dawn and Danny. And the two of them usually made working a riot, especially when their dad wasn't around.

I was supposed to work until 8:00, and for dinner we usually ordered in or picked something up. This time we didn't have to. Wes dropped off Thai food for all of us. Large containers of just about every sampling on the menu.

"You're so stupid," Dawn said as we carried it to the table in the back room.

"What are you talking about?"

"I would've been long gone with that guy. He can bring me Thai on a tropical island, *not* at Healey's Used Books."

"Dawn, stop it. You're out of control. Besides, he hasn't asked me to go with him to some tropical island."

We had the food containers spread out now, and she busily plopped a large portion of rice noodles on her plate. "That's too bad. I'll have to have a talk with him."

We both laughed and filled our plates with a little bit of everything. After a few minutes, Mr. Healey came into the back room and quietly took me up on my offer, fixed himself a sampling, and moseyed toward the door.

I called after him, in between bites, "Mr. Healey, tell Danny to come back and get some."

"Danny left for the night."

"What?" Dawn asked. "He's not supposed to leave until 9:00."

"He had some studying to do."

Dawn and I both laughed, although my laughter was a bit more restrained than hers.

She practically spit out her food and would've had she not had a napkin to cover her mouth.

Rolling her eyes, she replied, "Yeah, right, Dad."

Mr. Healey wasn't smiling. "Dawn," he said, authoritatively pointing his plastic fork at her, "maybe you ought to try studying sometime."

Pointing her finger into the air as if a light bulb had just blinked on, she answered, "You know, Dad, I will. I have a test tomorrow, so I'm not staying until 9:00 to cover for him."

He shook his head and, choosing not to continue with the way the conversation was headed, reminded us to clean up after ourselves and left the room with his food. Dawn was making it overtly obvious that she really didn't want to work at Healey's anymore. I wondered what was up, but figured I'd leave it alone for now.

"Why did Danny just leave without saying anything? And since when does he pass up food?"

She shrugged. "I don't know what Danny is up to these days, but it ain't *studying*, that's for sure."

"So what do you know?"

She shook off the question. "He's just been hanging out with some weirdos. Ever since we went to that party, he's had some losers over at the house all the time. Like they have nothing better to do than hang out in our basement. They're fronting like they're starting a band, but whenever Mom and Dad are home, they all leave. Dad actually buys into the studying bit."

"Maybe he is. Studying, I mean."

"No, Danny has always gotten good grades, even if he sleeps in class. It's sickening. He doesn't *need* to study, and I'm sure he wouldn't start now."

"Hmm. Well, maybe he's helping out his new buddies."

She laughed again. "Yeah, maybe...if they were *in* school at all. He's the only one still taking classes." She shrugged. "It doesn't matter. Danny can do no wrong in Dad's eyes." Some newfound resentment was in Dawn's tone.

I figured she'd spill when she was ready and moved to a lighter subject. "Well, what am I supposed to do with all this food?"

"Take it home, or better yet, leave it here. We'll eat it again tomorrow!"

I took a bite of some chef's rice and agreed. She stabbed a shrimp and popped it into her mouth, seemingly unfazed by her spontaneous display of tension.

We put the leftovers in the fridge and both of us worked until 8:00. Mr. Healey ended up closing by himself since Dawn wasn't about to cover for Danny, and I simply didn't want to stay. Working my normal shift was one thing, but staying late was another.

I had things to do and they began when Wes picked me up as part of the agreement. My mom was not ready to let me drive with my broken hand and she was still worried about my safety. And, since I refused to let her drive me, she was happy to let Wes help. He pulled up right as I walked out, and I hopped into his car too fast for him to get out and open the door for me.

"If I didn't know better, I'd think you were happy to leave that place."

I leaned over and gave him a kiss. "No, just happy to see you." I buckled my seat belt and turned my body toward him. "Drive me somewhere, anywhere," I ordered.

"Your mom is expecting…"

"So what?" I countered.

He just looked at me, his stare as still as a statue's. I tried to return one of equal intimidation, but it didn't work. He wasn't budging.

I rolled my eyes. "Fine, I'll call her." I dialed her number and the second ring was cut short as she eagerly answered the phone. I let her know we were grabbing dessert somewhere and then I put the ball in his court. "Now take me somewhere." I smirked.

The statue came to life as his lips parted, at first with a smile and then with the words I was waiting to hear. "Where do you want to go?"

"Anywhere. I don't care. I just don't want you to take me home yet."

Smoothly putting the car in motion, he confidently said, "I have an idea." He shifted through the gears with ease and directed the car away from my house. I smiled in reaction, but of course, curiosity got the best of me.

"Where are we going?" I asked, feeling myself swell on the inside with hope of it being someplace alone.

Without taking his eyes off the road, he answered, "To get dessert. That's what you told your mom, right?"

I frowned. "Are you *always* such a goody two shoes?"

He laughed. "Aren't you?"

"Only because you make me that way."

After a few moments, he interrupted my silent sulk. "So how was it being back at work?"

"Weird," I answered, looking out the window.

"Weird how?"

I looked over at him and he was still watching the road, unaware of my silent wish to head off to that island Dawn had been talking about. I guess it was unreasonable, but being close to him made my desire for it all the more real. I snapped out of my secret dream.

"Well, Dawn is acting like she wants to run away, and Danny left early to *study*." I laughed at the last part. Saying it out loud made me hear how untrue it sounded.

Wes smiled in response. "Where does Dawn want to run off to?"

I rolled my eyes. "I have no idea. She just kept saying I was stupid for not riding off with you on your white horse into the sunset." He studied me briefly for my reaction to the idea. I looked out the window again. "Then she said she'd rather be on an island somewhere instead of at Healey's. She couldn't understand why I was still hanging around."

"And what did you say?" His voice was softer, as if he realized he'd missed something in my mood.

"I told her you hadn't invited me to any island." Then I thought I'd lighten the mood. "And that you are keeping me prisoner in my mom's house forever and that Healey's is my parole." He didn't laugh, so I nudged his thigh. "I'm just joking."

Giving me a smile that I was sure was forced, he pulled into the parking lot of a run-down pizza parlor.

"Pizza?" I asked.

"Stay right here. They have dessert. I'll bring it out to you." He kissed me on my cheek and got out, locking the doors behind him, and ultimately reminding me of my vulnerability. I shuddered and then ran down a list of Italian desserts in my head and came up empty on anything I would be in the mood for. But, as usual, he knew exactly what would make me more than happy.

Tapping on my window, he motioned for me to get out of the car. We sat on an iron bench facing a dark, wooded area, and had I not been with him, I might have been a little nervous. But I *was* with him, and I felt safe. And once he slid his purchase out of the bag, I felt elated.

"Funnel cake?" I smiled.

"For you," he said. "But you have to let me feed it to you this time, with your hurt hand and all."

"Yeah, right. You just don't want to wear it."

"Not true. You can do it if you want."

"No," I interjected. "I want you to."

I ate almost all of it before I felt like I was going to explode. He finished what I didn't eat and then he started talking.

"We used to eat here all the time, you know."

"We *did*?" I perked up and turned, completely facing him.

"Yes. It was the only place where your dad didn't know anybody."

"You mean Lenny's dad. The evil dad?"

He nodded. "Yeah, that dad."

Frank was my dad when I was Lenny. I had come to learn that I'd lived at least twice before. Amazing, unbelievable, but true. Not something I would've ever known had Weston's life not been unnaturally altered to near immortality in 1916. But, because it had been, he had known me then and assuredly identifies me now as the same person.

Lenny was born Lenore Lee Emerson in California in 1944. Maria and Frank were my parents. I have no memory whatsoever of that life, other than one dream and details that Wes tells me from our time together. And those all occurred after I met him in 1963.

Up until now, we hadn't had much time to talk about all the things we've really been through. I knew that Lenny's dad didn't like Wes because of his absentee parents. Of course Wes had no parents because they had died decades before, but Lenny's dad just assumed he was a misfit. Lenny had actually gotten into a big fight with her dad on the night she died.

Wes pulled me from my thoughts. "So we used to come here all the time because no one would ever be able to tell your dad you had been here. You used to love the pizza *and* the funnel cake." He smiled. "Anyway, it's family owned, and the owner might remember you, so I didn't want you to go in."

"What about you?"

"You know I can get away with resembling my 'dad,' but with the two of us together? Well, you know how that panned out last time."

"Right."

I didn't need the recap. I knew that Andy pieced together part of the puzzle when he thought I was just some girl who 'looked' like Lenny, until he saw me with Wes, and then he knew it wasn't a resemblance, or a coincidence. I shuddered a little, and Wes wrapped his arm around me.

"I thought you might like to see the place. Are you ready?"

I wanted to see if I remembered anything. I turned around on the bench and stared at the shack. That's what it was. A pizza shack. Rectangular building with a flat roof. One neon sign that spelled out Spitony's. I looked up, hoping something would bring my mind to pleasant memories with Wes, and got nothing. Instead, thinking of Lenny having to sneak around to get away from Frank annoyed me. I stood up and nodded and Wes walked me back to the car. I was about to get in when he stopped me.

"Sophie?" He was so close to me, I could've kissed him. He started wiping powdered sugar away from the corners of my mouth.

"Yes?" I answered softly.

"I *am* going to get that white horse and take you to that island."

I leaned in now, only millimeters from him, and I could feel his breath. "Now?"

He shook his head gently. "No. You're not ready."

"Yes, I am. I just want to be with you."

He kissed me in a tender way that reassured me of his affection, and also in a way that told me he would always be there for me. But it wasn't enough. It wasn't binding, like a plane ticket would be if it was purchased for us tomorrow.

I broke away. "We're not going any time soon, are we? I have to keep waiting for you to pick me up or come over to my mom's?"

That all sounded too immature and shallow for us. What we had become was so much more than that. A century of belonging to each other was undeniable. Our lives were connected, and even though the purpose of that had yet to be discovered, there was no doubt that I was born to be with him. Our destinies were intertwined, and I wanted to own up to it. Make it ours to mold. I wanted a place where we didn't have to hide our affection, a place where we could do whatever we wanted, whenever we wanted.

He kissed my forehead and drew me to his chest. "We'll go when the time is right. I promise you."

I thought about pressing the when and where, but I knew it was better not to. Wrapping my arms around him, I gave in to the idea that Dawn would just have to see me again at Healey's tomorrow, and I was fine with that, for now. I knew deep down that he was right. I was overreacting in my desire to be with him, and only him, right now. My mom would freak and that wasn't fair to her, but it didn't change the way I felt.

"You're staying with me again tonight. Right?"

He smiled. "Of course."

Chapter 4
DAMAGE CONTROL

O n Saturday morning, I was awakened by the smell of breakfast. I took a big whiff. Bacon, cinnamon, but there was more. Sausage? Yum, but not normal. I smelled a ton of different things and was hungry, so I dragged myself out of bed, brushed my teeth, and picked up a bounce on my way downstairs.

Mom was laughing, and then I heard Tom's voice. *If they are in their pajamas, I am going to be ill.* I turned the corner. Fully dressed, the pair were making breakfast.

"Hey, sleepyhead," my mom chirped. "We thought you'd never wake up. Come on. Tom came over to eat breakfast with us."

"Hi, Tom."

"Hey, Sophie. You look good. It's nice to see you feeling better."

Tom and my mom had been dating for almost as long as Wes and I. She met him on the Berkeley campus where she worked in one of the medical centers, and although he was 17 years older, he had enough energy to keep up with a toddler if he needed to. And he had a full head of hair. I wasn't into the salt-and-pepper thing, personally, but I was happy for her. I just didn't want to imagine them sharing a room. I was definitely glad he was still sleeping at his own house.

I sat at the table which was already set. "Thanks, Tom."

"You have perfect timing, sweetheart." My mom came over to the table, juggling platters of food. Tom freed one of her hands.

"Wow." I wanted to ask if all of this was for me, but I knew it wasn't, and that was okay.

I liked the idea of Tom hanging out here. Somewhere in the back of my mind, I still worried about Mom being alone. I couldn't shake the thought of my leaving, and then realized why I was so ready to go away with Wes.

I sensed I was leaving, and it was better to think of it in terms of "leaving" rather than "dying." If I only had a year left, why shouldn't I want to spend it with the one I loved?

"Sophie, honey, what would you like?" She was standing over me with a spatula. My eyes surveyed the spread. Eggs, bacon, sausage, biscuits, grapefruit, pancakes, hash browns.

"I'll take some of everything."

"Wow. Hungry, are we?"

Once we had our plates full, Tom offered to say a blessing. It wasn't something we normally did with breakfast, but we weren't going to object. We both felt comfortable with him around, but I noticed my mom looked extra perky.

"You're in a good mood." I took a bite.

"Me?" she asked.

"Uh-huh. Seems like you're back to normal."

"Well, I thought about what you said, and you're right. Wes is a nice young man, and it's not *his* fault some lunatic went nuts." I was about to say exactly, when she continued. "Plus, Tom helped me see things a little clearer. He remembered his father and knows how much Wes' uncle's research means."

My gaze diverted to Tom. "Really? That's pretty cool."

"Yeah, I'm just glad to see things worked out. Honey, did you show her the paper?"

My mom dropped her fork and hopped up. "No, I almost forgot! I'll go get it."

She returned with a folded *California Chronicle* and a huge smile on her face. Curious, I opened it to big, bold letters.

Case Closed in Kidnapper's Death

I read further, unsure whether or not I wanted the recap. I felt both sets of eyes fixed on me as I read, so I was sure to not give way to my reaction.

Police have determined the death of 61-year-old Andrew Walters of Orinda, California, to be an accidental drug overdose. It is unclear as to what type of drug was used, but it is speculated that it was related to stolen lab samples from several well-known research labs, including the California Blood Research Lab owned by 19-year-old heir Weston Wilson III.

Further reports confirmed that Wilson knew the unidentified victim whom Mr. Walters allegedly abducted in exchange for drugs, but no reports as to Wilson's connection with the deceased have been released.

Police will not confirm if there was ransom involved, but they did state that Mr. Walters had been in search of a cure for a possible illness he may have had.

Wilson, lab owner and heir, is expected to make a public statement regarding this incident.

At that point there was no hiding my expression. My mouth dropped open.

My mom reacted. "What? It's great news isn't it?"

I looked at her like she was speaking another language, then I blinked and cleared my throat. "Um, yes. It is."

"What's wrong? You don't seem happy about it. I thought you'd be ecstatic. The police have closed the case."

"I know. I am. It's just that Wes doesn't like a lot of attention, and I'm not sure he'll like it now."

"Oh, he'll be okay."

I forced a smile. "You're right."

Only she wasn't. This was *not* okay. Wes spent his life trying not to be noticed. He was literally the one and only walking medical phenomenon, and if people found out who he truly was, society would go cuckoo for Cocoa Puffs. Media attention was one hundred percent the last thing he wanted, or needed, and I brought it right to him. I was so stupid.

Tom interjected, "He does seem like a shy kid, and he has a lot on his shoulders. There aren't many veteran doctors worthy to sit in the same room as Dr. Thomas, including me. I can't imagine the pressure that boy feels."

My mom gave him an evil look. "I don't think that's helping matters, dear."

He casually kept eating. "I'm just saying he shouldn't have to address anyone regarding matters like that. He should leave that to one of the lab reps. Surely he has a spokesperson."

My head was starting to spin. Information overload. All I wanted was to speak to Wes and not on the phone. "Mom, I'm done. This was good. Thanks." I started to grab my plate but she took it.

"No, no, honey, you go rest. I'll get it."

I didn't want to rest. I needed to get out of the house. "Okay, I will," I lied. "But, in a little while, I want to visit Wes."

"But your hand. I don't want you to drive. He can come here, right?"

"No, I really want to surprise him. He's done so much for me, and I'm sure he's not admitting how much this attention really affects him. I'd like to go see him. I can drive. Really."

She looked at me, contemplating.

Tom came to my rescue. "Gayle, we're both medical people here, and I think we can attest that people drive with broken hands all the time."

She dropped her shoulders and exhaled before submitting, "Okay. But please be careful and rest first."

"I will! Thanks."

I kissed her on the cheek and went to my room, clearly not about to rest. Something awful was picking away at my insides. I couldn't identify exactly what I feared at that moment, but I was terrified. There was just an awful feeling that things were going to get real crazy, real fast, and it was all my fault. If only I had let Wes ride with me to see Lenny's still-living mother at that nursing home, then none of this would be happening. Andy wouldn't have been able to take me, Wes wouldn't have had to come rescue me, and there would be no police or media involved.

Ugh, I just wanted the nightmare to be over. Frustrated, I shifted to thoughts of getting out of there. My closet was in disarray. I hadn't had a chance to do laundry since before I was in the hospital and I hadn't asked my mom to do it, so my choices were limited.

After scrounging around, I found some jeans and a three-quarter sleeved pink sweater that was appropriate for January weather in California. The soft color also made me feel calmer. I eyed my black-and-white Converse sneakers and decided tying them wouldn't be fun, so I settled on my handy-dandy flip-flops instead.

After about an hour of pretend rest, I went downstairs and assured my way out the door, promising to call her when I got there. My mother's eyes were burning a hole in my back as I walked to my Jeep.

Feeling her stare, I tried to swiftly and smoothly slide into my seat. That part was easy. It was inserting and turning the key in the ignition with my left hand that tripped me up. I dropped the keys and felt the clock count down to the moment my mom would come bursting out of the house and tell me it was too dangerous. *Come on, Sophie. Get it together.*

Determined not to appear incapable, I shoved the key in and turned it. My baby roared to life. Within seconds, I was driving away, happy to be a free bird and anxious to get to my destination.

About halfway there, I realized that I'd done it again. *Darn it. I am truly an idiot. What was I thinking?* I had just left my house to go to Wes' without telling him, placing myself in the same position my overconfidence had put me in before—alone and vulnerable. He was going to be so mad.

I couldn't help it. I've always been a person who knows what I want. I set my sights on something and go get it, and right then my sights were on Wes. *Okay, who am I kidding?* I could convince myself that I was right to take my spontaneous solo trip, but the fact was, he was still going to be mad. I drove like a granny the whole way there, just hoping to earn some brownie points for safety. I rang his bell at about noon.

He practically yanked me inside and spun me around to see if I had any limbs missing. "Sophie, what are you doing?" he pressed, cornering me in his foyer.

"What does it look like?" I kicked off my flip-flops and brushed past him. "I'm visiting you."

He was hot on my heels. *Who was I kidding?* "All right, all right. I'm sorry. *Really* sorry. I should've called, but I just wanted to see you."

His face was conflicted. I'd seen it like that before but couldn't pinpoint where. Regardless, I didn't like it.

I stepped closer. "Come on, Wes, I'm here. I'm fine. I'm sorry. I'll call next time."

He turned one corner of his mouth up to acknowledge the apology, but the lines of his face were still hard and heavy. I reached up to touch his face with my palm and he turned his cheek into it.

"I just wanted to be with you. I wasn't thinking about you worrying. I saw the paper and I—"

"I don't care about the paper. I care about you."

Yep. This is why I came. I needed to see him, to see his genuine, loving expression that made me feel warm and fuzzy, but I was about to ruin the mood with some business to handle.

"Yeah, me too," I said. "Now can you tell me why in the blazin' inferno you're going in front of the media? Wait, don't answer that. No, I mean, do answer that. What the—?"

"Sophie."

He stepped closer to me, and I stepped around and to the side. He followed suit, and before I knew it, we were practically dancing around each other.

"Stop it."

He smiled. "Well, if you'd stop running away from me, I wouldn't need to chase you. Now come here."

"No, I don't want you to distract me. I need to know what you're thinking."

"Fine," he said.

"Fine?"

47

"Yeah, fine."

"What's that supposed to mean?"

"It means if you're going to be difficult, then I'm going to have to take you there by force."

I opened my mouth to speak and was shocked to see him lean over like he was going to tackle me—then swiftly put me over his shoulder.

"Wes! What are you doing?"

"I'm taking you to relax. Don't worry, we're not going far."

I wanted to demand that he put me down, but the words wouldn't come out. My laughter betrayed me. Then I thought about taking my good hand and beating on his back, except I had seen damsels in distress do that in a zillion movies. I decided to let myself dangle instead. The view, upside down, was good enough for me to note we were headed to the basement.

"I don't want to play, Wes."

"We're not playing any games." He set me down.

"Then what are we doing?" I shook my bangs out of my eyes as I stood upright.

"We're going to swim."

I turned my eyes toward the metal door with the small square window at the top then I looked back at him. Seeing him standing there so confident and relaxed, I couldn't help but buy into it.

"Okay. I'll just go grab my bathing suit. Oh, wait. That's right. I don't have one."

"Sophie, I'm serious. That's what I was planning to do before you came." His adorable half smile returned.

"Well, I came over to talk to you. I want to know what you're going to do." He traced his finger along my forehead to slide stray bangs away from my eyes. "Stop distracting me, Wes. I've been a wreck all morning about the article. Please."

"Which is why," he interrupted, "you need to swim."

"Wes."

"Sophie." He crossed his arms now. "I was planning to swim to clear my head, and would very much appreciate it if you joined me, because dancing around the foyer with you was not helping." He tilted his head and brought in those dark eyelashes. "Please?"

"I don't have a suit."

"Yes, you do."

I looked down at myself. "No, I don't."

He bit his lip, which was way unusual. "Remember when I told you that cars were the best way to keep memories alive?"

"Yes," I said slowly.

"Well, they're not the only things."

"Okay." That word lingered even longer.

"Lenny left some things at my house, and I've always kept them."

"Shut up." I smacked his arm. "Let me see."

He smiled slightly and walked past me toward a basement door I hadn't noticed before. I followed so closely that I almost bumped into his back as he paused to open the door.

He turned, as if having second thoughts. "Are you sure?"

"Yes, I'm sure. I need to relax. I want to swim, now come on."

He turned the knob, opening the door to a wine cellar. Only the space was filled with boxes. I shuddered a little because it gave me the impression of what a cold-case file room would look like. I stepped closer to him instinctively as we hovered over one particular box which was sitting right on top.

"What's in all of these?"

He shrugged. "Some things of Dr. Thomas', some of my mother's belongings, and this one is yours."

Remembering my hasty mistake of previously jumping into his 1963 Mustang, I decided on a more subtle approach. "What's in there?" I asked.

"Just some things you used to keep at my house."

Now my curiosity was killing me. "Let me see."

Without further delay, he lifted the top to reveal a combination of yellow, pink, red, and pale blue fabrics. *Yikes, Lenny.*

"Oh, my," I said out loud.

I stepped closer to the box and he moved aside to give me plenty of space. It was sort of creepy, because the items were from someone who was both missing in the flesh and standing there in the body. After taking a deep breath, I bent down and pulled out the first item. Pale blue bell-bottom slacks. Suddenly, creepy images were replaced by a *Brady Bunch* episode.

"Wes, please tell me I didn't wear these."

He laughed and reached into the box. "Yeah, you did. With this."

He held up a baby-blue and white horizontal-striped long-sleeved shirt. I cringed.

"Sophie, you looked really good in this. Trust me."

"If you say so." Next, I reached in and picked up some pajamas. Pale yellow pants and matching sleeveless top. Not too bad, other than the pleated seam going across the chest. Then it registered. "You mean I stayed with you?"

"Sometimes."

I smiled deviously, plotting how I could continue with tradition. A few more cute but like-to-forget garments later, I came to a bikini, a skimpy yellow two-piece that tied in the center of the chest and the matching bottom which tied at the hips.

I'd certainly worn two-pieces before, but I preferred something a little more sporty now. "I don't guess they did sporty in the sixties?" I asked.

"Not really," he answered. "I have a T-shirt if you want to swim in that."

Our eyes locked and the oddness of the moment was building. I was starting to see regret in his eyes, as if he wished he hadn't suggested I swim half naked. Then I started thinking about seeing him in his trunks and I instinctively licked my lips.

"I'll go get you a T-shirt to—"

"No, don't. This is good. I like it."

And at that instant, I decided this would be a good time to start working on his clarity. As if he could read my mind, his shoulders dropped, and he cleared his throat. His eyes confirmed he regretted the suggestion.

I smiled and stood up. "Where can I change?"

Chapter 5
FIFTEEN MINUTES

I almost didn't want to look at myself in the mirror, afraid I'd chicken out at flaunting it around, but then couldn't resist. Aside from the fact that I was lacking my summer tan, I wasn't bad. I smiled slightly and then adjusted my cleavage for added effect before turning for the door.

I came out in just my bathing suit only to be greeted by a wall of terry cloth.

"Are you ready?" he asked, wrapping it around me.

"Yes." I frowned as I was being transformed into a burrito.

"Good. Let's go."

I followed him toward the pool room, wondering how I ended up in this position. I had come over to settle a major concern, and was now plotting on how to intimately provoke him. *I am so shallow.* I rolled my eyes at myself, glad he was behind me, and then remembered this was his suggestion. Swim, clear our heads, is what he said. *So*, I thought, *let's swim.*

I dropped my towel as soon as we entered the warm room, and walked over to the pool. I might have even attempted a little hip movement on my way, but my mind turned to mush as soon as I turned around and saw he'd removed his shirt. Sweat seeped out of my pores as I pictured myself being able to feel his perfect, smooth chest against my almost bare body.

He walked over to me cautiously, never blinking his inviting eyes. "You look unbelievably good in that bathing suit."

The words sang in my ears as I thought the exact same thing about him. I cleared my throat. "Thanks." And then my seductive façade was gone. I felt completely nervous and vulnerable to my immaturity.

As if once again reading my mind, he relieved my racing pulse and our intense faceoff. He stepped sideways into the pool, feet first and soundless. I moved to the edge just as he resurfaced. For some reason, I was hesitant to jump in right then, probably because I didn't want to make a clumsy splash. Instead, I sat down and slowly put my feet over the edge and into the room-temperature water.

Wes was treading water in front of me. "Come on, get in."

"I will. In a minute."

"Suit yourself."

Ever so smoothly, he disappeared and swam the length of the pool under water. "Get in," he ordered from the far end of the pool.

I shook my head, playing hard to get. Without another word, he pushed off the wall and swam toward me with the most perfect freestyle I had ever seen. Watching him glide his way to me made my body temperature rise, and I was ready to get in. He stopped right in front of me, threatening to pull me in.

"You wouldn't," I said.

"Only if you want me to."

And I did want him to. I reached out my arms and he placed his hands on each side of my ribs and lifted me into the water. I instantly wrapped my arms around his neck, realizing I couldn't touch the bottom. I flinched, trying to keep my cast out of the water.

"I've got you," he assured.

Slowly, he turned himself around until my arms were wrapped around his neck from behind. Pressing myself against his back was complete bliss, and I was one hundred percent sure there was no place else on earth I'd rather be.

"Feel better now?"

"A little." I answered truthfully, but still on edge about why I had come over. "I still don't understand why you want to do a press conference."

"I don't *want* to."

"Then why?"

"Because if I don't give them something, they will snoop around for things I may not want them to find."

"But why do *you* have to do it? Don't you have people who can do that?"

"Yes, but it's the same thing. If I seem like I'm hiding something, then that will spark reporters to dig."

"I hate this. This is my fault."

"No." Still holding my arms, he turned to face me again. "This is not your fault. It's just part of life."

"But, if I hadn't—"

"Sophie, if you hadn't done a lot of things, I wouldn't even be here right now. This is nothing. Just a small speed bump."

I smiled softly enough to spark one from him in return, and with a calming energy that reached my toes, he leaned in and kissed my lips. The sweet taste of his mouth mixed with chlorine reminded me that I was in a pool, pressed against the bare chest of perfection.

It didn't matter that I almost died. It didn't matter that I might die. It didn't matter that we were two freaks of nature. All that mattered was that he was mine.

I put my fingers through his wet hair and absorbed each kiss until I felt like I was floating, and then realized I was. I looked around and noticed we had drifted away from the edge.

"What?" he asked, looking around too.

I thought of a few pointless remarks and then decided to kiss him instead. Which I did until my head was completely void of worry. At least for the moment.

We ended up swimming for a while after that, but the insistent ring of my cell phone brought me back to reality. I'd forgotten to call my mother. Lifting myself out of the pool, I wrapped my towel around me and found the phone. Apologizing for my whereabouts was getting old and my frustration was obvious by the time I hung up.

"Is that what I'm like?"

"Geeze." I exhaled and turned around. I hadn't even heard him come up behind me.

"Sorry. You didn't answer my question."

"Sort of but not really."

He raised his eyebrows, waiting for an explanation.

"You're not high-strung like she is, so you're not that bad."

"I'm sorry."

"Sorry for what? I can handle my mother."

"No, I don't want to make you feel like that. Like you're being interrogated." He put his hand to the side of my face and I leaned into it. "I'll still worry about you all the time, but I'll try not to make you feel like you're in trouble."

I smiled. "If that's what I was in when I got here, then please, by all means." He let go. "What?" I asked innocently.

He smiled and leaned down to give me a quick kiss. "I'm going to change."

"But—"

Oh, well. I suppose dry clothes were good. I went upstairs to change as well, and by then, it was lunchtime. With two plates of sandwiches and chips, we sat on the couch. We rarely watched TV. Our conversation usually filled up the space around us and also seemed to make our time together more valuable.

I took a bite of my sandwich and watched him pop some chips into his mouth. "So when is the press conference scheduled?"

Unfazed, he answered, "Tomorrow."

"Tomorrow?"

Still eating and not looking my way, he nodded casually.

"Where? When?"

"At the California Blood Research Lab." I waited for the rest. "Ten a.m.," he continued.

"That soon?" I put my plate to the side. "So let me get this straight. Tomorrow morning, you are going on television to talk about the very same stuff Dr. Thomas kept hidden, and you're enjoying a sandwich right now?"

Finally making eye contact, he put his plate aside and turned my way. "Yes, but I'll starve if you want me to."

"Wes! I'm not playing around."

"Me either. I will."

"You're impossible."

"Only to you."

I rolled my eyes.

"Come on. Stop worrying." He moved closer. "I'm not concerned. It'll be fine."

That was easy for him to say. I was a wreck all that day and through the night, worrying and wondering what he was going to say. And the morning was worse. He wouldn't let me go with him and I didn't blame him. But that meant I was stuck in my house with my mom and Tom, who were both hovering around the only decent-size TV we had in the house. Not good for settling my nerves.

"Sophie, sit down. Stop pacing, will you?"

No, I couldn't. An escape was needed. "Mom, I'm going upstairs. Call me when it's over."

"Are you kidding? Sit down. Wes is going to be on *TV*. You can't miss that. He's going to have his fifteen minutes of fame. That only comes around once in a lifetime."

She was clueless. I looked at Tom, whose expression was much more intense.

"Gayle, he's just a kid. He's not winning an award. He's talking about important stuff here. Even I don't know what goes on in those labs. It's very interesting."

"Hmm. If you say so," she said. "Sophie, sit down now. You're making me dizzy."

I plopped onto the couch with my arms crossed, biting my lip, waiting for the inevitable.

Just then, the Channel 7 live news flash graphic grew on the screen, spun around, and twisted one time before disappearing to reveal Topper Harris, a morning newscaster I'd seen many times throughout my mother's morning coffee sessions. Now he was going to be talking about my Wes. I flinched at the thought.

"Good morning, this is Topper Harris coming to you live from the lobby of the California Blood Research Lab, a facility rumored to be on the fast track to possible cures for cancer, HIV, and other diseases. As some of you may already know, last week, Andrew Walters, a security guard at the UC Berkeley campus, was found dead after allegedly kidnapping a young woman and holding her in exchange for experimental serums believed to be from this lab.

"Reports indicate that he had previously stolen rare samples belonging to the lab in a desperate attempt to cure his inoperable cancer. He later died from an apparent overdose of those stolen samples.

"All reports indicate that his victim is now safe and has returned home, but one question still remains. What, exactly, is going on in this lab that would make someone desperate enough to kidnap an innocent girl and risk his life to obtain it?

"In just a few moments, we are expected to hear from Weston Wilson III, the current owner and nephew of the legendary Dr. Oliver Thomas, a man remembered for his great contributions to blood research and new discoveries in that field."

Shortly afterward, Topper turned his head in acknowledgment and the camera shifted to a podium and microphone. It was a basic setup with nothing distracting. A plain gray backdrop read California Blood Research Lab in navy blue lettering, and nothing else. All eyes would certainly be on the speaker who, I cringed at the thought, would be Wes. After what seemed like the longest amount of time, a door to the right of the platform opened. Filing onto the raised landing were two older men wearing white lab coats with pocket protectors. Following were three younger men in lab coats, then finally Wes, also in a lab coat.

Shockingly, he looked mature and professional—*and* nerdy. His hair was doing some crazy parted-on-one-side thing and was brushed forward a little, and his perfect face was hidden behind a pair of rectangular black-framed glasses. I almost laughed out loud, but I was too intrigued and mesmerized by the images on the screen. He was perfect. It was still clearly him to anyone who knew him, and not so shockingly different that his friends would question his motives. They might pick on him for turning into a medical nerd, but nothing here was too different to raise an alarm.

"Ah, look at him. He looks so professional." My mom beamed at him like she was admiring her child at an elementary school play.

"He certainly does," Tom added. "All the weight he's carrying, he must be sweating bullets."

No, Wes doesn't sweat, but I wasn't about to fill him in on that.

"No, Tom, I think Sophie is doing enough sweating for him. Look at her. She's so nervous. Don't worry, honey. He'll do fine."

I took a deep breath, eyes fixated on the screen. The first five men walked to the far side of the platform, standing with their arms at their sides. As soon as their gazes shifted to Wes, I knew it was coming.

Unlike them, he strode to the podium. Cameras started flashing like crazy. He cleared his throat, and softly, in a steady voice, he began, not quite making eye contact with the camera, but rather looking at people throughout the room.

"Thank you all for coming. This has been an odd few days for me and quite an ordeal for other innocent people. I want to first apologize for any hurt that recent events have caused anyone. When my uncle began his research, he had only the best of intentions, to end suffering. It would sadden him to know that his work caused someone harm.

"Unfortunately, there have been rumors that our lab is conducting experiments and hiding groundbreaking results from the public. This speculation led a desperate man to seek something he could not find.

"I can assure you that this lab is working every day to find what Mr. Walters was looking for, but I can personally tell you it does not yet exist. We are close to finding cures for many ailments and will guarantee that as soon as we have anything substantially beneficial, the public will know. It is what my uncle lived for. Thank you."

As soon as he finished, questions began flying in from every direction. "Mr. Wilson, is it true Mr. Walters blackmailed you? Is it true he killed himself with alligator blood? Is there any merit to alligator blood in medicine? What does it heal? Did it kill him?"

Wes waited patiently for the barrage of questions to end. "You all have very good questions. Unfortunately, I am not the person to answer them. I am proud to support and carry on something my father and uncle began, but I will have to defer to the professionals on the rest of your questions. I give you first Dr. Dwight Lyon. Thank you."

He nodded respectfully and took his place among the five men standing behind him. Dr. Lyon, the oldest doctor, stepped forward with an intimidating demeanor that caused the reporters to step down their tone and eagerness a notch.

He immediately filled them in on several cancer studies they were working on, as well as HIV, and then addressed the important alligator blood question. He told the world that they had begun to extract antibodies from alligator blood for a topical cream study and had seen some benefits in using it on burn victims. He assured, very convincingly, that it was merely a topical application and injecting it in any way would be out of the question.

"Wow," Tom said, shaking his head in what appeared to be both admiration and disbelief. "They're working on some very advanced treatments. Wes is an impressive young man. His father would be very proud."

"See, Sophie. Now you can stop gnawing on your lip. He did great, and he might get an offer to do a billboard ad for pain reliever or something."

"Not funny, Mom."

"I'm just saying."

"I'm going upstairs. I have to work today."

"Okay, honey. Love you."

"Love you too."

By the time I reached the top step, I had gone through the press conference twice over. There was nothing that stuck out as far as I could tell. It had been perfectly done and there weren't any red flags I could see that would make people think something secretive was going on there. I still shuddered at the thought of the whole thing. Then I started to wonder how much those doctors really knew.

Surely, in order for the lab to find the cures Dr. Thomas had hoped for, they had to know the blood could be injected. Maybe not. I decided I'd ask Wes another time. I really didn't care right then. I just wanted to talk to him. I debated how long to wait before I called, but he called me first, only minutes after I got upstairs.

"How was it?" he asked, sounding nervous.

That took me by surprise because his tone was opposite from what I'd heard just moments before.

"You did great." I answered, still trying to decipher the worry in his voice.

"Are you sure?"

"Yeah, I'm sure. It was perfect. Or at least as perfect as it could be, considering."

He sighed. "Good."

"What's wrong? I thought you would be much more upbeat than me about it. What happened?"

I could almost picture him shaking his head. "I don't know. I thought it went well, but then everyone watched me the whole time. Even when the doctors were at the podium, they were all looking at me."

Now I was the one to calm the worry. "Wes, the reporters were probably watching you because you have such a camera friendly face. I'd look at you too."

He laughed. "Well, remind me not to do that again."

I snorted. "You'll have no problem from me on that."

Chapter 6
TEARS

I was in a much better mood after the press conference, and my hand was feeling fine, but I still solicited a ride to work from Wes. After he went home to change out of his Clark Kent look, he was coming by to scoop me up. I was on the lookout, knowing if he came inside that my mom and Tom would want to talk about the press conference, and I just wanted the drama to be done and over with.

And it seemed like it was. He was much more relaxed, and so was I the moment I got into his car. Leaning over to give him a kiss was a must, and although it was brief, it was enough to make me wish he wasn't dropping me off at work. *Focus, Sophie, focus.* Oh, what the heck? I was elated. I leaned over to kiss him again.

"To what do I owe all this?" he asked, laughing between kisses.

"You don't know?"

"Apparently, I don't."

"Mom says you're famous now. Might get calls from agents for commercials. I've always wanted a famous guy."

He laughed. "Yeah, right."

"Okay, you got me. I'm just so happy that it's over. The investigation is closed, the press conference is over, my mom is relaxing, and I'm with you." I was beaming.

His lighthearted laugh turned into a more serious but content smile. He leaned over to kiss me again and told me he loved me, then smoothly headed the car toward a destination I really didn't want to reach.

On the way there, I asked a few questions about the doctors from the press conference. He told me about Dr. Dwight Lyon. Apparently, Dr. Lyon was a hemophiliac who was treated by Dr. Thomas before he died. Wes said Dr. Thomas' research in the 1950s, using various animal plasmas and experimentations with variations of temperature and concentrations of saline and alcohol, led to the development of factors used to clot blood in home treatments. Dr. Thomas' findings didn't cure hemophilia, but led to a revolutionary way that people suffering from it could be treated.

Since Dr. Lyon was a beneficiary of Dr. Thomas' findings, he vowed to help continue with his research. I asked why there wasn't a larger focus on curing hemophilia in the lab and Wes said that they were working on that too, but current medications already allowed for hemophiliacs to live a relatively normal life. What they want to focus on more is finding cures for terminal illnesses.

"It's what Dr. Thomas wanted," Wes ended.

"I wish there was a cure for everything." I almost became melancholy again.

"Maybe one day." Wes smiled and lifted my chin with his finger.

"Right. One day."

A few moments passed and we pulled into the parking lot. A police cruiser sat right in front of the bookstore.

"What is going on here?" Wes asked.

"That's odd," I said.

Although Wes normally would've dropped me off, this time he parked and got out with me. Together, we walked to the door, curious and anxious. Inside were the same two police officers who had questioned me a few days ago. The sight of them made me tense as I tried to remember any possible slip I'd made in my story.

They were talking to Mr. Healey at the counter. I saw Mr. Healey dip his head and begin shaking it side to side. My thoughts drifted to Dawn and Danny, until I saw Danny come from the back carrying a small stack of items. Dawn.

I walked right up to where the officers were. "Is Dawn okay?"

"Yes, Dawn's fine," Mr. Healey answered. "It's Ms. Mary."

Ms. Mary couldn't have done anything wrong, that's for sure. She was just a quiet, elderly woman who worked at the store. Then it occurred to me that Mr. Healey didn't have a disappointed look on his face, he wore a shocked and saddened look.

"What's wrong with her?"

Mr. Healey cleared his throat, but the younger, thin officer spoke up. "Ms. Mary was found dead in her home this morning. She was murdered."

My heart fluttered and my muscles tightened. Wes stepped forward and placed his hand on my back.

I looked at Mr. Healey. "Oh, my gosh. Murdered? Ms. Mary?" At that point Wes put his hand on my elbow to steady me.

Mr. Healey said, "Officer, I don't understand. Why would anyone do that to her?"

"That's what we're going to find out." The officer reached out his hand toward Danny.

"Are these her belongings?" Danny nodded and handed over her cubby items. "We'll check these against the items her family says are unaccounted for."

"What happened?" I asked.

This time the rounder one spoke up. "We received a call this morning when her house alarm went off. Upon arrival, we found her dead."

It was all too much. This was the kind of stuff people see on TV. This didn't happen to someone who worked in the same little bookstore where I worked. This was some sort of nightmare.

The thin officer spoke up. "Speaking of this morning, do you mind telling us where you were?"

I looked up, about to answer his question, but noticed his eyes were fixed on Wes.

"Me?" Wes asked, confused.

"Yes, you. I find it a bit odd that two major crimes have occurred in the last week involving people you are somehow connected with."

"That's ridiculous!" I snapped, switching from shocked sorrow to anger.

"It's okay, Sophie. The officers are just doing their job." He squeezed my elbow and looked directly at them. "I was at a press conference this morning."

"Yes, the one that was televised live." I added, just to be sure it was clear that Wes was in *no* way responsible for killing poor Ms. Mary.

The officers nodded and wrote in their notepads.

"Thank you for the information. Please call us if you can think of anything else." The thinner one, Officer Petty, I had taken notice of his name tag by then, handed over a business card. Then they each gave a brief nod to Mr. Healey, Danny, and Wes, ignored me altogether, and walked out.

I turned to Mr. Healey. "I don't believe it."

"I know, Sophie. It doesn't make sense."

Wes made a more sympathetic comment. "I don't know who could be so cruel."

Danny added, "I know. It's crazy."

"So what now?" I asked.

"I'm not sure. I'm going to reach out to her family. I know she has several daughters in the area." Mr. Healey pressed his lips together, as if holding back emotion, and then walked toward the back room, leaving us to let the news sink in.

"Ms. Mary worked here for twenty years." Danny sighed. "She used to babysit us."

"I feel terrible." In fact, I was starting to feel all cruddy again.

"Do you want me to take you home?"

I looked at Wes. "No, I'm okay. I just think it's really tragic. She was so nice."

"Are you sure? I can take you."

He looked as if he didn't want to leave, and I almost didn't want him to, but I knew he couldn't hang out with me at the store all day. "I'm okay. Really. You need to go to class. Pick me up when I get off. I'll be all right."

He leaned down and kissed me on the forehead. "Call me if you need anything." Reluctantly, he turned and headed for the door.

I gave him a genuine smile, considering the circumstances, and turned to Danny. He appeared almost as shaken up as his father. "You okay?"

He shook off the concern directed toward him. "Yeah, I'm all right, but it just won't be the same around here. She kept my dad organized and me in check. We'll miss her, that's for sure."

I wanted to offer a hug, and then thought it might be awkward. Then I wondered who would hug him. I had never seen Danny with any girl. No one ever brought him lunch or dinner. I never saw him on his phone or texting or anything. And he was good-looking.

Then again, before I met Wes, no one would've ever seen me with anyone, and I had been just fine. I still would've needed a hug if someone close to my family had died. Still, it would seem forced, so I just walked around and patted him on his shoulder gently. He turned and gave me a soft smile.

Interrupting the awkward I'm-here-for-you-if-you-need-me moment was a gust of air as Dawn burst through the door. "What the hell, Danny? I'm not due in until 4:00."

"Well, little sis, Dad wanted you here, so he could tell—"

"Oh, please."

"Dawn, will you shut your mouth for two seconds?"

They were about to go back and forth in a sibling spat when I interrupted. "Ms. Mary died this morning."

Her mouth froze, her face flashed through the same expressions of confusion mine had, and then she asked almost the same questions.

Needless to say, the afternoon was not a joy. It felt cold, sad, and empty in the store all day. It seemed that we were the least busy we had been all year, like the customers knew to stay away and give the store some healing time, only it made matters worse. No one wanted to make small talk or discuss the awful news, so we were silent most of the day.

Finally, Mr. Healey went home early, and at closing time, I did too.

It wasn't surprising when my mother freaked out over the incident. By morning, she was actually considering moving. I had no choice but to fully engage in the conversation because she waited until I sat at the breakfast table with a bowl of cereal. No quick escape.

"You know, Sophie," she began, "I'm not sure living in this area suits us anymore."

"What? Are you kidding, Mom?"

"Well, no. Think about it. Danger never followed you like it seems to be doing since we moved here."

"Danger did not follow me. Ms. Mary is the one dead, remember? It followed her to her house. Not to mine."

"But, Sophie, how many young girls your age can say they almost..." She elected not to finish that sentence. Instead, she shook off the thought. "I just think you've been too close to too many incidents involving crazy people for my taste. We wouldn't move far. Maybe closer to the coast. Just somewhere new and fresh."

This was so like her. She'd always had the itch to try new places whenever she got bored, or didn't like something about where we were living. Now that we had moved back to the place where I was born, where I had found Wes, I was not about to move again. Not a chance. Plus, I was eighteen. She couldn't make me move, even if she wanted to.

"Mom, I'm not moving anywhere. I like it here. And so do you, for that matter. And what about Tom? What happened to Ms. Mary was crazy, but it doesn't have anything to do with us."

Which it didn't. Danny had given Dawn and me details. The police said there had been a few reported break-ins in her neighborhood in the past few months. That was why Ms. Mary had installed the alarm system that alerted the police to the intruder. It was an unfortunate situation, and Ms. Mary would probably still be alive if she hadn't been downstairs when the intruder broke in.

I had heard all the "if onlys," so I knew them well. If only Ms. Mary had been upstairs when the alarm sounded, she could've locked herself in her room until the police arrived, and maybe the intruder would've taken what he

71

wanted and fled without ever knowing she was there. If only it had been five or ten minutes later, Ms. Mary would have already left for work. But since she was downstairs, in the house, the police believed that the intruder panicked and strangled her. It was simply a matter of being in the wrong place at the wrong time.

My mom took a deep breath and a sip of her coffee. "It just makes me nervous. It's been one thing after another. I don't like it."

"Me either, but I like it here. I don't want to move."

"Maybe you're right. But I think we need to be more careful, pay attention to what we do. I'm seeing how crazy this world really is." She took a few more sips of her coffee and then her eyes went wide. "You know, I might get us an alarm too. I'd feel safer."

I finished my last bite of cereal, put my bowl in the sink, and quickly came up with an alternative. "Maybe. Or we could get a dog."

She pondered a minute. "A dog? That might not be a bad idea."

I knew she would probably forget about a dog or an alarm in a few days. This was just her typical whim. At least I hoped. An alarm would put a kink in Wes' late-night visits. I wasn't sure how I'd get around that. If she kept pressing the issue, I'd push for a dog for sure.

The following Monday was Ms. Mary's funeral. It was a small service at a little white church on a hillside over-looking the bay. At 9:00 a.m, I arrived with my mom and Tom, and Wes met us there. The high temperature was expected to be in the mid- to upper-60s, but the morning air felt even cooler. It was chilly enough for Wes that he wore a long black coat over his suit.

Although the atmosphere was somber, I couldn't help but smile at his handsome appearance. His coat was far enough open to reveal a black suit jacket and pale blue dress shirt, with no tie, peeking out at the center. His hair was back to normal, without the part, and slightly curled at the tips.

"We match," he noted, as I approached.

I looked down and saw he was right. I had chosen a fitted navy blue quarter-sleeve dress that fell to my calves. The dress had a wide ribbon around the waistline that was the same pale blue as his shirt. Oddly, we looked like we were going to a homecoming dance. I smiled softly, getting that we-belong-together feeling, and reached up to give him a kiss.

We filed into the church and sat near the back. I elected not to go up to the front and look into the open casket. I had no desire whatsoever to see Ms. Mary's lifeless form. Some people believe the viewing gives them closure. Not me. Remembering what Ms. Mary looked like when she was alive was all the closure I wanted.

The funeral service started out a little bitter, for which I couldn't blame anyone. I would be angry too if my family member had been brutally murdered. Ms. Mary's son read a letter, which challenged anyone who was considering taking someone else's life to look inward and reconsider. He read about how the family missed their mother and grandmother, and could not understand why someone had taken away the best-hearted person they had known.

The pastor preached a eulogy that piggybacked off the idea that this was not for us to understand, and then the momentum and mood quickly picked up when the pastor invited everyone to raise their faces toward heaven, because this was a celebration of a "homegoing," a home-going to heaven. By the end of the service, people were almost applauding.

Strangely, I didn't realize my situation until the interment. The only other funeral I'd attended had been my grandmother's, and I had managed to block out the actual sadness of it. Maybe if I'd allowed the sorrow to come out then I would've accepted that a death had actually occurred.

The small crowd of mourners gathered on the hillside beside the church. The bumpy slope made it difficult to walk in heels, so I clung to Wes the entire time. His hold on me as we walked was comforting, but nothing out of the ordinary.

What was different was the weighted feel of Wes' arm around me by the end of the service. He usually held on to me with a comforting and secure hold, but this felt different, heavy and limp. It was enough to cause me to look up at him. His face was pained and his head was tilted slightly to the side, as if he was having a hard time holding it up.

I turned back to see what had him so entranced. Ms. Mary's children had stepped up, one at a time, to toss a flower into the grave. When I looked back at Wes, I saw him blink slowly, releasing one small tear.

I watched it roll all the way down his cheek without him flinching or attempting to wipe it away. By the time it dripped onto his jacket, I realized that Wes was not just crying for Ms. Mary. A brick pulled my heart to the ground as I turned back to the grave.

In slow motion, the next flower left the hands of Ms. Mary's loved one and disappeared into the deep hole where her body would lie forever. I was very sure at that moment that this hole resembled the ones where Amelia and Lenny lay. A hole similar to where Wes may have dropped a flower for Lenny. A hole that Wes would surely never want to see again. And, unfortunately, one that I wasn't so sure I could avoid.

I wrapped both arms around Wes' waist, and tears escaped my eyes as I squeezed them shut. Wes pulled me to him in the firm hold that I remembered well and kissed me on the top of my head.

I refused to open my eyes but instead pressed my face against his side, absorbing him and every ounce of hope I held on to and feared losing. In reality, we are such little beings, insignificant to the greater powers of the universe, and suddenly I felt like I had no right to defy fate. No right to think I could beat the odds to remain in that moment, forever, with the one I loved.

I shook off all doubt, wanting to believe that a different future was meant for me. I willed it, even wished it. But an aggressive, overwhelmingly sad aura consumed me as I held on to him even tighter. And then, behind me, the last flower was tossed. I could almost hear it land six feet below the hand that had let it go.

Chapter 7
MAKING THE MOST

The strange thing about what happened at the funeral was that neither Wes nor I talked about it afterward. Even though we both knew my uncertain future was hovering over us like a low, dark cloud, there was no need to discuss it.

We tried to keep ourselves busy. I'd never eaten so much ice cream or seen so many movies in the two weeks following Ms. Mary's death. We were constantly doing something until it turned into such a routine that we had to change up, or both of us would burst. It was his idea to expand our horizons. We had just finished eating takeout one evening at his house when he suggested it.

"Let's do something different," he said.

I was stuffing our trash back into the bags. "Like what?"

"Like get away."

Tropical island? Was this it? I was beyond thrilled. "You mean, like, go away. For real?"

"No, not *go* away. *Get* away. I want to take you somewhere. Not too far. Just somewhere different."

"I'd love to." I curled up next to him on the couch, practically bouncing up and down on the cushions.

"Where would you like to go?"

"I don't care. Anywhere. You pick."

He smiled and shook his head. "No, I've picked where we've gone since the day we met. It should be somewhere you want to go. Pick a place."

"I'd love to see Kerry again, but that's too far and too cold. Hmm." I thought about it for a minute. "Fishing." The weather had warmed up nicely by then, so it sounded perfect, but he laughed.

"Fishing? Sophie, be for real."

"I am. We can't really go to a tropical island. It's too hot, and I don't snorkel."

"You don't fish either."

"Well, that's because no one takes me. My dad and I used to fish all the time, until he left. I haven't been since I was little. And it's different."

Still unsure, but seemingly content, he answered, "Okay. Fishing it is."

"Yay!" I gave him a kiss, and he shook his head. "What?" I asked.

"I had no idea you were so outdoorsy."

"See, you don't know everything about me after all."

The truth was, he did. I wasn't all that outdoorsy, but I remember enjoying fishing. The only reason I was such an indoor girl now, was because I preferred to be holed up in the house after all the new places my mom moved us. Heck, for all I knew, I might have an outdoor girl waiting to burst out of me.

He planned to pick me up at 8:00 Saturday morning, so I had to request off work, which I was hesitant to do since coverage would be thin. It turned out to be no problem. Mr. Healey had already hired someone new. Dawn said it was one of Danny's new friends and he was scheduled to come in and train on Saturday anyway, so it wasn't a big deal that I wouldn't be there.

I waited in the living room for him to pull up and when I heard a car, I snuck out without saying good-bye to my mother. She knew I was going fishing and it brought back memories of my dad that she'd rather not visit, so she didn't ask too many questions.

I opened the front door then almost shut it again, because a very intimidating vehicle was sitting where Wes' car should've been. Just as I was about to step back into the house, Wes got out. *Huh?*

I closed the door behind me and walked toward him. "What's this?"

"We can't go camping in a Maserati."

"Who said anything about camping?"

"Well, not overnight camping, but we are going to a campground. It's where the best part of the lake is, and I can't go four-wheeling to it in a sports car."

"So what is this?"

He had taken my bag by then and tossed it into the back. "It's my new car."

"New? You bought it? Where's the other one?"

"It's at home."

"But why buy this? We could've taken my Jeep."

Opening the door for me now, he said, "I thought about that. Then realized I'd rather have this. It's safer, and I have other ways to seek a thrill now. Don't need a sports car."

I smiled at his sly grin in suggesting new thrills. I was all for that. "Does that mean you want to work on your clarity?" He shut the door without responding.

"That was rude." I accused, as he slid into his side. He leaned over and kissed me on the lips. "Sorry."

I pouted. "So what is this anyway?" All I knew was that it was another black, shiny vehicle with black leather seats and large tires.

"Range Rover."

It was nice. I liked his taste, that was for sure. He knew how to look good, but classy, without blazin' in someone's face about it. We drove toward town and I wondered where we were headed. It turned out he needed to stop at the sporting goods store.

"I don't fish," he said. "So we need to buy equipment and supplies. You'll have to show me which ones."

"What? I can't remember." This was going to be the blind leading the blind.

He wasn't concerned. "We'll ask someone, then."

And we did. Within twenty minutes, we had all the fishing supplies we needed. After seeing them, I remembered the basics enough to have a shot at actually catching something.

We were about to check out when Wes asked if I had packed a swimsuit. *What the heck would I need that for?* The thought sounded so appropriate that I said it out loud.

"To swim, Sophie. What do you think?"

"Swim in what?" I asked, still not getting it.

"In the lake." He had a look on his face like he wanted to say "Hello?" after the comment.

"You don't swim in a lake."

"Sure, I do. I'll swim anywhere there's water."

Oh, geez. "Wes, I've fished in a lake, but never swam in one."

"Well, we're supposed to be doing something different, right?" He put his hands on my shoulders and lowered his gaze to mine, holding back a smile. "Besides, you said you were outdoorsy."

I let out a low grumble. He might have been able to woo me with those dark brown eyes before, but not anymore. Okay, who was I kidding? *Fine.*

I looked at the sales associate. "Where's your swimsuit section?"

Who was I to care about dirty, slimy lake water. I was with Wes, and we were going to have fun. And since that was the only way to make the most of what time we had, that's what I was going to do—swim in the lake. *Gross.*

Two hours later, we arrived at a wooded park area. A Fishing Docks Ahead sign blatantly beamed at us as we entered the parking lot. Wes' GPS system told him to make a right onto a paved, narrow lane. Instead of following the pavement, Wes turned again onto a dirt road. The GPS lady didn't like that. In a calm, stern voice, she told Wes to turn around in point three miles.

"You're making her mad."

"Oh, she'll be fine." He reached over and turned her off.

"Where are you going anyway?"

"There's a more private water entry this way."

I noticed faint tire tracks, so I knew we weren't the only people to upset their GPS lady. "How do you know what's up here?"

He looked at me as our bodies bounced around in our seats as we made progress over the rough terrain. "Research," he said.

"Research."

Turning his attention toward navigating our narrow, rocky path, he casually continued. "Yeah, I looked around for some good fishing places and this one had an aerial map, so I was able to see they had an off-road section."

"Uh-huh. I see."

After a few more minutes of bobbing up and down and left and right, we rolled to a stop just short of an embankment. I was impressed.

"Wow, the view is perfect. Look at it."

It was amazing. The water was calm, and a dark blue-green color that reflected the sunlight beautifully. There was no one else in sight. Just us and trees everywhere—behind us, beside us, and surrounding the lake on all sides, at least as far as I could see.

I waited for him to get out first, to check and make sure it was safe. For some reason, I was apprehensive. It could have been because swimming in a lake still didn't sound all that appealing. Luckily, he got out and went straight to the back and pulled out all our fishing supplies.

I carried the rods and tacklebox down to the water and he carried everything else, including a cooler I hadn't seen before.

"What's in that?"

"You'll have to wait and see."

"Oh, come on, Wes, you know I don't have patience for secrets or surprises. What's in it?"

"Just drinks, lunch. Stuff." He set everything down without looking at me.

I put down my load and smiled. "Aw, you packed us a picnic? That is so romantic."

His shyness was surprising, and I was getting a kick out of it. I stepped over to him and turned his face to me by holding his cheeks. I gave them a slight squeeze.

"You are so sweet. I just want to kiss you all over."

He smiled and pulled his head back just far enough that I couldn't reach it anymore. I jumped up, and he turned away, laughing. I wasn't ready to give up, so the chase was on. He started to run and I jumped on his back, wrapping my arms around his neck. He placed his hands under my legs to hold me up.

I was doing some sort of embarrassing laugh by then. I'm not sure why, other than this was a lot of fun. At least it was until he headed toward the water and then it registered. I tried to put my legs down, but he held me to him even tighter.

"Wes! What are you doing? Stop." Now he was the one laughing. "It's not funny, Wes. Don't go in there. I have my clothes on!"

Somehow, he pulled me around to his front, so he was carrying me. I was wriggling, but he was winning. Once we got to the edge, he held me out over the water.

"Wes, I swear. Please!" He moved as if to toss me. "My clothes!" I yelled.

He tossed and I closed my eyes, screaming. I braced for the impact, but there wasn't one, only the sounds of him cracking up. I opened my eyes and he still had hold of me. I smacked his chest and wriggled my way down.

"That's not funny." But I couldn't contain a smile, even though I was trying very hard.

"I don't understand why you're so concerned about your clothes."

"Because they're all I brought. What? Am I going to go home naked?"

He raised his eyebrows and shrugged. "You could."

"Yeah, right." I was still smiling, but I brushed past him in an effort to get away from the water before he changed his mind.

He followed after me. "What? You're the one who said you wanted to kiss me all over."

I smiled, but kept walking. Once we got back to our little spot, we unpacked the supplies.

He leaned toward me, all puppy-dog-eyed. "You don't want to kiss me anymore?"

"Nope."

"No? Why not?"

The truth was, I did. *Really* bad, but I was hoping that playing hard to get would spark him to kiss *me*.

"Because, I just don't," I answered, not sure if my face was serious enough.

"Okay."

I knew him well enough to know that he had called my bluff, but I wasn't going to cave. Acting satisfied with his giving up, I situated myself with the fishing supplies. I remembered a lot from the times with my dad. I baited the hook and everything. Even Wes watched me so he could learn.

"I'm impressed," he said.

"Why?" I asked, casting out.

"It's nice to watch you do something I've never seen before."

"There are a lot of things you've never seen before." I wanted to smile when I said that, but I remained serious.

"Is that so?" He cast his line into the water with ease.

"Uh-huh."

"Like?"

I was holding my rod steady and looking out over the water. "Well, let's just say you'd need to have a clear head before I showed you." I was cracking up inside.

"Is that right?"

I nodded.

"Well, I have a clear head now," he said, still calling my bluff.

My next move would be pivotal, so I had to think. I knew my hormones were bottled up, and he was just messing with me. Or maybe he wasn't. Either way, he had given me a chance to drive the train.

"That's good." I said, reeling in my line. "Because I'd like to show you. In fact, I'm ready for a swim. How about a change of clothes right now?" I started to take off my shirt.

"Whoa." He frowned. "What are you doing?"

"Showing you something you haven't seen before."

He jumped up. "Okay, okay. I get it. Ha-ha. You win. Keep your clothes on, Sophie."

"What? I'm just changing. Where's my swimsuit anyway?"

"It's in the truck. I'll get it." He turned away nervously, before I could stand up to take off my pants too.

I have no idea how I was able to take off my clothes so freely. I was so not a flamboyant person, and in truth, I was completely nervous at the idea of Wes seeing me naked. But I knew it would freak him out, so for some reason, that made it easier for me. Maybe if he was hawking me like a pervert, I might have been less open to it.

He brought my suit back just as I was pulling off the last undergarment. Although he now appeared much calmer with my nudity, he kept his eyes from wandering below my chin.

As I finished putting on my bathing suit, he went back to the truck and changed into his at the tailgate end, as far away from me as possible. By the time we were suited up and he was making his way to me, I felt I had lost the upper hand. *For crying out loud,* I thought.

Having had enough, I walked up to him, cutting short his approach. "Would you just kiss me alrea—?"

He grabbed the back of my neck and pressed his lips to mine before I could finish my sentence. My eyes closed instantly as the familiar fire spread through my body. I locked my arms around his neck and my mouth opened hungrily, allowing his tongue to meet mine in a long-overdue encounter.

With one smooth motion, he picked me up. I felt secure with his arms under my bottom. What I did with my legs is a mystery, because the only part of my body I felt at that moment was my brain burning in complete bliss.

I gasped as I felt a built-up flame explode from within. He kissed me over and over. Eventually, a cool sensation overtook the fire running from my toes. By the time the coolness reached my back, I realized it was water and opened my eyes.

"Water," I squealed.

He kept kissing me.

"Green water," I croaked between breaths.

"Sorry," he said, shrugging, "I was about to lose time."

"Ah." That was part of his clarity issue.

We had been in a zone where neither of us was thinking about time, and he needed to cool off. Literally. I understood and wasn't going to press him. We were both still breathing heavily, but a calm sensation was returning.

I looked around the lake for something else to focus on. "See? I *am* outdoorsy."

He smiled. "Yeah. You are. I like it." He turned us around, giving me the better view of the entire lake.

"Why is that?" I felt him pulling me farther into the water, so I kept the cast on my arm raised.

"I don't know. I think it's because I honestly never knew that about you. It's like I'm meeting you for the first time, and I like it. It makes me feel…"

I knew what he meant. Even though he couldn't find the right word, I understood. If he was getting to know me for the first time, then maybe things could be different. He was still searching for the word when I filled it in.

"Hopeful. You feel hopeful that things are new and different between us."

"Yeah. I think so."

An idea popped into my head. "You know what? I think we should make it a point to be different."

"How?"

"Well, let's not fall into the trap of history. Let's make a new beginning for Sophie and Wes."

"And how do you propose we do that?"

"I think we should keep doing different things. Let's not give fate the weapon of routine. Let's make it a point to deviate from what is anticipated. Like this. You didn't expect me to like fishing. And look how much fun we're having."

His face was starting to harden. "I don't think we can trick fate, Sophie."

"I don't want to trick anything. I just don't want to walk right into it. What do we have to lose? Maybe we can take the long way around."

He kissed me again, but differently. It was more of a comforting kiss. "You're right. It's worth a try. Sophie and Weston—outrunning themselves." He rolled his eyes.

"Hey." I scrunched up my brows.

"I'm just joking. I like the idea as long as I get to spend time with you. Which reminds me. If you're finished with your theories, I'd like to spend time with my *new* girlfriend."

I obliged and kissed him again. He asked me if I was hungry, and I wasn't, so I passed. But I was curious. I got him to tell me what was in the cooler. Ham-and-Swiss sandwiches, chips, strawberries, and sparkling cider. The sound of it all *was* making me hungry, but I preferred the closeness I had with him at the moment, so I chose to stay in the water a little longer.

"Do you mind if I float?" he asked.

"No, of course not. But can I touch the bottom? I can't float with my arm."

"I'm not going to let go of you. I just want us to float."

I couldn't figure out how he was going to accomplish that with me, but I trusted him enough to know he would keep me and my cast above water.

"Put your legs down," he instructed.

"Huh? Oh, sorry." I realized I still had them clamped around his waist. I slowly let them drop, and once my body was vertical to his, he pressed me up against him and tilted himself backward.

Slowly, I felt myself rise out of the water until I was lying on him. "Whoa."

"I've got you."

Once I relaxed, I felt weightless. He was floating on his back effortlessly and I was lying on top of him like he was a raft. I propped myself up on my forearms and studied his calm, perfect face in the sunlight. His eyes were closed and I could see that he was completely comfortable and relaxed. I looked around the panoramic view of the lake and couldn't help but feel relaxed too.

It was perfect. Absolutely perfect. I was floating in a beautiful lake with the only person in the world that I wanted to be with. My soul mate, my love, my everything. There was nothing else I wanted in the entire universe. What I wanted, what I needed, was right there with me.

I rested my head on his chest and closed my eyes, feeling the sun on my back. I felt us rock ever so slightly and sway back and forth with the gentle current, listening to the slow, steady beats of his heart.

That lake had no doubt become one of my new favorite places. Not Amelia's, not Lenny's, but Sophie's new place. *My* place. No, not just mine. It was *our* place—our lake. Our lake of complete happiness.

Chapter 8
IN WITH THE NEW

I could've stayed on that lake all day, but the temperature wasn't warm enough for Wes. It was okay for a short time, but then I felt his body getting cooler.

"I'm okay, Sophie." He kept saying, and he was for a while.

But I wasn't oblivious to the coolness beneath me, so I ordered him to float us on in. It was almost invigorating. I felt in charge, guiding and leading my ship to the dock. In command of my vessel. A very cute one. I smiled the whole way, wishing we could stay connected like this forever.

After drying off, Wes began unpacking our picnic. I laughed as he unfolded a red-and-white checked blanket. "Wes. You've been watching way too much TV."

He smiled without commenting and organized everything in a neat display of fine dining by the lake. Opening a bottle of sparkling cider, he poured us each a glass. He handed mine over as I watched the fizz settle, trying to determine if the glass was half full or half empty.

It bothered me momentarily that I hesitated before committing to my normal optimism that it was indeed half full. Shaking away negative thoughts, I smiled, touched my glass to his, and took a sip. He was less conservative with his, downing it in one gulp.

"Thirsty?"

He poured himself another glass. "Yes. *And* hungry."

Watching him eat had become a common thing for me. We had been dating long enough that I wasn't nervous eating around him, but for some reason, I was never really thinking about food when we were together. There was a different kind of fullness within me whenever he was near, so I usually found myself content with nibbling.

He, on the other hand, usually ate all his food. I couldn't help but become curious. "How do you eat?" I asked.

Taking a bite of his sandwich, he looked at me with a raised brow. "Is this a trick question?"

"No, silly. I mean, what is food to you? Do you need it? Is it just habit?"

Figuring out what I was dancing around, he smiled. "You mean, do I hibernate and go without food for long periods of time?"

I shrugged a little. "Yeah, I guess."

"Sophie, I do believe you read too much of that book."

He was referring to something I had read a few weeks earlier on understanding the cold-blooded creature, not that I thought he was a creature. I was just frustrated that he had broken up with me without an explanation, and I was coming up short with every other attempt at finding answers, so I thought that might work. Stupid, I know.

And he wasted no time laughing at me when he found out. *Whatever*.

"No, I did not read too much. I was just wondering. You say your metabolism has slowed down so much that you don't age. So it just occurred to me that you may not *need* to eat very often."

Taking another bite, he said, "I do need to eat. A lot. It's sort of like you people."

I scrunched up my eyebrows at the reference to my being a "you people," even though being a "you people" is normal. I just didn't like the designation.

He continued. "Normal people have to eat frequently if they want to speed up their metabolism, and if they don't eat often, their metabolism slows down."

"So you're worried about gaining weight."

He laughed. "Oh, my goodness. *No*. That's impossible. You can just call me Adonis forever."

I smiled and blushed at the same time. It was a first glimpse I'd been given of any sort of self-awareness that he was hot. And not only did he seem to be acknowledging his hotness, he was smiling about it.

"Or gator boy," I said. *Who's laughing now?*

"Good one."

"Yeah, so anyway." I bit off the tip of a strawberry. "Seriously, what about your metabolism?"

He nodded as if remembering the focus of our conversation. Then he leaned over and bit off the rest of my strawberry. "I don't have to eat for long periods of time if I don't want to. But if I don't, my metabolism gets even slower, which makes it harder to manage the time around

92

me. And, in the winter, my metabolism could get so slow I could go dormant. Then time would be nothing because I would miss all of it."

"Yikes." I nodded, getting it.

If his metabolism got too slow, he could fall asleep for a whole winter? And in those few months, his body might age a few hours while months of activity went on around him? His mind could miss all of it. I shuddered.

"It's not that big a deal, really. I just eat regularly. And if I get bored with something, or the daily routine. I just stop eating, and zip, it goes by."

Seemed simple enough. Except that ever since I met him, he has been eating. Now would his constant eating be a reminder that he was trying to savor the moments he has left with me? I was starting to feel full.

"What's the matter?" he asked, moving our already tilting glasses to a safer place.

"Nothing." I looked down. "I just don't want you to constantly be shifting your life or habits around for me. I just wish you could be you."

He tucked my bangs behind my ear. "Sophie. This is normal for me. When I'm not happy, I don't want to do anything. I don't want to eat, or drink, or take care of myself. All I can do is hope I can slip into an eternity that I won't remember when I wake. Are you kidding me? Being me, the person I *want* to be, means being with you. All the time."

He had a way of making me feel like I was a wanted addition to his life, and not a ticking time bomb. I reached over and gave him a soft kiss on the lips. And, knowing how to fully make me forget my worries, he gently pushed me back onto the blanket and softly kissed my mouth, and then my ear, and then my neck. I stared at the blue sky, feeling a tingling sensation spread throughout my entire body. I wanted to cry. I wanted to smile, to sleep, to live. I wanted everything all at once with him.

I was in complete bliss following that trip and felt like I was on a natural high every day. Until the following Thursday. It was my first day back at work since the funeral. Wes drove me again but not because I really needed him to. My hand was feeling fine, other than the annoying cast smothering it. I had just grown used to him taking me and it meant more time with him.

Plus, he didn't like it when we were separated and neither did I, so I let him take me places all the time. My mom was growing concerned that I was becoming dependent on him, but I didn't care. If I could've moved in with him, I would've, but my hands were tied. I was eighteen, but still in high school and that meant I was still a minor in my mom's eyes. It was a fine line, and she was very good at showing just enough concern without pushing me to challenge my adult status.

When we arrived, Healey's looked devoid of life. I'm sure it looked exactly how it always had, but on that day, it seemed weird. There were no cars out front. Every crack in the bricks showed, every flaw in the roof, and everything bleak stuck out like a sore thumb, like the building itself was in mourning. It was creepy.

"Are you okay?" Wes asked.

I blinked and realized we had been parked a few minutes and I hadn't moved. "Yeah, I'm just wondering what kind of day it will be." I leaned over to give him a hug and got out, walking into a bookstore filled with somber air. Mr. Healey was at the counter, as usual, but he looked a little annoyed.

"Hi, Mr. Healey."

I walked to the back where Danny was on break, eating Skittles. "What's up with your dad?"

He laughed. "Oh, you mean you haven't heard? Dawn sneaked out last night and he still hasn't seen her."

"Well, where is she? Is she okay?" I put my purse in my cubby and pulled up a chair next to him. I leaned in intently, to listen.

He casually responded, "Oh, yeah, she's fine."

"How do you know?"

"Because she called *me* to call in sick today. She's avoiding dad like the plague." He was smiling.

"Are you serious?" *She is so dead.* "What is she thinking?"

"That's one of Dawn's biggest problems. She doesn't think."

"What is your dad going to do?"

"Dad? He'll take her favorite toys away and then ignore her. She hates that. It drives her crazy."

I thought about that for a moment. It seemed so strange to play games like that. I was suddenly really glad my relationship with my mom included communication.

"Why does he want to drive her crazy?"

He popped in another piece of candy. "He just doesn't buy into her tactics anymore. She's always been spoiled and one day he just woke up."

The word dysfunctional bounced around in my head. Between Dawn thinking Danny was the smart apple in Daddy's eye and Danny calling Dawn spoiled, I was glad I didn't have any siblings to cause drama. I was thinking of a response when I heard the bell on the front door.

Danny spoke up. "That's probably my boy."

My boy? Since when did Danny's "boys" visit him at the bookstore?

"A visitor? *For you?*" I didn't mean for it to come out like he wasn't popular, but I feared it did. "I mean, since when do your friends come here?"

"Since they work here now, and since my baby sister abandons her post."

"Oh, right." I remember Dawn telling me that one of Danny's friends took Ms. Mary's place. I turned toward the door as soon as I heard it swing open.

"Wassup, Danny?"

I recognized the face, but couldn't pinpoint it. Not wanting to stare, I smiled slightly and turned away. As he walked by, I felt the hairs on the back of my neck stand up, like electricity was flowing past me.

"Nothing much," Danny said. "I gotta go to work."

He hopped up and headed back to the front to resume his shift. It seemed liked perfect timing, because the doorbell started chiming with customers coming in. I wanted to go out there too, but I didn't want to seem rude by clearing out the room on the new guy.

"You're Sophie, right?" He hung up his jacket and turned to face me, reaching out his hand.

I stood up instinctively. "Yeah, you look familiar," I prodded, hoping he would fill in the missing pieces.

"Yeah, we met once at a party, I think. I'm Chase."

I took his hand and gave it a shake. That was it. I remembered. "Right." The guy in my personal space at a party last month. The guy who was still in my personal space, because he wouldn't let go of my hand. I pulled it back.

"Oh, sorry," he said. "I just can't get over your eyes."

Now it was all *really* coming back to me. Wes and I were broken up when I first met him. He was good-looking, but something was missing. Aside from the fact that I don't really like guys who purposely look mismatched, his pick-up lines were unoriginal. Flashing his blue eyes at me, he attempted a crooked smile that couldn't even compare to Wes'.

Between Chase, Ms. Mary's death, Dawn's tantrum, Mr. Healey's mood, and Danny's *studying*, the bookstore was going to be one weird place from now on. I just wasn't sure how weird, but I was glad that the Chase part was going to take place on days I didn't work. That was *if* Dawn could get her act together.

I cleared my throat and planned to text her the first chance I got. "I gotta get to work," I said pointing toward the door, backpedaling.

With the same unnatural half smile, he replied slyly, "No problem."

NOT COOL DAWN. WHAT THE HECK ARE YOU
DOING?

I closed the phone and waited in the aisle. Within a
minute or two, it started vibrating in my hand.

OMG. DAD'S ON A KILL MISSION. SORRY.
NOT COMING IN.

WHAT DID YOU DO?

THE QUESTION IS WHO.

??

JACKSON. AND FREAKIN DANNY TOLD ON ME.
HE IS SO DEAD.

HOW DID DANNY...

Okay, texting was meant for quick messages, not a
soap opera script. I dialed her number and moseyed my
way to the farthest aisle. She didn't even say hello.

"That little prick told on me. I'm *so* mad."

"Dawn," I was half whispering. "Why would he do
that?"

"I don't freakin' know, but I slipped out to go see
Jackson, and at freakin' one o'clock in the morning my
dad comes knocking on the Jones' door, asking for me.
Jackson's mom comes to his room, I hide in the damn
closet, and Jackson lies his tail off that I'm not there. *Then*
dad sends me a text, telling me he's at my car around the
block, waiting for me."

OMG, is what I was thinking, but I tried to keep my
voice low. "What did you do?"

"Nothing. I stayed in his room all night. I wasn't going out there."

I was holding back a smile now. "How do you know Danny ratted on you?"

"Because Dad didn't know where Jackson lived. Danny *had* to tell him."

"So what are you going to do now?"

"I don't know. I'm going to make up something, I guess. He never actually saw me there. My car doesn't mean anything."

Good luck with that, I thought. Dawn was still highstrung and irritated when we hung up. But for some reason, I was still slightly amused. I slipped the phone into my back pocket and turned to get to work, when I bumped into a rather hard chest that didn't budge.

"Oh," I said, ricocheting off of it.

"My bad."

"Chase," I greeted him, wondering why he was dipping into my conversation.

"Yeah, sorry. I didn't mean to scare you. Mr. Healey wanted me to put these back. Any idea where they go?" He was holding *Green Eggs and Ham* and *Put Me in the Zoo.*

"Yeah, the children's section is about ten aisles the other way." I raised my eyebrows, waiting for him to move. He didn't.

The trying-too-hard smile appeared again. "Right, I'll remember that. I see you broke your hand. I didn't notice that before. Does it hurt?"

"Oh, it's nothing. Just an accident." If he was hoping for some long, drawn-out story where he could swoop in and make it feel better, he didn't know me very well. Not one for sympathy. "I have to get back to shelving," I said, trying to drop the hint and be polite.

As if a 120-watt light bulb went off, he quickly moved aside. His dirty blond bangs were covering his blue eyes and he shook them off with one quick shake of the head. "Sorry."

"No problem." I walked past. "And don't forget. They go in the children's section."

"Right."

Once I finished shelving, I wheeled the cart up front. By then it was almost time to close. Danny had been working the register, and Chase had been sucking up to Mr. Healey all evening. They were actually in the back while Mr. Healey was counting money for the deposit. I finally had two minutes alone with Danny.

I pulled up a stool next to him. "So why did you rat out your sister?"

"What?" he spit out as if it was ridiculous. "Dawn rats herself out."

"Come on, Danny. You guys are like my best friends here. I don't want to see you two fighting."

"Don't worry. Dawn will figure out how to get herself out of this. She always does."

I wasn't convinced, but was distracted by a flash of headlights as a vehicle pulled into one of the parking spaces out front. My smile overpowered any confusion I had with what was going on at the store.

"Looks like your ride is here," Danny said.

"Yep." I hurried to the back to grab my purse, which was not where I put it. I specifically remembered putting it into my cubby. I looked around and Mr. Healey and Chase were chatting away, ignoring me. Frustrated, I stood on my tiptoes and found it two cubbies above where it had been. That's when Chase spoke up. "Oh, sorry, Sophie. Your purse fell out and I wasn't sure which cubby was yours."

"Thanks." I skeptically put it on my shoulder, checking to see if it was zipped. "See ya tomorrow, Mr. Healey."

"Oh, bye, Sophie. Have a good night, and be safe."

"Yeah, be safe," Chase added.

I turned and nodded, not sure what to say back to the new guy. Nothing came to mind, so I walked out into the presence of the only person who made sense to me. Waiting for me by my door was Wes.

My Wes. Yummy, yummy, and yummy. The weather had warmed up, so he wasn't wearing a coat. He had on a long-sleeved, buttoned-up, collared shirt that he wore untucked. He had just the right amount of bagginess to his jeans and bright white tennis shoes that screamed clean. What I couldn't take my eyes off of was his collarbone peeking out from the few buttons that he had neglected to close. I gave him a huge hug.

Wrapping his arms around me, he gently lifted me off the ground in a strong, perfect squeeze. "I'm going to have to pick you up every day if this is how you always greet me."

I smiled. "Let's get out of here."

He set me down and opened the door. Knowing him and his patience, I knew he anticipated my spilling every detail of my mood as soon as we got into the car. Which I did. I told him all about Dawn and Danny and, of course, the new guy. Wes didn't seem surprised or fazed by any of it.

"Don't you think it's weird?" I finally asked.

"I've seen a lot of weird things over the years. Sibling rivalry and teens not getting along with their dads is nothing new."

Something about the reflective tone in his comment made me think back to how Lenny died. I vividly remembered a dream where Lenny fought with her dad over Wes, stormed out, and died in a car accident shortly afterward.

And all I did was remind him of that by rambling and complaining about the bookstore. Something that had nothing to do with us.

I leaned over and kissed him on the cheek. "I'm sorry."

"Sorry about what?" He was looking both ways, waiting to pull out onto the highway, but I knew him well enough to know he was thinking back.

"I'm sorry about reminding you of Lenny. I didn't realize. Dawn's stupidity really isn't that stupid." Fighting with your parent over someone you love is serious, especially if you're willing to give up everything for someone. I wanted to take Wes' mind off of Lenny's decision to come see him over her father's wishes. So I tried to change the subject.

"I don't know what you're going to do about Chase."

He looked at me for the first time since pulling onto the highway. "What do you mean?"

"Well, Mr. Chase thinks I have pretty eyes." I batted them trying to be funny.

Wes smiled. "You do."

"Yeah, but that's your job to remind me. Don't you think?"

"Sophie, anyone with a brain can see that. I can't get mad if another guy notices."

"Yeah, but he intrudes into my personal space."

Casually, still driving and focusing on the road, he replied, "Now that's another matter."

I smiled. Why is it that girls get a kick out of their boyfriends being jealous? I don't know, but I liked it. I bounced and shifted closer to him.

"Are you jealous?" I prodded, leaning over to kiss him on his ear.

"No." He answered confidently.

"No?"

"No, I'm not jealous. But if he violates your personal space again, let me know."

He turned toward me and kissed me on the tip of my nose, looking ever so confident and strong. *Yum*, was all I thought. Well, that's not totally true. I was also thinking about not wanting to go back to work. Unless Dawn was going to be there, it was going to be too weird. In the meantime, I resumed kissing Wes on the entire right side of his face and neck until he broke out into a laugh.

Chapter 9
THE FIGHT

A mazingly, Dawn managed to get herself out of major trouble. She ended up telling her parents that she and one of her friends, Jenny, met up to hang out with Jackson and his brother, and when she got tired, she just went home with Jenny. She said she never got her dad's calls because she left her phone in her car.

It was a ridiculous story, and I'm not sure Mr. Healey believed it, but he only grounded her for a week for sneaking out. He also told her that Jackson was off-limits until she learned to become responsible.

I was just glad that she was at work. Things were almost back to normal, other than Danny's strange *studying* behavior. He started leaving work earlier and earlier, until sometimes he took the whole day off. The story was that he had major tests coming up and wanted to start thinking about grad school for an MBA. None of us could picture Danny in a suit and tie, but Mr. Healey was just tickled pink at the idea.

Besides making Dawn sick, and making me curious as to what he was up to, I had no problem with Danny taking off work. Until Chase started filling in. He was extremely annoying. Just one of those guys who feeds off attention. It seemed like he expected girls to swoon over him and when they didn't, he shamelessly attempted to turn the chips.

When it came to Dawn, he managed to find ways to infiltrate her boundaries by doing something to make her laugh. He often walked by her and taped something onto her back, and once he put a dead cricket on the stack of books she was putting away. Dawn found him amusing. He was like a big brother who didn't know it all. Sometimes he got on her nerves, but the two of them couldn't go five minutes without cracking up about something.

I always ended up being the mature one. Maybe I just wasn't the horsing-around type, or it could have been that my history made me more serious. Either way, the bookstore was becoming a bit of a downer. All I thought about was Wes, all day, every day. Was I obsessed with him? Probably. Was that wrong? I don't think so.

If he wasn't meant to be the center of my world, then why did I keep coming back to be with him? No, obsessed was not a bad thing in my mind. It was simply the truth. He was my past, my present, and my future, and other than the safety of my mom and friends, nothing else mattered, including an annoying new attention sponge named Chase, who was cramping my style.

I had to separate the bookstore from my personal life, because if I didn't, I found myself griping about it the entire ride home with Wes. So I learned to block out the annoyances of work as soon as I got into his car. Wes wasn't even in the same league as a regular teen or college boy, and he made it a point not to even step onto the playing field. That was until Chase pressed his buttons.

Wes dropped me off one day at work, as usual, and Chase was outside smoking a cigarette. We pulled right up to the front, and I leaned over to give him a good-bye kiss.

"I miss you already," I complained.

He smiled softly.

I kissed him again and turned to get out when I noticed Chase staring intently through the windshield. *Peeping Tom.* Then I realized this was something different because, when caught, peeping Toms look away quickly. Chase was still staring—but not at me.

I followed his gaze to Wes, who was staring back.

"See you later," I muttered, dreading going in, wondering who called in sick this time.

Without taking his eyes off of Chase, he said, "Call me."

"Will do," I said, shutting the door.

I walked past Chase, wondering what his problem was. He took one long drag on his cigarette without looking away from Wes. Once inside, I turned back to see Wes backing out of the space, certain that Chase was still watching him. Dawn was there, which meant Danny was the one MIA.

"Where *is* Danny?"

"Where *is* Danny?" she repeated. "Since when are you Danny's keeper?"

"Since it means I have to work with *him*." I tilted my head toward the door.

She laughed, following me to the back room. "He's not that bad."

"Yeah, right." I checked to make sure he wasn't coming. "He gives me the creeps."

"Why? He's just a goofball."

"Yeah, with you. With me, I don't know. He's always looking at me like he's trying to figure something out. Not to mention he just spied on me and Wes kissing in the car." Maybe I was being overly sensitive. But still. "I just miss Ms. Mary."

"Yeah, me too. But, you have to admit, he brings some flavor to the store. It was getting way boring for me before."

She may have had a point, but I kind of like boring. There's nothing wrong with peace.

I relished the thought and put my purse away.

As if on cue, Chase interrupted. "Is one of you going to work the register, or what? A lady wants to check out, and I can't count, so it's one of you two."

Dawn laughed, as always, and that time I couldn't help but join her. Even though it was probably true, that was not why he wasn't able to check people out. Mr. Healey never trained him on the register. He only used him for stocking and inventory-type stuff.

Actually, the more I thought about it, Mr. Healey probably didn't trust him at the register. How did he get the job anyway? Oh, right. Danny.

I volunteered for the register and was reminded of his filthy habit when the fresh scent of cigarette smoke wafted off his shirt as I passed him in the doorway. I had never liked the smell of cigarettes, and now I hated it since Andy had reeked of it.

"Excuse me," I said, holding my breath.

Pretending he didn't know he was in my way, he stepped back, then forward, then finally to the side, his square dance over. Dawn probably would've found that funny too. Not me. I preferred to breathe, which I resumed doing after I passed.

After ringing up the sale, I started straightening up behind the counter, something Dawn hated doing. Thankfully, Dawn kept Chase occupied by playing hide-and-seek in the aisles when there weren't any customers. After about an hour, I got a text:

HOW'S YOUR PERSONAL SPACE?

I smiled. It seemed Mr. Chase's little staring episode got on someone else's nerves.

Taking the time to think of something clever, I responded:

TOO EMPTY. WANTS YOU.

SHOULD I COME NOW?

Mr. Healey wasn't in. Sometimes he left in the evenings and came back to close if Danny wasn't in. I could've asked Wes to come by, but it felt sort of selfish, especially when he was picking me up in a little while. Plus, for some reason, I didn't really want him there when Chase was there. So I went with patience.

TWO MORE HOURS, TWENTY MINUTES, FIVE
SECONDS AND COUNTING.

☺ SEE YOU SOON. LOVE YOU.

U 2.

"Who's that?"

"Geez." I jumped and snapped my phone closed. *Oh, my gosh.*

"Sorry. I didn't mean to scare you." His unapologetic expression and continued proximity near my shoulder told me that he wasn't.

"It's my boyfriend."

"Oh, I wondered. You looked so intent with those lightning-fast fingers."

I turned around and straightened the already straightened flyers on the counter, hoping he'd take the hint. He didn't.

"Actually, I came over to tell you I'm fighting this weekend. I think you should come."

What? "Fighting? Um. I'm not really into that."

"But it's fun. You should come. I think Danny and Dawn are coming."

"Maybe."

"Okay."

I turned in time to see him wink before walking off. The truth was I had no intention of going. None. Not until I got sucked into it.

After Wes picked me up, he drove me home and waited in my room while I took a shower. I no longer savored the bookstore smell anymore. Maybe it reminded me of all the unwanted changes there.

When I climbed into the bed, he was waiting with open arms. I unwound in no time, again reminded of my heaven on earth.

Unexpectedly, Wes jerked upright into a sitting position. "Oh, man. I forgot to e-mail Dr. Lyon."

I glanced at my alarm clock, and it was 12:30 a.m. "About what?"

Sitting on the edge of the bed now, he slid out his QWERTY keyboard and began e-mailing from his phone. "I signed up last summer for a medical conference in Arizona. I need to cancel. I meant to do it earlier, but it slipped my mind."

"Cancel? Why?"

He was typing away by then. "Because it's this weekend. It's on the use of alligator blood in creams. The lab is presenting."

"So why aren't you going?"

He turned, looking me in the eyes, and calmly and confidently answered. "Because I'm not leaving you for a weekend."

As much as the reality of that sucked, I couldn't let him give up all he had worked for to babysit me. "Wes, you shouldn't cancel. You need to be there. It's a huge breakthrough, and you shouldn't miss your lab's presentation."

Pulling me over onto his lap, he put one arm around my waist and the other hand kept clicking away. "I have plenty of people who can go in my place. It's not a big deal."

I put my hand over his. "It is a big deal,Wes. Finding medical cures is your whole life. It's your purpose."

"No, you're my purpose now, Sophie."

"*No*, finding cures for the sick is your purpose. You are *my* purpose. And my duty tells me you should go."

He stared at me in the blue glow of my alarm clock. I knew a million and one things were going through his mind, all related to my safety, so I used the only thing I could think of.

"Besides, Wes, I'm not nineteen yet."

Though I felt him tense at the mention of the age Amelia and Lenny had died, I knew he got my point. Even if I was going to die, as far as we knew, I still had at least six months.

"Why are you so set on my leaving you?" he asked, unsettled.

I scrunched my brows together. "Well, when you put it like that, it sounds awful. But seriously, how long would you be gone?"

"I'd leave tomorrow evening and come back Saturday night."

"So we're talking about twenty-four hours?"

He squeezed my knee. "It's not the hours that bother me, it's being that far away from you that I don't like."

I wrapped my arms around his neck and kissed his cheek softly. "We can do one day, as long as you don't break up with me when you come back this ti—"

He kissed me before I could finish. But I pulled back.

"As long as you don't break up with me."

He kissed me again, and between kisses whispered, "I don't know what you're talking about."

Before I could protest, he lay back with me on my bed. Making out with him was getting easier. He was much more relaxed when it came to being close to me, but it seemed that his momentary seducing episodes were very well calculated. He knew exactly how to make me forget any unwanted thoughts and only allowed them to return under much more peaceful terms.

Breaking our moment, he said, "I will not break up with you ever again. I'm yours every single day, forever."

I melted into his chest, but not in a passionate way. Hearing something like that only makes you want to be cradled in the arms of the one who said it. No kissing was necessary. All that was needed was the closeness of his entire body against mine. And I stayed there, just like that, for the rest of the night.

The morning brought much greater disappointment than I'd anticipated, since he had to be at the airport by 6:00 p.m. That meant I had to drive myself to work on Friday.

I was fine. I wasn't depressed about it or anything, but it only highlighted the fact that Wes was gone. I pulled into the parking lot, glad to see both Dawn and Danny's cars there. It was a perfect greeting to an evening of work, and just like old times, things were great. Danny and Dawn were actually getting along and even Mr. Healey was in good spirits.

I made it through work in a good mood, and had even picked up a new book to keep me busy that night. *Not.* Wes called me as soon as his flight landed in Tucson and I wouldn't let him get off the phone. Okay, *let* is a strong word. I simply talked my head off until my eyes were too heavy to stay awake, and he listened.

I heard, "I love you. Good night." Then I dozed off to dream of coconuts and a white horse.

Saturday was a drag. Not because anything was wrong at the bookstore. I just didn't like feeling the separation. For some reason, it makes a difference when you know the person you want to be with forever is only a few *minutes* away. I did things to keep myself busy all day, and thankfully the normal crew was at work again.

Mr. Healey was out running errands. Danny was shifting around some shelves and Dawn and I were hanging out at the register. She was extra bubbly as she twisted around on her stool.

I caved and opened a can of worms I wasn't sure I wanted open. "What are you so happy about?"

"Me? Hmm. Let's see. I'm off restriction and my dad is letting me go out with Jackson tonight."

"Really, so soon?" It was good news, but a little surprising. Her dad must've really believed her bogus explanation.

"Yeah. Well only because Danny will be with us."

I scrunched up my nose. "Danny is going with you...on a date?"

"No, I don't need a chaperone, thank you very much." I still wasn't following so she continued. "See, Danny and his friend Jared, who happens to be Jackson's older brother, are going to a boxing match tonight. Jackson is going too. Sooooo, I asked Danny if I could come, and he said yeah."

"Why would he let you come to a boxing match with him?"

She was getting a kick out of where the story was going and made me wait while she pulled a piece of gum from her pocket. Unwrapping it and folding it in, she said, "Because Chase is in a match and Danny owes me for ratting."

I was trying to picture the whole circus when she grabbed my arm.

"Hey, you guys should come too. Wes would probably like it. It's a guy thing."

I shook my head. "No, Wes is out of town."

"Then you come, Sophie. Please. It'll be fun. I'll probably be the only girl there."

"I don't think so."

She was squeezing now. "You can't stay home alone tonight. What are you going to do, have phone sex? Come *on*. It'll be cool."

"No."

"Sophie, seriously. What else are you going to do?"

"Nothing."

"Then come. Aren't you even the least bit curious? This is supposed to be big time. Danny says the guys are pretty good." She paused. "Hey, you might get to see Chase get his ass kicked." I perked up. "See? Now you want to come."

Although it did momentarily sound appealing, I didn't want Chase or anyone else to get beat up. "I don't want to see anything like that."

"Then do it for me. I don't want to feel like Danny is babysitting me. If you come, then it'll be like we're all hanging out—to watch Chase get beat up." She smiled.

I knew I should've just held my ground, but for some stupid reason, I have the hardest time telling people no. I thought it was a product of Wes' chocolate brown eyes, but I was learning that it was just a weakness of mine. I told her yes, but that I'd drive myself. I wasn't going to get stuck waiting for a ride home. She was thrilled and asked if she could ride with me.

Wes had told me his conference was an all-day thing, with a dinner to follow. Then he was heading straight to the airport. I had already told him to come over no matter what time he got back, and of course, he agreed.

In the meantime, I couldn't call him to tell him where I was going. Instead, I texted him:

DAWN IS DRAGGING ME TO A BOXING MATCH TONIGHT ☹.

He texted right back:

??
I KNOW. I MISS YOU.

I pictured him texting a hundred miles an hour, because all the questions, like where, what, when, who, came flashing across my phone. I quickly let him know that Danny, Jared, and Jackson were chaperoning. I neglected to tell him about Chase, only because I didn't want to distract him from the conference more than I already had.

At any rate, he seemed much more relaxed to know that big brother was coming. My phone buzzed one last time.

BE CAREFUL. SEE YOU SOON.

I knew by his choice of words that he wished he could be with me right then, and hidden somewhere in the undertone was a, "You probably shouldn't go without me." But I figured I'd be perfectly safe with Dawn and her older brother, so I didn't think much of it.

I turned to Danny, curious. "What do you wear to a boxing match anyway?"

He laughed. "Well, we don't have front-row, celeb tickets, so I would say whatever you're wearing now is fine." He seemed glad I was going, and I was starting to warm up to doing something new. That's one thing I could say. I'd never been to a boxing match before.

I went home to change, despite Danny's advice. I changed out my blue shirt and white sneakers for a black shirt and black Converse low-tops. Then I drew my hair up into a ponytail, applied a little bit of eyeliner, and drove over to Dawn's.

"You got directions, right?"

"Of course," she said with a *Duh!* tone as she hopped up into my Jeep. "But we have to get Jackson first."

"He's not riding with Jared and Danny?"

"No. They went out for drinks first. Plus, we thought we could make out in the back of your Jeep on the way." She winked in a joking way, only she wasn't.

They absolutely sat in the back of my Jeep, kissing and carrying on as I drove them around like a chauffeur. It felt odd to be around the two of them together. They seemed so young. They were seventeen, but for some reason, their carefree mentality made me feel older. Plus, they're complete opposites. She's dark-haired, outgoing, and bold at times, including the heavy eyeliner she likes to wear. Jackson's laid-back, usually dresses in light colors, and has perfect blond hair that nearly covers his eyes. The bangs sweep themselves perfectly in one direction. I wanted to take a pair of scissors to them, just so I could see his eyes. Then, realizing I sounded like my mother when it came to my own hair, I nixed that thought.

The venue was in Albany, and the only thing Danny gave Dawn was a street address. Computer mapped and ready to go, we headed to the location. All was smooth until I realized the computer printout was navigating me to an area of clubs and bars. No large arena or anything. I drove by a few dilapidated buildings and was about to turn around when I saw Danny standing on a corner with his hands in his pockets.

He flagged me down and pointed around the corner while waving his other hand to signal a nearby space. *This can't be right,* I thought.

All Dawn kept saying from the back seat was, "Cool."

We got out and met up with Danny and Jared. We heard club music pounding around the corner, and I thought we were headed toward it. Instead, Danny turned down a dark, narrow alley behind the buildings. It was just wide enough to fit a Dumpster and have enough room for one person to walk between it and the brick wall.

Danny stepped through the narrow passage first, and I followed close behind. Not because I was eager to go, but because I was not about to be the last person in line. Once we were past the Dumpster, the alley opened up to a dark, pothole-ridden path leading to what looked like a dead end. The deeper we went, the more I imagined rats and dead bodies at my feet.

"Danny, where are we going?" I asked, starting to get the creeps.

"Chase said it was around back." His casual voice was not calming my nerves.

We finally reached a metal door that read "No Trespassing."

Danny knocked on the door three times before it opened outward, toward us, tempting me to cover my ears as the weight of it scraped the asphalt. A rather large, bald, sweaty guy with tiny, birdlike eyes stood before us. His tight black tank top pressed against his man boobs and beer belly. And even though it was still very dark, I could see that tattoos completely covered his arms and neck.

"What?" he hissed with a deep, scratchy voice.

Dawn and I exchanged shocked glances and then she weaved her arm through Jackson's for protection.

Danny, seeming a little out of his element, but nevertheless prepared to negotiate his entrance, mumbled the words, "The red sun rises."

The guy looked at Danny and then at the rest of us. "There are too many with you."

Danny cleared his throat. "We were all invited."

"By who?" The man spat back. "Four max. That's the rule."

Counting Danny, Jared, Jackson, Dawn, and me, it was clear we were one person over the limit. I stepped up, about to volunteer to leave when Danny pointed to me.

"Yeah, she was a last-minute addition. Chase personally invited her."

Baldy raised his dark brows and gave each of us an intimidating look-over. Then he tilted his head toward the inside. "Hurry up."

The invitation felt more like a threat and caused me to jump a little. Temptation to leave overcame me, so I glanced down the dark alley and saw a group of men filing in past the Dumpster. Walking toward them alone was not an option for me, so I decided to cling to Dawn's other arm instead.

Once we were inside, a narrow hall led us down steep stairs and then to another metal door below. Hard-rock music was pounding on the other side. Danny pulled it open to a stench of sweat mixed with cigarette smoke. Instantaneously, I held my breath as I tried to figure out which was worse, the smell or the noise. After about thirty seconds, I decided it was the smell.

A few turns later we entered a large basement area with about twenty guys standing around. They were much more fit than the bouncer but had just as many tattoos. There was no ring, no ropes, and certainly no one in a tux announcing the impending rounds.

"Um, this is not what—"

Dawn cut me off. "Yeah, I know. Just stay close."

"Danny, what is this place?" I demanded.

"It's a fight club."

"A what?"

Before he could answer me, a stocky, shirtless guy about our age, with a dark buzz cut, slid past us. Danny's attention was fixed on him with an envious smile. I watched as the guy, wearing dog tags and camouflage pants, walked toward the center of the room. His torso was shaped like a perfect V and his stagger was confident. He looked in charge, but something about him looked weathered.

The crowd parted like the sea for Moses as he made his way through. At the center, he turned, and in a shocking, military boot-camp style chant shouted, "Are you rrrrreaaaddddy?" I thought he was about to drop and start doing pushups.

Instead, my senses were overpowered as the entire room of men shouted back, "Yes. We. Are!"

Suddenly, it was a chant, back and forth, with each round getting louder and louder until the leader was hopping up and down. Just when I didn't think it could get any louder, he stopped and crouched low to the ground.

His voice grew softer, and he said, "Let the fighting begin."

A movement to the right caught my attention, and a man stepped forward. He, too, was shirtless. Though taller, he was ripped and defined like the leader. Pale and already sweating, he had a fire in his eyes. Danny and Jared were nodding as if in respect for the guy. No doubt he was a familiar face there.

I knew nothing about fight clubs, but I suspected he'd been around awhile. He was probably thirty and had multiple scars on his face, including a nasty raised one going across both shoulder blades. He spit, then showed his teeth, raised his arms, and completed a three hundred sixty-degree turn.

As he stepped aside, a figure moved in from the left side of the room. Everyone's gaze diverted to a much smaller guy with a blond buzz cut and flannel shirt.

"There he is," Dawn whispered.

Once my brain finally caught up to my eyes, I realized it was Chase with a new haircut. Drastic, bold, vicious. I almost didn't recognize him. He'd been annoying before, but had never looked so intimidating.

Once he stepped to the center and turned our way, I noticed his unbuttoned shirt revealed a tattoo traveling from the center of his chest, all the way to the line where boxers were peeking out from his jeans. He was equally ripped, like the other guys, but more lean.

His introduction was less of a production, only releasing a small smile before turning toward his opponent. Once they were chest to chest, it was clear that Chase was just a kid. He couldn't have been older than twenty and he came up to the guy's collar bone.

I thought it might be nice just to see Chase get punched good one time, but this was not cool, not fair, and nothing I wanted to see. The leader had other plans. He clapped his hands together, and in an instant, the other guy was all over Chase like white on rice.

Within two seconds, Chase was in a headlock and getting punched in the face by the man's bare fists. Then he rammed Chase's head into a metal support pole and kneed him in the abdomen. I closed my eyes until I heard an unsettling cackle. I opened them to try to find the moron who thought this was funny, and to my shock, the odd laugh was coming from Chase.

The man kept punching him, over and over, and Chase was laughing the whole time. Blood began dripping from his mouth and then, out of nowhere, he spun out of the guy's hold and rammed the guy's head into the same pole that had been used on him. For a minute, I felt relieved, and then I saw Chase twist the guy's arm behind his back. In a swift motion, he lifted the man off the ground and slammed him onto that defenseless side. Everyone in the room saw and heard his shoulder pop out of its socket.

I expected the leader to jump between them. Instead, a smirk appeared on his face as he looked entertained. This was not entertainment. This was stupid and cruel. Chase, meanwhile, swelled like a beast, puffed out his chest for the audience, and then rammed his foot into the guy's side.

Unable to defend himself, the guy tried to stand, but Chase pounced on his back like a monkey, grabbing his hair in a violent grip. With no mercy, he began banging the guy's face into the concrete.

I looked away for what seemed like forever, and when I turned back to see if it was over, Chase was still ramming his face into the floor. The guy's eyes were swelled shut to the point that you couldn't tell if he had passed out or not. At that point, the expressions on the faces of the crowd began to change from being impressed to somewhat concerned.

It took three guys to pull Chase off his wounded victim. I turned my head as soon as I saw the man's bloodied face and mouth, both seeping dark, syrupy, thick blood.

"Oh, my God." Dawn said.

I covered my eyes. "He's missing teeth. Oh, my gosh." I felt sick. "I can't stay here," I said, starting to push my way through the crowd.

"Me either," she replied, just as grossed out. "Are you guys coming?" she asked, turning back toward Danny, Jared, and Jackson, who appeared more surprised than anything.

"No, we're gonna wait to see Chase. We'll be out in a minute."

We wasted no time shoving our way through the conversing crowd. Once out in the hall, Dawn said she needed to go to the bathroom. The hall reminded me a little bit of the one where Andy held me. I cringed as visuals of a bathroom with tea-colored toilet water flashed through my brain.

I convinced her to go alone while I waited right there. I stepped back with my shoulders against the wall. The hall started to get crowded with drunken spectators filing in and out. I lowered my head, trying not to make eye contact. I couldn't believe anyone would come to participate in or watch something like that.

After a few minutes, I started mentally cursing Dawn for taking so long when I felt my phone vibrate in my pocket.

"Wes!"

"Hey, you." His voice could've melted butter.

I pressed my ear to the phone, trying to hear better. "Are you back?"

"Yes. I just landed. What's all the noise?"

"Oh, my gosh. It's a *fight*."

He didn't sound concerned, and I suppose he wouldn't be. He was probably envisioning me at a regular arena, and surely there would be noise.

"Is it almost over?"

"Uh, yeah." The uncertainty in my voice was enough to raise a flag.

Concerned now, he asked, "What's wrong?"

"Nothing. It's just that I'm ready to leave and Dawn went to the bathroom, and I'm waiting for everyone."

"Where's Danny? Where are you?"

I scrunched up my face. "I don't know. Some crazy place."

He was getting agitated now. "Where exactly?"

I didn't even know where to begin to describe it. "I don't know. Some club." I didn't want to have to explain the situation in a shout over the noise around me so I was glad when I heard my name.

Thank goodness. "Dawn! She's back. Okay, we're about to leave." I hoped the newfound tone in my voice would calm the storm I'd started within him.

"I don't like not being there, Sophie."

"I know. Me either." I spoke softly and truthfully. At that point, Dawn was pulling me toward the room again. We weren't done with the conversation, but I knew we didn't have much time before it got louder. I squeezed in the most important issue at hand. "You're coming over tonight, right?"

He answered assuredly, "I'm on my way."

Dawn pulled harder on my arm. "Would you come on already? We have to find the guys. Hi, Wes," she shouted into the phone. "I know it's you. She's been thinking about you all night, but she's gotta go!"

"I'm sorry, Wes. Ignore her. I'll see you soon."

"Not soon enough," was all I heard, and felt, before he hung up.

Chapter 10
ON EDGE

O n the way home, Dawn tried to get me to take her to Jackson's, but I refused. I was obviously annoyed. After reminding them of her probationary status, they both slumped back in their seats.

"Geez, Sophie. You sound like my mom."

I hoped I didn't annoy my mom that much and realized that I was being too harsh with my friends. After all, they weren't the ones beating people's brains out.

"Sorry." I said, sounding sincere, but still firm. "But you're not getting into trouble on my watch."

My attention was divided by thoughts of the fight and trying to maneuver my way through side streets, looking for a way out. Dawn was, of course, unconcerned with our safety. I could've been driving her down a rat-infested, dead-end alley, and she would have still been focusing on Jackson.

Once I made it back to the highway, I let the agitation from what I'd witnessed pour out.

"I can't believe what we just saw. I mean, it was disgusting. Don't you think that was the most horrible thing? How can people even watch that stuff?"

Dawn spoke up quickly. "I don't know. It was pretty gross. I agree."

I continued my rant. "I mean who does that?"

It was quiet for a minute, but I needed some clarification. "Jackson? Is that, like, something you guys do all the time?"

Sounding much less appalled than I was, he answered, "Nah. We've been a few times. The first time we went, Chase got beat down. Then T took him under his wing and he's been vicious ever since."

"Who's T?"

"Oh, he's the leader."

My hands squeezed the steering wheel as thoughts of being dragged to that falsely described boxing match resurfaced. "Well, that'll be my last time. I'll probably have nightmares just thinking about it."

Dawn leaned forward. "No, you won't. Wes will be with you." She laughed deviously.

I rolled my eyes, but she was right, which did spark a small smile from me.

I got home around 11:30, left my terrace door unlocked, and took a shower. I felt ten notches better just getting the sweaty basement smell off of me. Eleven notches once I came back to my room and saw Wes.

I shut my door, locked it, went straight over to him and climbed onto his lap. I kissed him a hundred times all over his lips and face. He broke away only to press himself against my neck. In a secure hold, I held onto him for a long-overdue reunion.

"I missed you so much," I whispered.

He squeezed me just a little bit tighter and whispered back, "I'm not leaving you again."

Selfishness kicked in as I agreed that no matter what else came up, we would not be separated again, even if that meant I had to wear a lab coat and a pocket protector to the next conference. It just wasn't worth it.

Everything else seemed trivial compared to the time I had with Wes, especially when compared to egotistical guys trying to bloody someone else up just for kicks. I was so glad Wes was different. He was so full of substance, maturity, and purpose.

"You have no idea how much I missed you," I told him again.

"I think I'm getting a pretty good idea."

I yawned and that prompted him to carry me to my pillow, which was just for looks. My real pillow for the night was the inside of his bicep. I curled up to my linen of preference—his T-shirt, which smelled extra fresh and clean.

"You took a shower?"

Surprised by my accusing tone, he replied, "Yeah. I've been on the go all day. I wanted to freshen up."

"Please. You don't sweat. You don't get *un*fresh."

"I still need a shower. I deserve one too."

"Yes, but that meant it took you longer to get here." Every part of me was pressed against him now. Even my toes. I felt a gentle vibration in his chest as he held in a laugh.

"Aw," he said, "you really did miss me." He kissed my forehead. "You mean you didn't like the boxing?"

"Ugh. You mean fighting."

He pulled back slowly so he could see my face in the darkness. He wanted clarification.

"Yeah, it was *fighting*. Like back alley, underground, illegal, bloody, sweaty—"

He popped upright. "You went to a fight club? Danny took you to a fight club? Why would he do that?"

Now I had no choice but to spill the beans. Actually, I was looking forward to it. I don't think I could fully let go of the bad experience without sharing it with someone.

"Well, Chase was fighting. Only Dawn said it was a *boxing* match, and she begged me to go because she didn't want to be the only girl, and she didn't want Jackson to think Danny was babysitting her, plus she said Chase might get beat up and—"

He was laughing now. "Okay, okay. I get it. So were you able to see Chase get punched in the face?"

I exhaled the bottled up regret but rolled my eyes.

"What?" he asked.

"That's the thing, it was weird. He got punched a lot, but he wasn't fazed at all."

"Hmm. Tough guy, huh?"

"Yeah, but it was almost like he was on something." As soon as I said it, I remembered back to the party. His arms had needle marks and his eyes had looked like he was high for sure. "Now that I think about it, I remember needle marks on him at that party."

"Wait a minute. What party?"

I'd forgotten to mention to Wes that I'd seen Chase before, so I filled him in on my first encounter. Wes didn't comment, but I could tell he was thinking.

129

"Go on," he said, taking note of everything I said.

"So I noticed both those things then, which only heightened the fact that I was not interested in him. And now that I think about it, his arms were covered during the fight."

"That doesn't mean anything."

I shook my head. "Yeah, but you should've seen and heard him. He was insane. He actually laughed at the pain. Then he beat up that guy relentlessly until some guys pulled him off." I stopped. I felt myself getting all worked up, and I didn't like it. "I'm just never going to one of those again."

Wes started rubbing my arm with his palm, as if warming me up, but it was calming me down. "I wish I could've seen your face," he said.

"Oh I'll show you what it looked like."

I raised my face to demonstrate what I was sure it had looked like. It was a cross between how I imagined a person would look when a complete stranger puked on their shoes (disgust) and when someone realized they ran over someone's dog (horror). All of those emotions bottled up into one expression. That's what I showed him in the darkness.

"That bad, huh?"

"Yeah."

He pulled me close, still chuckling at my horrible evening.

The next morning I woke up to my mother on the phone in the kitchen. By the time I fixed myself a bowl of cereal, I figured out she was revisiting the idea of an alarm system. Apparently, Tom had knowledge of different types and was recommending a company to her.

As soon as she hung up, I jumped right on it. "Mom, we don't need an alarm."

"Yes, we do," she stated matter-of-factly.

Did I miss something? I knew she had been throwing the idea around, but now she seemed set on it. "Did something happen that I don't know about?"

As if I'd opened the flood gates, she shifted in her chair, looking at me head-on. "Well, I have a strange feeling I can't shake." That was nothing new. I kept eating. "I think I hear things at night."

"Like what kind of things?"

"Like noises on the terrace."

I almost coughed up my cereal. My mom's room was on the main level, right under mine. The only noise on the terrace would be Wes coming to the second-level deck to my room. But he was too quiet for her to hear anything. Plus, if there had been any noise, other than him, he would've surely heard it from my room.

"It was probably just animals."

She sipped her coffee, but still leaned intently toward me. "That's what I thought, but last night I heard a noise outside my window, and I got up. I didn't see anything, but I went to check all the windows and when I looked out the front, I saw a gray car drive by real slow."

She was so intent in her description that even I started to suspect something evil. Then I snapped out of it.

"Mom, a lot of cars drive by."

"Not at 2:30 in the morning."

I really didn't have anything to say after that. The only thing I was thinking about was that if my mom got an alarm, I'd be locked in at night, and Wes would be locked out. Even if we punched in the code, it would make enough noise to wake her. That thought was not how I wanted to start my day.

It put me in a grumpy mood, and I had a ton of homework to do. I had missed two online lessons with my teachers last week, so I needed to watch the recorded lessons to get caught up. It took me just a few minutes to log on and pull up the links. Still in my pajamas, I cuddled up in my chair and watched a lesson on Jonathan Swift's essay *A Modest Proposal*.

By the time I finished reading it myself, and submitting the assignments, I was ready for a nap. I'd been on the go for a few weeks by then, and exhaustion was catching up with me.

With dragging feet, I went over to my bed and wrapped myself in my sheets. My brain was feeling funny with all the thoughts that were bouncing around. Between my mom and her alarm, Wes and the police, me and my life, and work and its drama, I was amazed that it had taken me this long to crash.

The next thing I remember was popping up, wondering how long I'd been asleep. I was supposed to go to Wes' house around noon and was positive it was later than that. I just knew it.

I glanced at the clock—1:30. "Crap."

I threw off the covers and reached for my cell. Quickly dialing his number, I just hoped he wasn't too worried. I closed my eyes to block the light when I heard a familiar ringtone coming from my reading chair.

Confused, I opened my eyes again. "Wes! Holy crap."

He was sitting right there. "Sorry. I didn't mean to startle you."

"I fell asleep."

Smiling softly, he said, "I know."

"Why didn't you wake me?"

He moved over to the bed now. "Because I didn't want to."

"Because I was completely out of it?"

"That too." His hand was on my knee.

We were both holding back smiles. I was hesitant to fully commit to mine because of my disappointment in a wasted afternoon. His hesitation was different.

"What?" I asked. "Why are you looking at me like that?"

"You are just the most perfect thing ever. Even with huge circles under your eyes."

My hands went up to them immediately. "What kind of compliment is that?"

"An honest one. It's okay to need rest, Sophie. A lot has happened in the last few weeks. You don't have to be on the go all the time. You need to take care of yourself."

Now I tried to rub the bags from beneath my eyes. "You're right."

I pulled him down and nestled up to him for at least another hour, getting more needed rest.

By Monday morning, I was feeling better. Energized, no dark circles. I finished most of my work for the week, had lunch with my mom on Thursday, exchanged some kisses with Wes before I left campus, and then headed to work. And that's when the downer came. Its name was Chase.

I was shelving books when the doorbell chimed. Usually, it would've been Dawn in the store, but the little hussy called in sick, leaving me to work with him. I glanced at him as he walked to the back, expecting his usual smirk and flirty look, but instead I was greeted by a cold stare.

At first, I thought it was his new haircut that was making him look less friendly, but when he didn't look away, I knew he was purposely giving me an intimidating stare. I gave him an uncertain look then turned away, still feeling his stare as he passed. An odd, creepy feeling climbed up my back.

I was so disturbed by the encounter that I went up front and asked Danny to shelve for me. Mr. Healey was gone for a few hours, leaving us to man the counter. I started flipping through a comic book, trying to shake the annoyance that was building within, when a body slowly closed in on my personal space.

"So, I saw you on Saturday."

Was that a question? Not sure, so I kept it simple. "Uhh…"

"What did you think?"

That was easy. Without looking up at him, I answered, "I thought it was gross."

"Gross? Why is that?" He had positioned his elbow on the counter and was leaning in.

I looked at him now. His face was perfectly fine. No bruises, no sign whatsoever of the fight he had been in. But there was a coldness in his eyes that screamed viciousness, and then I remembered it fully.

"It was gross because it was bloody, cruel, and barbaric."

He looked like he wanted to smile, pleased with the memory. Not backing off, he said, "You know, Sophie, everyone has something they like to do. That's not a bad thing."

"It is when you thrive on hurting people." I was flipping back and forth through pages I had already seen when he stopped my hand. "You know all about that, don't you, Sophie?"

I was annoyed now. "Know about what?

"Hurting people."

"I don't know what you're talking about."

He patted me on my shoulder. "No worries. We all have secrets." Then he winked and walked away.

I felt the hours of rest in my body fade away as my nerves tensed all over again. I hated how my work environment had changed. It had been so perfect before. Now the tension, the games, the annoyances, the disruptions were all too much.

I was still frustrated when the bell chimed again. My heart tensed as Wes entered, carrying a big bag of Thai food. Although I was ridiculously happy to see him, today it felt uncomfortable. He could sense it too.

Walking directly over to the counter, he leaned over and whispered, "What's wrong?"

"Nothing," I whispered back. "I'm just tired of working here, with Chase."

He stood up straight, as if getting it now. "What did he do?"

Unfortunately, or fortunately, I don't know which, Chase hadn't done anything.

"Nothing." I sighed. "He's just so annoying. I hate talking to that guy. He gives me the heebie-jeebies."

"What were you talking about?"

"We were talking about hurting people." Chase interrupted, returning to his spot on my side of the counter, very much near where he had been standing before.

Wes didn't respond. Instead, the silence prompted Chase to keep talking.

"She thought it was cruel to beat up that guy on Saturday." He looked at me. "Barbaric? That's what you called it, right?" I didn't reply. Then he looked at Wes. "What do you think?"

Casually putting the dinner he had brought to me on the counter, he answered, "I think it's not so barbaric as long as it's an even fight."

Chase was about to respond when Wes cut him off. "Sophie, you want to take a break?"

I hopped off the stool. "Love to."

Brushing my way past Mr. Wannabe Gladiator, I hurried around the counter. "Let's go outside. I need some air. Danny!" I called into the aisles. "I'm going out front for a break."

Wes wrapped his arm around me, like a boyfriend might, but I recognized it as protective. As soon as we got outside, he turned me to face him. "I don't like that guy."

"Uh, *yeah*. I've been trying to tell you that for two weeks now."

"Well, you have my attention now."

Although glad, I was curious as to what sparked his distaste. "What did you see?"

Still leaning in very close to me and gazing seriously into my eyes, he said, "There's something about him that's off. Hatred oozed out of his muscles. He wanted me gone. I think he wants you and not in a normal way."

I didn't like the sound of that. "What does that mean?"

He looked back into the store then led me farther away from the window. "He was acting territorial, competitive. Like he wanted to challenge me right then and there. I want you away from that store. We don't need any more crazies, Sophie."

Okay, I had been thinking about how much I was beginning to dislike the bookstore, but he was acting way too hasty for my taste. "Wes, slow down. He's annoying, yeah, but I can't just quit."

"You said it yourself. You think he's on something. He's a loose cannon."

That was the first time I'd seen Wes ruffled and I wasn't sure how to calm him down. I was glad to see Mr. Healey pull up. Once Wes saw him enter the store, he seemed to relax at the idea of me finishing my shift.

"I don't want to go back, but I can't just quit because he's annoying. Besides, this is *my* job. Not his. *He* needs to get lost."

"Don't be trivial, Sophie. It's not worth it."

I reached up and put my palms against his cheeks and drew him in for a kiss. He pulled back, but I kept my hold and pulled him in. It was tense at first but, as always, I was able to relax him. "See? We're cool. Not going to let anyone annoy us." I kissed him again, before he could protest. "I only have an hour to go, and you can pick me up." Then I added, "Funnel cake? Please?"

He looked at me warmly. "Okay, but I'll be sitting out here until you get off."

Not worth the argue. "Fine," I conceded. "But now I'm hungry. So I'm going to eat my dinner, and maybe I'll see if Mr. Healey will let me off early."

I went back inside to find the bag missing from the counter. In the back, Danny and Chase were digging into my rice noodles. "What are you doing?"

Chase spoke up as he was spooning chunks onto his plate. "Oh, Danny said you wouldn't mind. He said you always share with everyone. It *is* a lot of food. And good too."

With compressed lips, I walked over and snatched my container from his hand. "It would be nice if you asked."

"Oh. My bad." Chase smirked. "You looked a little busy out there in your liplock and all."

I wondered how quickly Wes would come in here and wipe that look off of his face if I told him Chase took my food. Danny interrupted my thoughts by chuckling and I darted him a nasty look. He coughed himself into silence, and my gaze met Chase's again.

I could see it now. Chase got off on ruffling people's feathers. He obviously didn't get a lot of attention as a child. Now he thrived off of making people uncomfortable so he could feel more empowered. It was an ego boost. Once I figured it out, I decided to bring him down a notch.

I sat across from both of them and started eating. "So, Chase. Why were you the only fighter wearing a shirt?" The question took him by surprise. "I mean, there were a lot of hot, shirtless guys there, and yet you were covered up. What? No physique?"

He looked at me as if assessing my motivation. Then he smirked. "I don't need to show off my goods."

He started laughing and Danny followed suit.

"Is that why your shirt was unbuttoned? Because you didn't have to show off your goods? Or did you not want to show off your arms?"

His smile disappeared. He started moving his tongue around the inside of his cheek then picking his molars with his tongue, clearly agitated. I don't know what got into me, but I liked seeing *him* ruffled for a change. He was always the one bothering others and getting a kick out of it. It was time for him to get a taste of his own medicine. He moved his tongue to lick his lips, still watching me closely.

"Maybe you have a secret under there that you don't want the other fighters to know about?" I suggested.

It was twisted. My little attempt at a mind game. *Why am I doing this anyway?* I didn't thrive off bringing people down. Why was I so inclined to bring Chase down? It didn't really feel right, but it didn't feel all that wrong either. Until he answered, and then it felt eerie.

Leaning forward, he replied in a near whisper, "Now, Sophie, secrets aren't so bad. Everyone has them. Including you. *Especially* you." He started smiling. He was beyond irritating.

I looked at him with my eyebrows scrunched together, but didn't interrupt my chewing. "You don't know anything about me."

He chuckled. "I know you're the girl in that article. You're the girl whose boyfriend killed that guy."

I dropped my fork. "Oh, please." I looked at Danny and stood up. "You know, Danny. You really should find better friends. Ones who have a life and little bit of class."

I grabbed my trash and tossed it as soon as I reached the door. As I suspected, Mr. Healey let me off early and Wes was waiting.

I plopped into his car, trying to contain my irritation. "That guy gives me the creeps. Why is he so annoying? He purposely tries to irritate people." I was talking more to myself, but I wanted Wes to hear. I wanted him to chime in, but he didn't. He just listened and drove. "Something has to give. I don't need to work there if it's not fun anymore."

The truth was, I was starting to doubt myself. Maybe it was me. I'd never liked hanging out with people. Getting a job at Healey's was perfect. It was small. Dawn and Danny were great, and Mr. Healey and Ms. Mary stayed out of the way.

Ever since Chase came, he was always in someone's face. Maybe I was out of line to be so annoyed. He didn't seem to bother anyone else. Well, actually, he did. He bothered Wes too. And Wes could read people well. Wes knew when someone wasn't right. In a way, it made me feel better to know it wasn't just me, but at the same time, it put me on edge. I would have to decide what to do about the store.

Chapter 11
PARTY NUMBER TWO

W es took me to get funnel cake, like I had asked, except this time we picked it up and took it to the overlook. Now that he had the Range Rover, it made the overlook that much better. He backed in and opened the tailgate. That way we were able to raise the hatch and lie in the back. He had huge down blankets back there and we could get comfortable and look out over the hills and up at the stars.

The funnel cake was particularly good that evening because he fed it to me. I used my hand as an excuse again. Neither one of us mentioned the store. Instead, we laughed while we covered our lips with powdered sugar.

"You know," I started, "it's your turn to pick our next getaway."

He leaned back on the blanket with his arm behind his head. "You're right."

"So what's it going to be?" I lay back too.

"I don't know yet. Let me think about it. I want it to be somewhere good. And somewhere far away from here."

Chase must have really irritated him. Suddenly, I had visions of the white horse again.

"Dawn says they sell white horses down at Claggett Farms."

He laughed.

"I'm serious." I paused. "Okay, well not about the horse. But getting away. I'd leave, you know."

He pulled me in so I was lying on his chest. I could still see the stars. "What about your mom?"

I thought for a few minutes. I'd miss her and she would miss me like crazy, but she had Tom now. And they were happy. He'd take care of her.

"It's not like I'd never talk to her again. Or see her. I just want to be somewhere with you. Just us. No worries. Somewhere remote." I felt him exhale a small chuckle, but he was quiet. "What are you thinking about?" I asked.

"Ah, I'm just thinking about it. Where I'd take you. What we'd do. How happy that would make me."

I lifted my head to tell him to take us away then, but his phone rang. I hate when his phone rings, because it usually means he has to leave. Or worse, that one of his labs was broken into again. I wondered if we'd ever be able to stop worrying about that. Could we go to a place where we were surrounded by nothing? No phones. No connection to the outside world. Just me and him, together, like fate meant us to be. It sounded clichéd and selfish, but I didn't care. It's what I wanted. And the more time that went by, the more I realized it was what I deserved. I'd already lived two short lives without getting to experience a lifetime of love.

And I wanted that with him. *Is that so bad?*

He pulled the phone out of his pocket and the backlight lit up the space around us. He glanced at the number, made a confused face, and answered. Immediately, I heard a bubbly female voice. A few things went through my brain, like, *What the...? Who in the...? Wait a...!* Finally, I propped myself up on my elbow.

He spoke softly. "Oh, I see. Um. I might. I'm not sure. I'll see, but if I can't, I'll see you Monday for sure. All right, I'll try. Bye."

He put his phone in his pocket while I watched and waited.

"What were we talking about?" he asked.

"We were talking about who was on the phone."

He looked up. "Oh, that?"

"Don't be cute. Yes, that."

"That was Brandie."

"Brandie?"

He moved to pull me to his chest. I held back.

"Yes, Steve's girlfriend."

An irritated feeling crept through my body, tickling every nerve. I think it was jealousy. I shook off the thought. "Who's Steve?"

Acting like it was no big deal, he answered, "My lab partner."

"So why is Steve's girlfriend calling you?"

"Are you jealous?"

No shame whatsoever. "Should I be?"

He just looked at me and cocked his head to the side without answering. I was left to consider my insecurities. So maybe I was having a moment. He couldn't have made

144

it more clear to me that I was the only person in the world that he wanted, and I started to feel guilty for my insecurity, but not enough to quit.

"Just tell me why she's calling *you*?"

He smiled a little. "She was inviting me to a surprise party for Steve tomorrow. It's his birthday."

That's all? "Okay." I lay back down, getting relaxed again, and then I popped right back up. "Wait a minute. Your lab partner's girlfriend, as in that was *Blondie*? Brandie is Blondie? Blondie is Brandie?"

He let out a long sigh, probably realizing his plan to get me to ignore the connection hadn't worked. "Sophie, calm down."

"What? The girl you used to make me jealous after you broke up with me just called your phone?"

I was getting so mad, but not mad at him. Mad at her for enjoying it too much while walking with him on campus. And putting her hands all over Wes to make me think he wasn't into me was one thing, but calling him up, all bubbly, was another.

"Sophie, please. You're being so silly right now. If you don't know I'm not about anyone but you, then…"

I shook my head. "No. This is not about you and me. I trust you. One hundred percent. Really. It's her I don't trust."

I didn't think for one second she wasn't interested in Wes. She was way too convincing with him on that path. She had enjoyed leaning into his tall, hard, lean body way too much. I saw it. I remembered. She was evil. She *wanted* to hurt my feelings.

145

"When is the party?" I asked.

"Tomorrow night. Why?"

"Because I want to go."

"No, you don't. You hate parties as much as I do."

"So? We're going. It's your friend's birthday, and Blondie needs to know there's a new sheriff in town."

He laughed out loud. "You're not a sheriff."

"No, I'm your girlfriend, and you hurt my feelings by walking with her and letting her touch you. She needs to know you're taken. For good."

"Taken?" He was looking at the ceiling of the Rover now, considering the word. "What does that mean?"

"It means I'd like to consider you mine. For me only. Forever."

Smiling slightly, he whispered, "So I'm taken then." He leaned over to kiss me, pulling me to him by the back of my neck. He kissed me, holding back a smile, and in between kisses, he added, "Do you want me to wear a sign?"

I kissed him like I normally would and then I pulled back. "No. Just taking me to the party would be good."

"There's no need." He tried to kiss me again.

Oh, yes there is. I had cried for almost a half hour, sitting in my Jeep at this very spot, after I saw her "pretend" to be his new girlfriend. His attempt to change my future by separating us and making me think he was dating someone else had been hurtful. I wanted closure. If she had no interest in him and was all about Steve, then our going to the party together wouldn't be a big deal. Either way, one thing was sure, we were going, and he didn't argue.

The next morning, I woke up with a mission. It started with my calling Dawn to hash out some things about work. I mainly wanted to ask her why she kept calling in sick so much. She had no real answer.

"Dawn," I told her, "you can not keep leaving me with Chase." She laughed, but I was serious. "It's not funny. He ruins my whole day."

"Oh, stop it, Sophie. He's harmless. You have to just ignore him. I do."

"I don't want to have to ignore him. I just want to work in peace."

I wasn't all that convinced that she was paying attention, or had any intentions of working when she was supposed to, so I let it drop. This was something I had no control over.

When I had finished the conversation, I went downstairs to grab some breakfast. In the kitchen, I saw a man in a white utility shirt and navy pants. I blinked and took a step back.

My mom came up behind me. "Oh, hi, honey. It's okay. You can go in. He's just here for the alarm."

"Alarm?"

She brushed past me and went over to the coffeemaker, looking back with an excited smile. "Yeah. He's installing the alarm. Remember?"

"On the window?"

"Yes. He's installing them on every door and window. We'll be secure for sure."

She was stirring in her cream and sugar now. My shoulders drooped as I walked over to the pantry to get my cereal. Trying not to sound too bummed, I asked, "So does that mean I'm locked in?"

She laughed and went over to the table to sit. "No, silly. It means strangers are locked out."

Wes wasn't a stranger, but the alarm would mean he'd be locked out. This was not cool. No way could I sleep with him locked out. I had gotten so used to him being next to me. This was horrible. Filled with thoughts of loneliness, I immediately began to consider ways to get around it. Nothing came to mind, but I knew I'd have to figure something out. I was not about to go endless nights with us across town from each other. This was an issue that needed to be addressed, but I had more important things to get through first.

Later that evening, I needed to get dressed for the party. While not being a person who's concerned with her wardrobe, I have to admit that I stared at my closet for a long time. My outfit of choice suddenly became the most important outfit in the world. More important than what I wore on my first date with Wes.

I felt petty, but at the same time, I couldn't shake the motivation to look my best. I would be a high-school girl among a bunch of college girls, and I was sure I'd be with the finest guy at the party.

Ugh. I knew Wes loved me, and that what we shared was stronger than what anyone in that room would probably ever experience, but I also feared their hawklike gazes staring at me, trying to figure out who I was. So my outfit was not something to take lightly.

I weeded through a zillion shirts and jeans. *What color?* Black was too dark, brown was too bland, pink too innocent. Purple too immature. Yellow too happy. Blue too pure. That left green. I scanned the hangers until I found a sea green tunic and then moved onto the jeans.

I had nice jeans, but I didn't want to look too put together, so I settled on a pair of skinny jeans that were faded, with a vintage feel. I left my hair down. Somehow, I felt more protected that way, almost like it would shield me from the eyes I feared.

Wes came to pick me up at 8:00. He wasn't smiling as usual and I knew it was because he didn't like my motivation behind this.

"Would you relax?" I said, climbing into his SUV.

"I just think this is petty, Sophie. It's really not necessary."

I pouted, wondering if I was really that out of line. Then I started doubting why he was so set on not wanting to go. Maybe he was protecting Blondie, and that idea made me angry.

He glanced over at me, realizing I was starting to get mad. "Okay, we'll go. I just don't think we need to be drawing attention to ourselves."

Considering his reply, I ran through the potential chain of events and nothing of concern stood out.

"It's just a party, Wes. A bunch of college kids."

He breathed in deeply and exhaled, put his hand on my thigh, and started driving.

We arrived at a single-story house near the campus. There were a lot of kids spilling out onto the lawn and into the street. Wes crept through them, being careful not to run over anyone, and we found a parking spot about two blocks away. Even houses that far down had students lingering on the front porches.

"Are these fraternity houses?"

He nodded and walked around to my side and opened the door. I hesitated. I think I was starting to regret the whole idea. Only my stubbornness caused me to get out of the car instead of suggesting we go.

He took my hand, interlocking our fingers and led me toward the party. I could hear the house boom-boom-powing from around the block.

He ignored it, leaning in toward my ear. "You look beautiful tonight."

I blushed and looked down. My hair fell forward, covering my eyes.

He reached over and moved the bangs behind my ear. "You know you're going to be the center of attention here, don't you?"

"Why is that?" I asked, confused and fearful all of a sudden.

Maybe I didn't realize how popular he was. Maybe I didn't realize how many people would probably crowd around him, wondering who he was with. Wondering who that girl is. *Oh, crap.* I felt my stomach tighten with an awful feeling of nervousness and cringed.

He pulled on my arm until I was pressed against his side and then he wrapped his arm around me. Leaning down, he whispered, "Because you will, hands down, be the prettiest girl here." I smiled at his compliment, although still nervous. "I might have to keep the guys off of *you*. What did you call it? Sheriff? Yeah, I think I might need a badge tonight."

I had my arm around him now and squeezed, realizing how insecure and immature I had been for wanting to come here. What we shared was more powerful and more unique than anything at this party. Right then, I wanted to leave. To be alone with him. That's all I needed.

I was about to speak up when a tan, dark-haired guy, who looked about Wes' age, walked up to us with his hand out. He was dressed more casually than Wes usually was. Faded jeans that were frayed at the bottom, flip-flops, and a T-shirt, but by the wide smile he wore, I knew he was a friend.

"What's up, man?"

Wes smiled and greeted his outstretched hand with a low high-five that moved around a bit into some sort of shake before they lightly bumped shoulders together.

"Nothing much," Wes answered. "Happy birthday."

"Thanks. I can't believe you came. We never see you off campus."

The guy looked shocked; then his gaze moved to me.

Wes took the cue. "Steve, this is Sophie. Sophie, this is Steve."

Steve raised one brow and nodded his head in approval. "Nice to meet you, Sophie. She's even prettier than I imagined." He looked back at Wes with a sly smile. "Come on, man. Come inside. Everybody is here."

Wes still had his arm around me as we followed. My mind was going a hundred miles an hour about how much

I wished I'd spoke up about leaving just a minute sooner. But it was too late. We were there and his friend was way too happy to see him for us to leave then. I sucked up my regret and my heart started racing. I tried to slow its beat, but it only pounded faster and harder. I think Wes could hear it, because he pressed me even closer as we approached the open door.

It helped, but not enough. As soon as we got inside, people started greeting him. He worked the crowd like a professional. Smiling, introducing me, never letting me go. It wasn't so bad. Everyone was really nice. Everyone. Even Blondie.

She bounced out of the kitchen like a cheerleader. "Wes! You came. I'm so glad." She was so hyper she could easily be heard over the music.

I tensed at first. I thought she was going to hug him, but she stopped before she got too close.

"Is this Sophie?" I'm not sure who else she thought I might be, but I supposed it was the normal thing to say. He nodded.

"Sophie, it's nice to meet you. I've heard so much about you. We never see Wes anymore. He's obsessed with you."

I wasn't sure how to respond, so I just smiled.

"Anyway," she said, "drinks are over there and cake's in the kitchen. See ya, guys." And she was off, on her way to mingle with the crowd.

Wes leaned down smugly. "So, Sheriff Slone, will you be arresting anyone tonight?"

I nudged his chest with my cast. "Shut up."

He laughed. "Want a drink?" he asked. I paused. "Water or soda, of course," he corrected.

"Yeah, I think so."

He cleared the path toward where Brandie, I decided to use her name now, had pointed earlier. We reached the table and had eaten a couple of chips with dip and were about to get some soda when I felt his back stiffen. His hold on me tightened, he raised his head, and his eyebrows moved together a little.

I tensed too. I'm not sure why, but feeling his change made me uneasy. "What's the matter?" I asked.

He pulled me to his chest like we were about to slow dance. It was an odd hold since the thump of the blasting music didn't exactly constitute a slow dance, but I wrapped my arms around his waist anyway. I looked up and watched him look around the room.

"I don't know," he said. He was still looking around. "Something's off."

Confused, I tried to pull back to get a better look but he didn't let go. I was about to insist that he tell me what was happening when I heard a voice.

"Don't I know you two?"

Wes turned around to reveal Chase standing behind him, looking smug.

I rolled my eyes. "Chase? What are you doing here?"

He had on a white long-sleeved, fitted T-shirt with black jeans. I also noticed he was wearing dog tags and had a bottle of beer in his hand. Not making a move to shake hands, he stood still as a statue with his gaze on

Wes. Noticeably shorter, he tilted his chin up to highlight the fact that he was watching Wes.

He smiled slightly. "I go here, you know. Or at least, I used to. And I like parties, so I'm enjoying the festivities."

My thoughts ranged from annoyance to wondering why Wes was so tensed up. Then I remembered what Wes had said about feeling hatred flowing out of Chase. But what was there to hate? Neither one of them was speaking, so I tried to pave the way for our exit.

"Oh, that's nice. Well, we were just leaving."

At that point Chase looked at me. He tilted his head and leaned in closer. "Wow, Sophie. That shirt looks really nice on you. I like the way it brings out those eyes." He smirked.

I hated this guy. He was such a pest, and he was purposely trying to irritate Wes.

"Thanks." I said pulling Wes to the side. He obliged, but Chase stepped into our path.

"I bet people tell you that all the time." He was leaning in, trying to get closer to me, but Wes shifted me behind him.

"Uh, sometimes," I said trying to step around.

He looked at Wes. "You know, you should put a leash on her because someone just might steal her away and make a pet out of her. A pretty-eyed pet."

I saw Wes' jaw flex, but he maintained his composure and effortlessly moved Chase out of our way with a slow but firm swipe of his arm.

"He's just trying to mess with you, Wes. He gets off on the attention. Ignore him."

154

"I am. Let's go." He started moving toward the door. We were almost there when I heard a thud. I wasn't sure where it had come from, but Wes turned around. Chase had tried to sucker shove him from behind, but it ended up just sounding like a hard slap instead.

Chase looked a little stunned that Wes hadn't been propelled forward but refused to let up. He hustled up to Wes and got right in his face. I was stunned, but Wes' face was stoic. I couldn't tell if he was mad, surprised, or scared.

Then he calmly said, "Chase, I don't know what your problem is, but I'm taking Sophie out of here, and I'm going to act like you didn't just try to make a fool of yourself. Now, if you'll excuse us."

Chase just laughed and stepped even closer.

Wes lifted his arm from around me. "Sophie, go outside."

"What? No!"

"Sophie..."

"We're leaving together," I said.

I glanced at Chase and saw a look in his eyes similar to what I'd seen that night at the fight club. I knew right then that this was not going to end well.

"Come on, Wes," I urged. I looked at Chase and squeezed between them. "Don't be stupid, Chase. Leave us alone. I'll stop being mean at the bookstore. I'm sorry, okay?"

He smirked again, still looking at Wes. In a firm voice, he said, "You think this is about the bookstore? No. This is bigger than that. I know scum when I see it." By then a crowd had gathered.

"Sophie," Wes said. His voice was firm now. "Go outside, please."

"No, I'm leaving with you. Now let's go." Now *my* voice was firm.

I pressed against Wes' chest, trying to back him toward the exit. He started backpedaling, which made me glad. But then I felt my hair being pulled. Chase had grabbed a handful and yanked me to the side. The force was so strong that I stumbled. A bystander grabbed my arms and I instantly heard scuffling. My heart flipped around inside my chest.

I turned back to see Wes grab Chase by the throat, shoving him back swiftly. Within seconds, Chase's back hit the wall with such force that two large pictures fell, crashing to the floor.

Wes lifted him off the floor and pinned him against the wall. Chase was unable to speak, but he was flexing every muscle as he tried to pry Wes' hands off his throat. After a moment, he started kicking like he was running in place, but the more he kicked, the harder Wes squeezed.

Chase's grunts ceased and his fiery stare turned to shock when he realized he couldn't budge Wes one centimeter.

Wes leaned into his face and spoke slowly, making each word clear. "You are a little boy, with little aspirations. I suggest you find something else to do besides pick on girls and start fights you can't finish."

Chase was turning red. Wes lowered him so his feet were on the ground, but held tight to his neck. "I'm going to walk out of here, like I planned, and if you try to stop me or lay your hands on Sophie ever again, I'll have no choice but to finish what you started."

Chase was starting to fade, his eyes closed, so Wes finally let him go. He crumpled to the floor and grabbed his neck. Everyone in the room stood wide-eyed and quiet. Wes walked over and put his arm around me, guiding me to the door. We passed a few people, including Steve.

Wes spoke up. "I'm sorry, man. I don't know what his problem is. I tried to leave."

Steve, still a little shocked, patted his shoulder. "Are you kidding? I would've done the same thing."

I looked back to see people close the open space we had created and start dancing to the music again, still wearing looks of shock.

Chapter 12
NEW TO THE EXTREME

W es walked me to the car without saying anything and worry began to build with every step. I began stressing about how I'd dragged him here. None of this would've happened had I'd listened to him. But, once again, I had drawn attention to us.

He opened my door, and I couldn't hold it in any longer. "Are you mad at me?"

He looked surprised. "Don't be ridiculous."

I stepped closer to him. "Then why aren't you talking?"

"I'm just thinking." He leaned in to kiss me on my cheek and then signaled for me to get in. I didn't want to. I wanted to stand there until I knew he was okay, but my stubbornness had already caused enough trouble. I got in and he closed the door.

We drove for a few miles and the silence was killing me. "Wes, please tell me what you're thinking."

Still looking straight ahead, he said, "I don't know what that was back there. I'm trying to figure it out."

"It was just Chase. I'm telling you, he gets off on challenging people."

He shook his head. "No, Sophie. He was on something. He was crazy. He was…"

"He was what?"

"He was stronger than a normal person."

I didn't understand. "He wasn't stronger than you."

"Trust me, he was stronger than normal. He was almost like…"

He stepped on the brakes and pulled over. The abrupt deceleration propelled me forward, and without the restraint of my shoulder strap, I might've hit the dash.

"Almost like who?"

He turned to face me. "He was like Andy. I can't believe I didn't make the connection."

My heart stopped. "What? No. Wait. You don't think—"

"I don't know what I think right now, but I know you are not leaving my sight for a second. And you are not to go near that bookstore."

"Okay, wait. Let's think about this for a second. What's happening?"

"Sophie, this could be bigger than either of us realize. If Andy was on some sort of serum derived from what was stolen from my labs, then who knows who else is."

"Andy wouldn't have spread it around. He wanted it for himself, and for his—Oh, my gosh. His grandson."

Wes leaned his head against his headrest and closed his eyes. He started massaging his eyelids in a circular motion with his palms.

"Wes, Chase can't be Andy's grandson. No way. He's just on regular drugs."

He was still rubbing his eyes.

"Wes, you're scaring me."

He exhaled. "It all makes sense." He opened his eyes and turned back to me. "I can't believe I didn't see it."

"See what?" I was getting worked up now.

"The party. The bookstore. Ms. Mary. Chase messing with you all the time. Chase hating me. Chase challenging me."

"Wait a minute. What about Ms. Mary?"

"Think, Sophie. He approached you at that party you went to in January. Then, after Andy dies, so does Ms. Mary. Then he conveniently has a job at the bookstore. He always provokes you, and now he challenges me in public." He paused and closed his eyes again. After a minute, he whispered, "He knows."

"Knows what?" I grabbed his hands.

"He knows about the gator blood. He knows about us."

I froze. No. It couldn't be. There was no way. It was just annoying Chase. Or was it?

He was annoying, but he was also insanely inhumane. I had watched him beat that guy to a pulp without a single ounce of mercy. I watched him laughing as he was being punched in the face. I had watched him overpower that man with superhuman strength. And he told me I had secrets. He told me his hatred was bigger than the bookstore. I sank back into my seat. Now I was the one rubbing my eyes and it wasn't working. I couldn't settle my nerves with silence or thoughts. I needed facts.

I sat up straight. "Wes, take me home. We need to get to my computer."

He looked at me, confused. "For what?"

"Research. We need to find out about Chase. We don't know for sure. We can't assume. We need details."

He nodded, respecting my rationale, and put us in motion and back onto the highway. Once we were in my room, I quickly slid into my computer chair. I typed Chase's first name then realized I didn't know his last name. I only hoped it wasn't Walters. *Please, don't be Walters.*

I turned to Wes, who was pacing my floor. "I don't know his last name."

He stopped in his tracks and started biting his thumbnail. After a minute, he started pacing again. I sensed his frustration building.

I thought for a moment, my gaze following him. "Wait. I know."

I hopped up and grabbed my cell phone. Within seconds Dawn picked up. I didn't even say hello.

"Dawn, this is Sophie. What's Chase's last name?"

She was silent for a second. "Chambers. Why?"

"Thanks!"

I hung up the phone, realizing that I'd been rude, but was too concerned to call her back. I went back to my computer and typed "Chase+Chambers" into a search engine. Apparently there were a lot of people named Chase Chambers out there. It would take too long to sort through all of them, so I decided to try Facebook.

I didn't have an account, but my best friend in Virginia did. Kerry had given me her password because there were a few times she wanted me to go in and peek at some profiles of students at my old school.

Once I logged in, I searched for Chase Chambers. He was easy to find once I narrowed down the city. His thumbnail was a picture of him, shirtless, with a tattoo of a snake slithering down his abs.

I opened his wall and there were a bunch of comments from other guys with buzz cuts.

Nothing stood out linking him to Andy. I was reading through his profile when I realized Wes was now looking over my shoulder, reading intently.

I quickly scanned the posts and nothing seemed out of the ordinary. I closed out, trying to think of something else. *Andy,* I thought. As creepy as it sounded, I had heard of people's pages still being active after they died, so I took a shot.

Sure enough, Andy's page was still active. Wes quickly knelt beside me, reading the information on the computer screen. We opened Andy's profile photos and found several pictures of his family, most of his son in military fatigues, but only one of his grandson. The picture was old. It was taken in front of a Christmas tree. In it were Andy's son, a woman who I took to be the mother, and between them was a boy. He looked to be about ten years old. His hair was dark, unlike Andy's, and although it was hard to see his face clearly, it was easy to tell he was not Chase.

I relaxed instantly. So did Wes. Both of us exhaled. Wes looked at the floor and then stood up. He walked over to the bed and plopped down silently. I turned back to the picture for further confirmation. I looked closely, feeling relieved, but like I had seen the boy somewhere before. I looked even closer. The names under the picture read: Sally, Johnny, and Timmy.

I started to feel sorry for them. I had remembered Andy telling me that his son died in combat and his daughter-in-law died of cancer. That meant Timmy was the only one still living. I wondered about him. I remembered Andy saying he had wanted to make him the new Wes. *What is he doing now?*

I closed out the webpage, trying to block it out. I felt sorry for him in a way, but was so glad it wasn't Chase. Chase was just a messed up, attention-seeking, wannabe tough guy. I lay down next to Wes. He put his arm around me and gave me a gentle squeeze.

"What do you think?"

He let out a built-up sigh. "I don't know what to think. I still don't like how I felt around Chase. I still don't like you being around him. And I still don't like not knowing who else is out there."

I understood that. I felt the same way about everything he said, but I didn't want it to affect us.

"But you do feel better, right?"

"Much better." He definitely seemed more relaxed than he had been moments before, but still not completely himself.

I had an idea. "You know what?"

"What?"

"I think things are going nuts around here. My mom is locking me in once this alarm is activated. My job is really not fun any more. And Chase is a weirdo. I think it's time for us to have another getaway."

He pulled me closer. "I think you might be right."

"Good. Now where to?"

He started stroking my hair. "Wherever you want."

"No. It's your turn to pick, remember?"

"That's right. Let me think."

He was quiet. I tested him about how far he was willing to go. "Maybe the Bahamas? Hawaii?"

"You can't go that far. Your mom will never go for it."

"Yes, she will. I'm eighteen. I can do what I want. Okay, well, she will if I tell her it's a spring break getaway with a friend."

"You don't need to lie to your mother."

I kicked one leg, like a spoiled child. "Oh, come on, Wes. I want to go far away from this place. We need a *real* break."

"You're right about that." He was silent again. "How about Virginia?" he finally suggested.

"Vir*ginia*?"

"Yeah, you're always talking about visiting Kerry again. That's pretty far away, and I'm sure your mom would approve."

I was sure she would too. I went every summer to visit Kerry.

I sat up in the blue glow of my clock, looking at him. "You forgot one thing." I leaned closer, waiting for him to acknowledge it. He just stared back at me. "It's *cold* in Virginia," I said.

It was early March, and that meant it could still get really cold there. In fact, two of the biggest blizzards I remembered had been in March.

"I'm not afraid of the cold, Sophie."

I rolled my eyes and plopped back down. "Well, it can snow there in March too."

"Really?"

"Yeah, really."

He was quiet.

"I haven't seen snow in I don't even know how long."

I was quiet.

"I think it would be nice," he continued.

"Are you joking? Come on, Wes. You can't get cold."

"I can't get hot either, so Hawaii is out. Plus, it's a lot easier for me to keep warm than it is to stay cool when it's burning up outside."

"I am not taking you into the snow."

"Sophie." He turned to me now, and I was glad I couldn't see those chocolate browns in the darkness. "I'd really like it. You're the one who says we need to take the future on a detour. Try new things. What's more new than that? And I wouldn't go if I thought I wouldn't be able to handle it."

I shook my head. "Then why can't you remember the last time you've seen snow?"

"I didn't have a reason before. Now I do. I *want* to take you to see your friend and I *want* to go somewhere new."

I didn't say no, but I didn't say yes either. It was insane. Was he kidding? Visions of him in hypothermic shock after he jumped in to save that drowning girl last November flashed through my brain. I shuddered.

"I'll be fine."

"How can you say that when you almost died just by jumping into cold water? No way. I'm not going there again."

He moved my hair away from my face, and made me look up at him. He kissed my forehead. "That's because I wasn't prepared. Once you got me warm, I was fine."

"Wes, it's probably going to be forty degrees or lower, the whole time. No *way*."

He chuckled. "They have coats and hats and scarves. I *can* go out in the cold. Just not for long periods. They do have houses in Virginia, don't they?"

"Stop it. Of course they have houses."

"Then it's settled. You're taking me to see some snow."

I opened my mouth to protest, but he kissed me first. I pulled away, but he pressed further, rolling himself on top of me. I felt his wide shoulders hover over me, making me feel small and protected. Making me feel *good*.

He was *so* not playing fair. My eyes rolled back in complete bliss as I let him kiss me. His lips traveled down my neck onto the bare skin that was peeking out from the neckline of my tunic.

I shoved him. "Stop it."

He lifted his head. "What's wrong?"

"I know what you're doing and it's not working. I don't want to go to Virginia."

"Yes, you do." He kissed me again. Same spot.

"Wes, please. This is serious."

He stopped. "Don't you trust me?"

Catching my breath, I said, "Of course I trust you."

"Then believe me when I tell you I can go to Virginia. I'll be fine. I want to go away with you. *Please*."

"Well, get off of me then."

Taken aback by my request, he responded in a shocked voice, "What?"

"I need to think straight. And I can't with you seducing me."

Without argument, he rolled over so that no part of his body touched me.

I pondered the details. Okay, if he had a heavy coat that held in the warmth, and we stayed indoors most of the time, then maybe. Kerry's family had a nice ski chalet in Wintergreen. Wes would actually like it there. It reminded me of his place. We could stay nice and toasty in there, and the view was to die for. Well, not literally.

"Are you sure about this?" I asked.

"Yes, I'm sure. Does that mean we're going?"

As unsure as I could possibly sound, I answered, "I guess." It was almost like a question.

He quickly rolled back over and gave me a big kiss. I must say it was nice seeing his mood change. I no longer felt his worry, frustration, anger, or concern. He seemed much better. More relaxed, for sure. I only wished I felt the same.

Chapter 13
PLANS

I was so glad Wes had stayed the night, because Mom had the alarm activated the next day. No more sneaking in at night. At least, not until I could figure out a way to bypass my zone. It sucked. But it caused me to dive right into making plans for the trip. The more I felt locked in at my house, the more I wanted to get out.

I called Kerry on Sunday to feel her out about a visit, and she was stoked. She said we could use her parent's ski chalet for sure. She and her boyfriend Rich went up there with friends almost every weekend in the winter. I'm sure they all had a great time, but I honestly didn't want to mingle with anyone from my old school.

I had to ask. "Is it just going to be you and Rich or are you bringing others?"

"Oh, no. We barely hang out with anyone anymore. There's so much drama going on. I'm *so* over it. You can bring friends, though. I'd love to see a bunch of people with California tans."

We planned the trip for the following weekend, and once I finished talking to her, I moved on to Mom. It was surprisingly easy. I had gone skiing with Kerry several

168

times, so she was fine with it. She didn't even ask me if I was taking anyone, so I didn't have to go there. She was used to me flying back there alone, and just assumed it was the same old, same old.

The next morning, I called Mr. Healey and told him that I couldn't work with Chase anymore. I didn't mean to get Dawn in trouble, but I told him that if Dawn was going to be out and Chase was filling in, then I'd have to take off. He agreed, but asked why. I didn't go too far into detail, but I did tell him that Chase purposely distracted me at work.

No offense to Mr. Healey, but I thought it was the smart thing to do. I couldn't stand the tension between Chase and me anymore, and there definitely didn't need to be any more encounters between him and Wes.

While I had him on the phone, I requested Friday and Saturday off, assuring him it was only because I was going out of town to visit my friend in Virginia. Not that I was avoiding work altogether. He had no problem with that.

By the time Wednesday came around, Dawn was already in on my request off. I guess her dad was trying to find coverage. She called me first thing that morning.

"Why are you sticking me with him?"

"Who?" I asked, barely awake.

"Chase."

"What? What are you talking about?"

"Oh, don't play dumb. I know what happened last weekend. Chase told me that Wes attacked him."

"What? Dawn, please. Wes wouldn't attack anyone."

"Well, that's what Chase said."

"Well, *he's* a liar."

"So what happened then?"

"Chase was being Chase and purposely trying to get on my nerves. He was flirting with me in front of Wes, and then told Wes he should put me on a leash before someone steals me."

"No way."

"Yes, way. And when Wes and I tried to leave, he still kept egging him on. Then he sucker punched Wes in the back and grabbed my hair. Wes had no choice but to put that little punk in his place."

"Oh, my gosh. That is *so* not what he said."

I really didn't care what he said. I was over it. All I wanted to do was avoid him.

"Well, anyway, thanks to you, he's all over me now. Messing with me. Asking me what your problem is all the time. Ugh."

Sorry to hear it, but he isn't my problem anymore.

"So where are you going anyway?"

"Skiing." I answered, still not quite believing it myself.

"Where?" She shot back.

"Virginia."

"Oh, cool. You're so lucky."

There was a moment of silence.

"Well, the real reason I'm calling is because I was hoping you could give me a ride to work. My car's in the shop, and Jackson has to work."

"Sure."

I picked her up at 3:30. She usually arrived at work at 4:00.

170

She wasn't in the car two seconds before she started up with our earlier conversation. "So who's in Virginia?"

"My friend Kerry."

"Cool. Are you going *alone*?"

"No…"

"I knew it! That is *so* not fair. I want to come. And Jackson. Please take us with you. Please."

I looked at her and she had her palms together, like she was praying.

"Please?" she pleaded.

I did not plan on bringing anyone but Wes. I really didn't want company, but the more I thought about it, the more I realized that she and Jackson just might provide more company for Kerry and Rich than we could. We were going to a ski area, and I wouldn't be able to ski. Wes and I would mostly be holed up in the house.

Although that sounded wonderful, I considered the pressure we might face when Kerry and Rich wanted us to go outside a lot. Dawn would get along well with Kerry, and having her there might actually afford me more time alone with Wes.

"Kerry did say I could bring some friends."

"That's awesome! I can't wait to call Jackson!"

"How are you going to get your dad to okay it?"

She was already calculating. "Oh, he loves you. He'll let me go as long as it's with you. And let's just say he doesn't have to know about Jackson."

Oh, geez. I didn't want to be a part of her lie.

Oh, who am I kidding? My mom didn't know about my traveling companion either. I just hoped to goodness none of our parents came right out and asked.

We pulled up to the store and there was a gray four-door car parked out front. Chase was leaning in the window. I cringed and chose the farthest space I could. He looked up and then looked away as if he didn't know it was me. Dawn got out, completely excited about planning her newfound trip.

"Do me a favor, Dawn?"

She turned back. "Sure."

"Don't go talking about it, okay? It's no one else's business, if you know what I mean."

She smiled and then winked. "Gotcha. Lips are sealed."

As I backed out of the space, I couldn't help looking over at the car again. Two men in some kind of uniforms were talking to Chase. He was nodding and shrugging his shoulders. They appeared to be giving him instructions. By then I was out of the space and turned my Jeep the other way thinking only happy thoughts of not having to work with him anymore.

I told Wes that Dawn and Jackson were coming, and he agreed that having them might take the pressure off of us to ski. He immediately called for the extra tickets. Although I didn't mean for him to pay for all of them, he did anyway.

I worked on Thursday and, thankfully, Dawn showed. She was giddy all day. I thought she was going to blow it for sure. She couldn't stop talking about how excited she was. I was hoping to play it cool in case Mr. Healey started asking a bunch of questions. Luckily, he didn't.

Later that evening, Wes picked me up to go shopping. Neither of us had any real winter clothes anymore, so we both needed warm, rugged gear, and he knew exactly the place. Located near the mountains was an extreme sports shop. The parking lot was filled with SUVs with bike racks and two or three had kayaks attached to the roof. I laughed.

"What?" Wes asked.

"Well, I think this solidifies that I'm an outdoorsy girl."

"Oh, your getting into the lake solidified that."

His eyes were beaming at me with such pride that I couldn't help but remember how great it had been. Getting away with him, trying something new, it all came back to me about how wonderful this trip was going to be. I just wished I could shake the feeling that we were insane.

But, I have to admit, he did a good job of leading me toward sanity. He, as always, was thinking ahead. As soon as we entered the store, he walked right up to the counter and asked for help. The three employees standing there in their fleece vests and khaki pants looked well qualified to assist.

A little too quickly, the girl in the pea green vest stepped up. She looked like she was about our age, maybe a little older, and she didn't take her admiring gaze off of Wes for one second. A little possessiveness surfaced, but I quickly remembered my previous lesson in insecurity. *You can look*, I thought. *Just don't touch.*

Wes politely asked, "Can you tell us where to find your heated jackets?"

She looked at him with a smile that stretched from one ear to the other, but not in a friendly "I'm here to provide great service" way. It was an "I'm trying to look sexy in my pea green vest" way.

"Sure, they're right over here."

She walked ahead, and Wes motioned for me to go first.

"So," she turned back, disappointed that I was the one right behind her, "going camping or something?"

I glanced at Wes, realizing that my proximity to her meant that I was the best person to answer. "No, we're going skiing."

She looked back again and forced a grin. "Oh, that's nice." We arrived at a section of fleece jackets. "Here you are," she said.

"Thanks," Wes and I replied at the same time, which was awkward. She didn't know who to look at first. After she figured it out, she told Wes that she would be nearby if we needed anything. Once she was gone, we were free to shop.

"What are these?" I asked.

"They're heated, windproof fleece jackets. I read about them."

I picked one up. It wasn't very heavy. "How does it work?"

He picked up a different one, and flipped it inside out. "See, it has a battery pack that sends heat through these wires. It keeps the chest and back warm."

I smiled instantly. "You are so smart."

There I was, thinking he would be shivering to death on the trip, and he found a heated jacket. It was perfect. "What size?" I asked.

He flipped the one he was holding back the right way. "A large will do."

We both started looking through the coats for the right size when I heard that voice again.

"We have heated gloves and socks, if you like."

I turned to see the clerk lurking by the coat racks. "Thanks," I shot back, really meaning it. I looked at Wes. "You are *so* getting some of those too."

I was getting really excited now. It was sinking in that the trip was actually going to happen, and the best part was that it would really work. Wes could stay warm without being wrapped in a zillion layers of down.

We found the gloves and socks, along with some heavy sweaters. He wasn't interested in special pants or anything. He insisted he would be fine in regular jeans. I figured if we decided to hit the slopes, we could find him some ski pants once we got there, but I doubted that would happen.

When we finished picking out his outerwear, he insisted I get a few things as well. I just wanted a couple of sweaters and some boots. He wanted me to get a heated jacket too, but I passed.

"I'm used to the cold," I told him. "I miss it, actually. I'm looking forward to freezing my butt off."

"You should still get one. I don't want to watch you freeze."

"I'm an outdoorsy girl, remember?" He wasn't convinced. "Seriously, Wes, I lived in Virginia. Winter was one of my favorite times of the year. I love the snow. I want to embrace it. I'm not going to be a wimp about it."

He raised his brows and his lips parted almost like I'd punched him in the stomach. I looked at his face and realized I had insulted him.

"I'm sorry. You're not a—I mean you're *different*. That doesn't count as being wimpy."

He finally cracked a smile. I sighed in relief and then *my* lips parted when it hit me that he had been pulling my leg. He wasn't insulted at all. I smacked his arm with my good hand and then said, "Ouch."

"You're going to have two casts if you don't watch it."

He grabbed my hand and, laughing, kissed it.

A nearby cough from the eavesdropping sales girl brought our attention back to our mission.

I loved winters in Virginia and I liked to ski, but didn't care for fleece all that much. I preferred sweaters, so I picked out some that were really warm and cozy. I was excited, just thinking about being there. Although I still feared the cold because of Wes, I was kind of hoping for snow. It was beautiful, especially at Kerry's chalet.

The whole back was windows and you could sit around the fireplace, sip hot chocolate, and watch the snow fall. It felt like being in a giant snow globe. I missed it, and I guess it showed on my face. Wes smiled again.

"What?"

"I just know you're happy that we're going, even though you won't admit it."

I didn't respond, because I was still having major reservations, but I did reach up and kiss him on the cheek to show him that he might be right.

Then we, or should I say he, paid for our items and I nearly fell over when the guy behind the counter told us the total amount due.

"That'll be $592.76."

I was adding and multiplying frantically in my head while Wes casually handed over his credit card. Still mentally calculating, I snatched the receipt from the bag before he put it in the truck.

I felt like my mother, in a bad way. She always audited receipts whenever we left a store. I can only remember one or two times when she actually found an error, but that didn't stop her. And here I was doing it.

"What are you looking for?" Wes asked.

"A mistake. Oh, I don't know. I just can't believe it cost that much."

A thorough look-over of the receipt explained it. The most expensive items were the heated things. The coat alone was $230, and then Wes had bought gloves and socks. He had also picked out a couple sweaters, long johns, and warm pajamas.

One thing was for sure, we were prepared. We would be warm. We would have fun. At least, I hoped.

Chapter 14
THE FLIGHT

O ur flight was set to depart Friday at 6:45 a.m., so I picked up Dawn the night before. Mr. Healey actually did some fact-checking by calling my mom to talk about the trip. She let him know that I had made the trip a few times before, it was a safe place, nice people, blah-blah-blah.

So Dawn was fine on the parent front, and including her seemed to please my mother. The thought of me hanging out with my friends made her very happy. Little did she know I was just setting the stage for some alone time with Wes.

We packed the Jeep before we went to bed and a 3:00 a.m. alarm had us at Wes' by 4:00. Jackson had told his parents he was going camping for the weekend, and that wouldn't have included me giving him a ride, so he arrived around 4:15 in his own car.

By 5:00, we all climbed into Wes' Range Rover. I felt excited and nervous as we made our way to the San Francisco airport.

Wes took the initiative and struck up conversation with Dawn and Jackson. It turned out Jackson was a music buff and knew almost as much about artists from the '60s and '70s as Wes. By the time we pulled into the parking lot, I knew we would all get along perfectly.

Inside, we checked our bags, went through security, and headed through the terminal. Thirty minutes later we were boarding the plane. At my insistence, Wes had his heated coat in a carry-on bag, which he stowed in the overhead compartment.

"Window or aisle?" he asked.

"Aisle." No hesitation.

He slid into the row, taking up the spot closest to the view I wasn't looking forward to seeing. Jackson and Dawn sat directly in front of us, and no surprise, she hopped right in next to the window. She was eagerly staring out like an excited child.

I shook my head. "I hate flying," I whispered in Wes' ear, hoping not to alarm anyone else. There was no need to draw attention to the what-could-and-could-not-happen possibilities of flying.

"Really?" he replied. "Although, I don't know why I'm surprised. You're afraid of heights."

"I hide it well," I said.

And I do. I absolutely loathe flying in every way. In fact, my nerves were in a zillion knots at that moment, but I usually just sucked it up and took slow, deep breaths, not to mention the little pills my mom gets for me whenever I fly.

Like clockwork, I reached into my handbag and pulled out a sedative. I turned to see if I could flag down a flight attendant for some water, but the bottle was snatched out of my grip.

"Hey!" I turned to see Wes tucking it into his pants pocket. "Give those back."

He was smirking. "You didn't say 'Swiper, no swiping.'"

"This is not funny. I'm doing my best not to embarrass you, here. I need those. Come on." I reached over to try to dig them out of his pocket.

He moved my hand away. "You're acting like a druggy."

"I am not." I pouted. "I'm just trying to relax."

"You don't need a drug to relax on this flight, at least not while I'm here."

I cocked my head to the side and dropped my shoulders. "Wes…"

"I'm here. I'll relax you." He touched my nose with the tip of his finger. "Promise."

We locked eyes in a brief staredown until I gave up, thinking of an easier avenue to what I wanted. I scooted to the edge of my seat and stuck my head between Jackson's and Dawn's headrests. "Dawn, do you have any Valium?"

My brief moment of hope ended when she turned and looked at me like I had two heads. "Why on earth would I want to be sedated?"

It was useless. I flopped back into my seat and let out a huge sigh. I knew I wasn't getting my pills out of Wes' pocket, and I wasn't about to go asking other passengers for something. I was frustrated and irritated, and out of the corner of my eye, I could see Wes watching me, smirking. I refused to look his way.

"Swiper," I said, and then leaned my head against the headrest, buckled my seatbelt, closed my eyes, and tried to meditate.

I heard him chuckle, but refused to look at him. Within a few minutes, I felt him pull on my elbow until I was leaning into him. He wrapped his arm around my shoulders and kissed my forehead. I ignored him, but didn't pull away, and although I felt better on the inside, I wasn't ready to admit that yet. After a few minutes, he started talking, his voice soft so that only I could hear.

"Remember what I told you my father did for a living?"

I didn't answer.

"He flew planes, Sophie. He designed them."

I opened my eyes. "He also died in a plane crash. *Hello?*"

"Yes, because he was trying out new designs. Things weren't as controlled a hundred years ago like they are today."

I closed my eyes again and buried my face against his chest. "It doesn't change things."

He kept talking. "Not to mention I've flown for, what, seventy years now? If you could see the planes I used to fly... My point is that I wouldn't take you on a plane if I didn't believe they were the safest way to travel."

Eyes still closed, I muttered, "Not the point."

I didn't care about safety statistics. It just wasn't natural to be jetting through the sky a million miles up. I didn't like it. It wasn't that I feared dying, necessarily. I feared the fall.

And it wouldn't be such a big deal, if I could've just taken my pills. A little sedation was all I needed and I was good.

"All right, so I'll stop talking about flying. How about..."

"No. Just be quiet for a minute. I need to clear my head."

Giving me a gentle squeeze, he whispered, "Okay."

After a few minutes, he said, "Do you really need them? I'll give them back if you really..."

"Just shush...please?"

Call it reverse psychology or whatever, but I didn't ask for the pills. My stomach was still in an uncomfortable knot, but everything else felt more relaxed. My brain felt warm and fuzzy and I knew it was because of Wes. I would've much rather absorbed his tranquility than any prescription drug.

Takeoff was always the worse. I hated how the plane felt as it struggled to climb. I dropped my head and pinched my eyes closed. By the time it felt like we were floating, I knew we had leveled out at our targeted altitude. Slowly prying open each eye, I saw Wes staring out of the window. He looked content, like when he'd taken me to see his race car hangar last fall. He was in his element, and suddenly I felt curious. Flying was something he was passionate about. And I had buried myself in his armpit, being a chicken, when it was a perfect opportunity for me to learn more about Wes. Not the Wes I know now, but the one I couldn't remember or never had the chance to know.

I untucked myself from beneath his arm and repositioned myself so I was leaning on his shoulder. I tucked my arm under his and turned toward him. He looked away from the window, curious.

"So, tell me about your flying."

He turned toward me, noticeably pleased that I had asked. Then he leaned in closer to isolate our conversation. "Like what?"

"Like everything. Like why I should be so happy to be flying in this particular one."

"Well, my dad was part of the group of aircraft designers in 1896 that built steam-propelled models, and he also played a big role in developing the first planes to be propelled by an internal combustion engine. He was actually test-flying a gasoline-powered plane when he died."

I could tell he wasn't looking for sympathy, but I still gave his arm a soft squeeze.

"For a while, I envied my father's death. It sounds weird, but as a child, I always imagined him having an exciting, wonderful life. Remember how I told you my mother never let me go anywhere or do anything because of the hemophilia?"

I nodded, listening attentively and watching his expression closely.

"Well, my mother had pictures of him standing beside all the different planes with their mesmerizing wings. I wanted to be there, in those pictures. Even though I knew they killed him, it didn't matter. The pictures seemed so alive. So much more alive than I had ever felt.

"That was why I was so intrigued when I saw Amelia that day in London. The excitement in your eyes. They spoke to me and told me you loved where you were going. Almost like my father's looked in those photographs, but more. Watching you made me feel so much all at once." He trailed off, looking out the window again.

I squeezed his arm and snuggled closer to his shoulder. "That's sort of how I felt when I crashed into you." I felt him laugh, and then lean his chin into my hair. "So when did *you* start flying?" I asked.

"When I came to America. You know about the Ford Model T that Dr. Thomas bought me so I could loosen up, but I didn't tell you about the flying. I spent quite a few years looking for exciting things to try. I raced cars, rode motorcycles—"

"Wait. Motorcycles? When?"

"1923."

"They had motorcycles then?" I smiled, picturing what one might look like.

"Oh, yeah." He smiled, and I wished I could see what he was seeing behind those eyes. "I had a Harley-Davidson."

"What did it look like?"

"Well, picture a bicycle with a banana seat and tiny motor, without the pedals."

I laughed out loud. "I *so* wish I could have seen you on that."

He was about to continue when I thought of something else. "Why don't you still have that? You kept your first car."

He took a deep breath. "Because I wrecked it."

"You crashed?" I popped up, although I don't know why it bothered me now. Clearly, he wasn't severely injured, as he was sitting next to me. Anyway, I shook the feeling.

"Yeah, I did. Someone drove right into me and ran over the bike with me on it. The bike was toast. The guy just kept going, didn't even look back." He paused. "I liked that bike too."

"Were you hurt?"

"No. A little sore, maybe."

Unbelievable. "So you traded the bike for a plane?"

He shook his head. "No, I stuck with cars for a while and then, in the summer of 1933, aircraft engineer Arthur Raymond designed the first twelve-passenger airplane for TWA. It was a DC-1.

"I followed his progress in the '30s until he made the DC-3. It was a beauty. At the time, the Boeing 247 was getting all the hype because it took seven hours off the average 27-hour cross-country flight. But, when that DC-3 came out, that's all people were talking about.

"Seeing that plane, just in a photo, was the first time since Amelia died that I almost felt excited again. I pictured my father standing beside that plane. Then I pictured me standing beside it.

"That's when I told my uncle that I *had* to fly on one. So, in the spring of 1936, he took me to New York and back."

"And?"

"It was amazing. We had seven stops and it took almost twenty hours total, but it was the wave of the future back then. You'd laugh if you saw it now. There's so much more technology in the planes today. There's backup system after backup system, and they practically fly themselves."

Hmm. Well, I just hoped this plane would fly us straight to our destination and quickly.

Dawn unplugged her iPod and turned around. "Where's the flight attendant? I want some muffins or something."

I looked around in an attempt to help her spot one, but gave up quickly. I heard her suck her teeth as she put her ear buds back in.

"She might be waiting awhile," Wes said.

"Why?

"Times are hard. The economy and decline of people's trust in flight safety have airlines tightening their pockets. It's sad."

I was surprised to hear him talk about it as sad. I thought it was cheap, not really a big deal, but he had something to compare it to, and I didn't.

"In the '30s and '40s, airlines were competing for passengers, like today, but it's not the same. Back then, airlines took pride in being respectable. Today, they just want to be profitable. When passengers stepped onto a DC-3, they felt the pride of the airline, and the flight attendants took honor in making the passengers feel like they were on a vacation. Now, it's all about implementing rules and procedures and giving the minimum to gain the maximum out of passengers' dollars."

He had given me something to consider. He was talking about planes, but I couldn't help wondering what the world was coming to in general. Wes was sitting on the medical discovery of the century but no one could know about it because people would go nuts over it. I don't think

I was totally convinced before, but after my encounter with Andy, and the ruthlessness at the fight club, I was beginning to believe it.

Wes had seen so much greed and selfishness unfold over the decades, and the sad thing about it was I wasn't sure how or if it could be fixed. But I couldn't let go of the feeling that if anyone could change the way the world thought, it would be the person sitting next to me.

I heard Dawn snore, and by the tilt of Jackson's head, I assumed he was out as well. I looked at my watch and it was only 8:00. In fact, most of the passengers were resting. A few people had laptops out and some others had books. I thought about reading, or even picking Wes' brain some more, but I noticed he was gazing out the window again. He seemed lost in thoughts that I didn't want to interrupt. I decided to rest my head on his shoulder and close my eyes. I thought about being somewhere on the ground, hoping my dreams would take me to that place.

I didn't sleep well. There's no way I can sleep peacefully while in motion. It's the same with cars, but I must've been in and out, because Wes needed to tap my leg to let me know we were descending.

I lifted my head, hoping to see the ground. Instead, I saw clouds. "Why didn't you wait until we were on the ground?"

"You don't want to miss this. Look." He pointed out of the window.

"No, that's quite all right."

"Look. It's beautiful."

I shook my head, still not interested.

"You're missing Lake Michigan."

Although it did pique my interest a little, I still wouldn't look. He, on the other hand, was leaning into the window. "You don't get to see a skyline like that every day."

I remained staring straight ahead.

"And look at that. A carnival."

"Where?" I asked, perking up.

"Right there." He pointed.

"Wow." I smiled a big cheesy grin, not realizing I was lying across him to get a peek.

There it was, a carnival located next to a pier. A huge Ferris wheel, and a giant swing that was spinning like a merry-go-round, captured my attention in an instant. It looked unbelievably fun *and* far down.

Realizing how high we still were, I tensed and sat back in my seat. "I've seen enough."

Right about then, the pilot's voice came over the intercom, letting us know we were preparing to land at our destination, Chicago Midway Airport. I clutched Wes' arm until we touched down. Now it was okay to look outside.

Relieved and curious, I watched through the window as we taxied to our gate. I noticed right away the gray hue of the sky. It looked cold.

"Wes? Was Chicago the only layover option?"

He started zipping up his jacket. "No, I think there was Las Vegas too."

"Then why did you choose the coldest one possible?"

"Sophie, we're not leaving the airport. Relax."

I made a face that should've accompanied a growl.

"You're not going to be a big grump on this trip are you?" He smiled.

I nudged him. "I just might."

"Lucky me." He sighed.

"Yeah, lucky all of us," Dawn interjected.

"Shut up, will ya?" I shot back.

She scowled.

"Ignore her," Wes told Dawn. "She's having a moment."

I huffed, feeling like the odd man out. We were all holding back a smile.

"Fine. Let's go, tough guy."

We all walked off the plane and into the terminal. Wes was right, we didn't leave the airport, but it still felt cold. He was fine, or at least he was acting that way. Dawn and Jackson went their own way to check out food choices. Our layover was only about an hour, so Wes and I stayed close to our next departure gate. There was a little eatery nearby, along with a bunch of yummy dessert stands, but I passed, not wanting to upset my stomach for the flight.

We boarded our next plane as soon as they let us.

Wes decided to challenge me to a game of rock-paper-scissors during the plane's takeoff. It worked up until the wheels left the ground, and then I had to close my eyes and rest my head against the seat.

"You're just mad because you were losing," Wes said.

"Whatever." I smiled.

Things went smoothly once we leveled off, but apprehension was building. Our next stop was Virginia.

"So tell me what Virginia is like."

I looked at Wes, wondering if he was holding back some sort of mind reading skill. "Why?"

Taken aback by my tone, he answered, "I've never been. I thought you might want to tell me what I'm in for."

"You're in for cold."

He smiled and licked his lips in a way that I was sure was meant to distract me. "Other than that. What else?"

I took a few deep breaths, trying to let go of the horrible feeling that we were the stupidest people on the planet right now. Once I pushed that out of mind and thought about what Virginia had to offer, I started to feel better.

"Their slogan is 'Virginia is for lovers.'" I smiled.

He laughed out loud. "Okay, we'll fit right in. What else?"

"It has four seasons, which I love. Just when you get tired of a certain temperature, the weather changes for a couple of months, and when you get tired of that, it changes again. It's great." I felt myself smiling with each reflection.

"It also borders Washington, DC," I continued. "And where we're going is convenient to just about everywhere. Virginia Beach is a few hours away and, of course, there's the mountains."

"It sounds like a great place."

And it was. I couldn't deny that.

Right about then, the plane dropped and my stomach jumped into my chest. Several passengers let out nervous squeals. I grabbed my armrests as my heart started pounding. Deep breaths and Wes beside me were not enough to make me feel calm.

With my eyes closed, I heard a professional voice on the loudspeaker. "Attention, passengers. We're flying through a patch of turbulence, and as soon as we get through it, we'll turn off the Fasten Seatbelts light."

Before I could open my eyes, Wes was already buckling me in. He didn't look concerned.

"What about you? Have you nothing to fear?"

Straightening out my shirt beneath my belt he replied casually, "Only of losing you."

"Well, that might just happen," I huffed.

"We're not going to crash. It's just a little turbulence. It's fine."

"Right," I replied sarcastically. I closed my eyes and started counting, slowly. I reached seventy before the pilot came back on to tell us we were all clear.

"See," Wes said. "These planes are built to withstand a lot."

At that point, I was getting a little annoyed at his overly cool persona. "Have you never been scared on a plane? Ever? Seriously?"

Reaching over to unbuckle me, he said, "I never said that. I was scared once," he admitted.

"Really?" I looked at him, trying to tell if he was pulling my leg. "When?"

"Actually, it was in the eighties. I was flying a Cessna 152 with a flight instructor. I already knew how to fly, but I still had to go through the motions and get my license as Weston II. Anyway, my flight instructor's name was Dan. He knew right away that I could fly. He called it a natural ability that must've been in my blood."

That made me laugh a little.

"He was quick to show me new things, just for kicks. We became pretty good friends. He said I was his favorite student, because I never showed fear. One day, we were in a practice area, doing maneuvers. It started when he asked me if I wanted to roll the plane, so I said, 'Sure.'"

"How do you roll a plane?" I wasn't sure I wanted to know, but I interrupted anyway.

He put his hands out like he was steering a car. "Well, you make sure the plane is coordinated and you pitch the nose up, and then turn the yoke. Then you hold it until you come full circle."

I was staring at him and I don't think I blinked once. "In English, please?"

He laughed. "Just take the yoke, the handlebars," he clarified, "and pull up the nose by pulling the handlebars toward you, then turn the handlebars in the direction you want to rotate. It's sort of like a rotating backflip."

He was insane. "So what happened?"

"Nothing. We rolled the plane."

"And that scared you?"

"No, after that we started doing steep turns."

I raised my brows. He took the cue for an explanation.

"The point is to turn the airplane three hundred and sixty degrees with a forty-five degree bank, until you come back to your main heading, without gaining or losing fifty feet in altitude.

"On that day, Dan wanted to see how tight he could make the turn, so instead of gradually pulling the yoke, he pulled up on it." Wes took his hands and positioned them like he was driving a car again, and then he yanked them into his chest really fast. "Like that," he said. "And then we heard huge crackling sounds from the wings being stressed by the g-force." He paused. "That scared me."

"Why did he do that?" I asked, wondering what kind of loony person this Dan was.

"He just wanted to try new stuff, I guess."

"What happened next?"

"Nothing. He just cursed and straightened it out." Wes smiled. "Then he said not to tell anyone."

"What's so funny?"

"I'm just remembering the look on Dan's face. We laughed when it was all said and done."

I'm glad someone thought it was funny.

"But you see, we stressed the plane so hard that there were cracks in the paint on the wings, but the plane was fine. They're extremely durable."

"It scared you."

"Only for a moment."

I let the plane talk drop and started refocusing on our trip. We landed a short time later, and I could tell as soon as we touched down that it was cold. Cold enough for snow. The whole sky was the hazy gray color that snowy Virginia possesses in winter, a clear indication that it had either already snowed or was about to. And, considering I didn't see a speck of white on the ground on our approach, I could only assume it was coming. I sincerely hoped Wes had turbo batteries for that jacket of his.

Chapter 15

ARRIVAL

W e had arranged for Kerry to meet us in the baggage pick up area. Wes put on his regular overcoat when exiting the plane, insisting he would be fine. We filed out and headed to get our luggage. The airport wasn't very crowded, so it made it feel that much colder.

"I can't wait to ski," Dawn said. "This is so exciting. Where are the slopes?"

"The chalet and slopes are about four hours away."

She looked at me, disappointed.

We arrived at the baggage claim just as our luggage was coming through the conveyer belt doors. Wes recognized mine and reached out to grab it. His bag was the largest and also one of the last ones to come around. Just as he was reaching for his, I heard Kerry.

"Wooo-hooo," she called, with a higher pitch than her usual tone.

I smiled immediately, and turned to see her coming in our direction. She hadn't changed a bit since last summer. Her hair was still dark blonde and cropped very short on the sides and back. Her bangs were longer and fit perfectly behind her ears. She was cute and she knew it, but her hair was not what raised her shoulders the extra inch. It was her perfectly curved hips and behind, which filled her jeans in all the right places.

What made being her friend so easy was that we were both laid-back. She didn't care about being the center of attention, or being in anyone else's business. She was confident, not the type of person who collected friends just to feel adequate, and I really liked that about her. She walked up to me with a big grin and gave me a brief hug.

I turned and grabbed Wes' arm. "Wes, this is Kerry. Kerry this is Wes."

"Hi, Wes," she said, greeting him with a mischievous smile.

She reached out her hand for a shake, cocked her head to the side, and twitched it slightly, like she had a tickle on her neck. Everyone looked at her a little strangely, but I knew what she was doing. It was her secret signal when she wanted to say, "He's fiiine."

I tried to hold back a smile and took the attention off of her. "And this is Dawn and Jackson."

Kerry snapped out of her itch and turned to face them. "It's nice to meet you. I can't wait to get going and have some fun."

"I'm all about the fun," Dawn piped up.

Jackson stood shyly behind her, and I was surprised at how timid he appeared. Dawn was not timid, so the match-up was odd. Their relationship was one where that opposites attract saying definitely applied.

Wes and Jackson grabbed the bags and walked behind us while I played a little catch up with Kerry and Dawn soaked it up.

"So where's Rich?"

"He's in the car, circling, until we come out." We passed a coffee shop and she added, "I need a frickin' latte."

"Me too!" Dawn spoke up, interlocking her arm with Kerry's as they veered toward the line.

I set my gaze on the Cinnabon shop. Now that the fear of losing the contents of my stomach was gone, I was dying of hunger. "I'm getting one of those."

"I want one too." They both chimed.

Then Kerry suggested, "Grab two boxes and we'll take them with us, and I'll get the coffees."

Wes and I headed over and ordered some to go, and then we sat down and shared one right there in the airport while we waited for the girls. It was so good, and we were so warm. I wanted to put off our departure into the cold, but everyone else was eager to get going. I could no longer hold off the inevitable, and we all headed toward the exit.

The minute the doors opened, the bitter cold smacked us in the face. I wanted to hug Wes, but his hands were full of luggage, so I clutched the Cinnabons as if they were going to blow away.

"Geez," I said. "This is ridiculous."

"You said it would be cold," Wes replied, unsurprised.

My teeth started chattering, and we all hunched our shoulders in reflex to the chill. All, that is, except Wes. He didn't have a reaction to temperature. No sweating, and no shivering either. He looked completely comfortable, but I knew better. The longer we were out there, the more I risked another pier episode.

Rich saw us and pulled up. We approached the waiting car quickly, and Rich got out to open the hatch of Kerry's mom's Suburban. I could immediately see why Kerry was attracted to him. Tall, dark, and handsome, he had a natural tan, like me, but looked to be maybe Greek or Italian. His hair was cut short and brushed forward and his eyes were dark brown. Almost black. A lot deeper color than Wes' and not nearly as warm, but something about them drew you in.

I was glad to see the guys quickly loading the car while Kerry opened doors. It was ironic to see the two people who had a natural defense against the cold hustling their rear ends to get inside the warm car.

Dawn and Jackson grabbed the backseat, while Wes and I sat in the middle row. Wes was rather quiet and when I reached for his hand, he pulled it away. I was surprised by the withdrawal at first and then realized he was trying to hide his temperature from me. I scowled at him.

"I'm fine, Sophie."

I leaned forward and made a request. "Kerry, can you turn on the heat, please? I'm cold."

Dawn yelled from the back. "Yeah, me too. Heat would be nice."

"Yeah, sure," she said. "There are vents on the sides back there if you need them."

I immediately turned ours toward Wes and blew the heat right on him. Then I snatched his icy hand and started rubbing it between my own. By the time we got onto the highway, the vehicle had warmed up nicely, but Wes' hands were still cold. I kept up the friction.

He leaned over, and put his lips close to my ear. "I love you," he whispered.

I didn't respond. He knew I was mad and cursing myself for going along with this trip. *What was I thinking?* Right. I wasn't. I just wanted to get inside a warm, cozy place already. In three days this would be over. I tried to focus on that, but it didn't make me feel any better. Of course, the nickel-size snowflake I saw fall outside our window didn't help.

I wasn't the only one who noticed. "Look. It's snowing," Dawn squealed. "This is awesome! Real snow!"

I shook my head.

Wes spoke up in spite of me. "Look, Sophie. It's snow. This is going to be great."

I was on my third time of calling myself an idiot in my head when Kerry chimed in.

"So, Wes, Sophie tells me you haven't seen much snow."

"No. I can't remember the last time. And I've never skied. It'll be a first. I'm looking forward to it."

"It'll be a lot of fun." Kerry looked back and offered a smile and then reached to turn up the radio. Her head started bobbing to some MJ remix.

Wes pulled his hand free and patted my leg. Putting his lips against my ear again, he whispered, "If you don't relax, I'll open this door, while we're moving, throw myself out of it, and walk in the cold."

198

His lips were noticeably warm and I couldn't help but laugh at the visual. Or at the fact that he'd probably do it *and* be completely unfazed by it.

"Fine," I whispered. "But promise me you'll be honest about how you're doing. Please."

He nodded and put his arm around me.

We were headed straight to the ski chalet. Kerry hadn't outright lied to her parents about no boys coming, but they didn't exactly know either. She said I was flying in with my friend Dawn and we wanted to go skiing, so stopping off at her house with a car full of hot guys wasn't a good idea. That meant we jumped onto the highway and kept on going.

Kerry offered to stop for food and Dawn was hungry, but I didn't want to waste any time on the road. A four-hour drive meant we would arrive at Wintergreen around 7:30 or 8:00, so I was able to convince them to stop for snacks and grab pizza once we got there.

"Are you sure you don't want to eat now?" Kerry asked.

"Yes, I'm sure. Let's just get there before we're stuck driving in snow."

"Good point," Kerry replied.

With everyone in agreement, we continued on the road, past civilization, and onto the winding roads of the Virginia mountains. The snow seemed to dissipate the farther we drove but I knew that didn't mean much. Storms rarely hovered in one spot, so for all I knew, it could be chasing us. And, if it was, I hoped it wouldn't catch up until we were nestled into the warm, cozy house.

It was dark by the time we reached the foot of the main mountain. A small ski shop was located there, and Kerry wanted to stop and buy new gloves for her and Rich. Dawn and Jackson hopped out with them and Wes and I stayed in the car.

"So this is it?" Wes asked looking at the narrow road that would take us up. It was dark and there was nothing but trees and blackness ahead.

"Yeah." I leaned over his lap to get a better look out of his window. "The view will be so much better once we get up there."

I felt his breath in my ear. He inhaled into my hair, and I was about to point out where I thought Kerry's house was when a tickling sensation going down my neck sidetracked me.

The bridge of his nose was touching my cheek. I leaned into him, turning to find his lips. They were warm, soft, and incredibly inviting. I put my palm on the side of his face and rested my thumb in the crease of his smile line.

For the first time since we set out on this trip, I re-membered the reason we had wanted to come. This was for *us*. So we could spend time together without the stress of everything we left behind. At that moment, I was one hundred percent glad we had come.

"Disgusting," Dawn said as she opened the door. "Get a room, will ya?"

"You have a lot of nerve," I replied, sitting up into my own seat.

"I have no idea what you are referring to."

She climbed into the back while Kerry climbed into the front, saying, "Yeah, well, we'll all have time to get a room once we get up this mountain, and we'd better hurry. The lady inside said there's a winter storm warning. They're expecting anywhere from six to ten inches. I gasped. "You are kidding me."

Kerry turned around and looked at me like I had asked a dumb question.

"No, she's not kidding," Dawn continued. "Totally rocks. I can't wait. It's going to be awesome."

Rich backed up the Suburban and headed up the mountain. I was quiet, trying to process all of it. Concentrating was difficult between my ears popping from the rise in altitude and Dawn's excitement.

"Jackson, did you bring the camera? I think I forgot mine. Damn."

"No," he answered, "but I have one in my phone."

"Oh, that's right," Dawn said, relieved. "Good. I *have* to get pics of a blizzard. I've never been in one of those."

"A blizzard?" I turned to her, eyes wide.

Kerry chimed in from the front, "No, she didn't say blizzard. Just snow."

Dawn countered with, "I'm from California. Six to ten inches is a blizzard in my book."

My shoulders dropped a good three inches. Wes put his hand on my thigh for silent support. With a storm like this, we could be snowed in a day or two before they cleared the roads enough for us to get out. But, as long as we were inside, we'd be good to go. We weren't set to leave until Monday morning anyway. Being snowed in for the weekend might actually be our best bet.

I started thinking ahead. "We'll need to get food tonight, before we get to the house."

"Yeah, you're right, Sophie," Kerry said. Then, looking at Rich, she continued. "We'll need to stop for groceries. Get everything now. Just in case we can't go out."

Rich nodded. He'd been up here before and knew there was only one store and it was about three-quarters of the way up. I knew that store had everything, including fresh pizza, and that's where we needed to be.

The way up was unimpressive because it was impossible to see the view in the dark. Normally, you could see massive hillside panoramas, similar to the overlook back home, but on a grander scale, and the hills here were less interrupted by houses.

As we drove, I thought about two spots on the hillsides that I hoped to take Wes to see, but the weather prediction was making me wonder if I'd get the chance. Casting even more doubt were the snow flurries that had begun to fall.

"It's starting," I said.

Wes rubbed my leg again in hopes of keeping me relaxed.

"Oh, we're here," Kerry said.

Rich pulled into the parking lot. There was only one space left out of the five or six total. We weren't the only ones with the idea of stocking up. We all got out and grabbed a basket. The store was too small for carts.

Kerry and Dawn went straight to the junk food aisle. My two best friends. It figures they would think alike.

The Broken Lake

Rich and Jackson went for the drinks. Wes and I, the adults, were in charge of the actual food. According to my calculations we would need breakfast for Saturday, Sunday, and Monday mornings, at least. Then we'd need lunch and dinner for Saturday and Sunday. As a safety measure, we added in Tuesday and Wednesday, in case we really got snowed in and couldn't leave on time.

I picked up three dozen eggs, two packs of bacon, pancake mix, maple syrup, butter, and three cans of cinnamon buns. Wes grabbed all he could in the way of hot food supplies. They didn't have a huge selection, so he grabbed stuff to make spaghetti twice, hot dogs twice, and frozen pizzas once. Then we added bread, a bunch of sandwich meats, and several kinds of cheeses. Their produce section was nonexistent, so we settled on relish and ketchup for the hot dogs and tiny jars of mustard and mayo for the sandwiches.

Dawn and Kerry's baskets overflowed with chips, cookies, and candy. And Jackson and Rich gave up on the baskets entirely. They came around the aisle with arms piled high with six-packs of sodas and waters.

Kerry said her mom kept a stash of tea bags, hot chocolate, and cider at the house, so we were good on that. I added milk and cereal to the mix and then we checked out.

There wasn't room in the back of the Suburban for everything, so we all held some of the groceries on our laps the rest of the way up. The farther Rich drove, the larger the flakes became, and the more I couldn't wait to get inside.

Chapter 16
SETTLING IN

"It isn't sticking," Kerry observed. I looked out at the moving black pavement and she was right.

"What does that mean?" Dawn asked.

Kerry turned around, more than willing to fill in Dawn on a few East Coast weather tidbits. "It means it's not cold enough outside for the snow to stick to the roads. See? It disappears as soon as it touches."

"Oh, man. That sucks."

"I'd personally like to see it stick," Wes chimed in.

I ignored his comment.

"Yeah, me too," Dawn agreed, overly bummed.

Rich casually added, "It probably will. The temperature will drop tonight."

"Cool," Dawn said.

I rolled my eyes as Wes said, "Cool." He strengthened his massage of my leg.

"Oh, crap!" Kerry nearly shouted.

We all jumped, frantically looking around for whatever it was we missed.

"The pizza. We forgot the pizza."

We were just pulling into her driveway when she remembered it. We had been so busy stocking up on food supplies that we forgot to pick up the pizza for tonight's dinner.

"And we were *right* there." She grunted.

I reminded her of the frozen pizzas we had stocked up on, but neither she nor Dawn were having that.

"No way," Kerry said. "I don't want that junk. That's for emergencies. I want the fresh stuff."

Rich offered to turn around, and we almost did, but Kerry suggested that we unpack first.

"Actually," she amended, "let's let the guys unpack, and we girls can go back."

That sounded like a plan to me. It meant Wes would be inside the warm house and that was exactly where I wanted him to be.

"Sounds good," I agreed.

The guys unpacked the stuff from the back of the Suburban and we took all the groceries in. Kerry even went so far as to put the guys in charge of putting the items in the fridge and cabinets. I found it amusing to see them all taking orders from Kerry, like good little soldiers. It was cute.

I also noticed Jackson and Rich slip out of their coats right away while Wes was still walking around in his. "Kerry can you start the fireplace and turn on some heat in here?"

"Rich knows how. He'll do it."

I didn't even have time to see how soon Rich planned on doing that before Kerry pulled me by my arm right out into the cold. I soon discovered that she just wanted to get Dawn and me alone so she could pry.

We weren't even out of the driveway before she jumped on Dawn. "So, Dawn, how long have you and surfer hottie been going out?"

Dawn laughed, and so did I. It did seem funny to picture them that opposite. Jackson looks like he'd carry a surfboard, but he prefers the acoustic guitar.

"What's so funny?" Kerry asked.

"Kerry, do you assume all boys from the West coast surf?" I asked.

Dawn settled herself down. "I'm *so* not into surfers."

Kerry defended herself. "Hey, there's nothing wrong with surfers. That's who I'd be looking for if I moved to Cali. One in a wet suit, for sure." I looked over to see her twitching her neck again, just visualizing a fiiine one.

"Well, no offense, but surfers just aren't my cup of tea."

"Fair enough. Well, then, how long have you and the hottie-whatever-he-is been dating?"

"Not long. Almost two months."

I couldn't help but jump in. "Yeah, but you'd never know by the way they constantly cling to each other."

"Yeah, whatever, Sophie. He's a good kisser, and you've got nerve."

"What?" I said innocently.

"Oh, don't pretend that you and Wes aren't always all over each other. Just because you act like old people about it doesn't hide a thing."

"What's that supposed to mean?"

"It means you guys act like an old married couple. It's ridiculous."

Kerry was getting a kick out of us.

"What are you laughing at?" I countered. "What about you? 'Oh, Rich knows how to start the fire and turn on the heat,'" I mocked.

"All right already," Kerry said. "I just want to know who's going to get it on in my parents' chalet."

"Not Sophie," Dawn declared.

It was probably true, but the accusation still made me turn around with my mouth dropped open, making it obvious that I didn't appreciate the comment.

"It's true. Married people don't do anything."

Kerry laughed and looked at me. I didn't say anything to counter. "Okay, Sophie and Wes can take the loft upstairs since they don't need privacy." She was still giggling.

"The loft is fine with me." I crossed my arms.

The loft *was* fine with me. It was an upstairs rec room that had been converted into a third bedroom. It had its own bath, and aside from the open landing, it was plenty private.

We picked up three large pizzas and headed back up to the chalet. At Wes' you could tell his view was amazing even at night, because the distant hillsides were lit up with house lights. There was nothing to see on this mountain after dark.

As soon as we got back and I stepped inside, I was relieved to see and feel that Rich had started the fire like Kerry had asked. Even though it was a gas fireplace, whenever they arrived, they always had to light the pilot, and do something more than flip a switch, so I was glad to see that it was taken care of.

The main level was one large, open space with a kitchen, great room, and one bedroom on each end. In the center was the stone, circular fireplace that was exposed on all sides. The back of the house was loaded with windows and a mountainside view that was out of this world in the daytime.

Rich and Jackson were at the table playing Xtreme Takeover, with Wes watching, intrigued. It was a relatively new game and I hadn't seen one at Wes' house, so he was probably fascinated. It was a strategy game, and although Wes had seen just about everything, it was good to see him interested—and also down to a sweatshirt.

"Okay, guys. Time to put the Xiacons away," Kerry ordered.

"I'm almost in his bunker," Rich pleaded.

"Come on, I'm starving. Put it away."

Rich sighed, shrugged, and put the board back in the box. "We'll pick this up later." His glare challenged Jackson.

"Picking on the new people, Rich?" Kerry asked with a smile.

"I'm not. He's played this before. He's pretty good."

With the table cleared off, Kerry opened up the pizza boxes and grabbed some paper plates from the pantry. Everyone grabbed a Pepsi and we ate. All of it. We were all starving from the long trip. By the time we were finished, it was after 9:00 and we wanted to settle into our rooms.

Interestingly, the guys had left the bags at the front door. They were not even going there with deciding who was sleeping where. They had left that for us, and Kerry had no problem taking control. She put her and Rich in the master bedroom and Dawn and Jackson in the smaller room directly across the great room. Like she mentioned in the car, she sent Wes and me upstairs.

I tried to pick up my bag, but Wes scooped it up first and motioned for me to go ahead. I rarely went up to the loft because, usually, it was just me and Kerry or us and her parents, so we only needed one level.

I was impressed again with the layout and was glad we had been given the space. At the top of the steps the room opened up to a large area with a fireplace and huge floor-to-ceiling windows on the entire back wall. I smiled, imagining the view in the morning.

To the left was a queen-size bed. It was set back, away from the stairs, which allowed some privacy. To the right, and closer to the steps, was a small round table with two chairs positioned in front of the window.

In the center of the space was a cozy-looking, double-wide chaise lounge positioned in front of the fireplace. It called our names the moment we saw it. I couldn't wait to nestle into that with a fire going.

The bathroom door was right next to the bed and hid a small sink, shower, and toilet. The space was more than enough for us. One thing that was missing was a dresser, but Wes noticed a platform with built-in drawers beneath the bed. We went ahead and unpacked our clothes into those and tossed our bags into the corner.

I looked at Wes. "Are you thinking what I'm thinking?" My gaze traveled to the fireplace.

"Uh-huh."

He approached the fireplace as if he knew how to make it work. He lay down and opened the vent at the bottom, turned on the gas, and pressed a red button. Next, he stood up and flipped on the wall switch.

A fire roared to life. I happily hopped onto the chaise. My body sank into the cushions, and once I settled in, Wes walked over with a contented smile and climbed on top of me. He held off most of his weight with his elbows, but I put my hands around his neck and pulled him all the way down.

I touched my lips to his in an urgent yet still soft fashion, and fire began in my toes and moved up. This was it. This was why we came here. Whatever was happening in the clouds was of no worry to me at that moment, because there was no other place I'd rather be.

As if my body was trying to do what my brain was thinking, I wrapped one leg around his waist in an attempt to secure him to me for what could've been forever. In response, he let out a deep breath that blew onto my neck and toward my ear. I heard myself sigh as I found his lips again.

What came next was unexpected. He gently but firmly placed his palm over my forehead and pushed my head into the cushion. "Sophie, Sophie," he said.

Unable to move, I released the word "What?" between labored breaths.

"You know what. You're attacking me."

"What? *You're* on top of *me*," I pointed out.

"Well, if you unlock your leg, maybe I can move." He was holding back a smile.

"Maybe if you release my forehead, I will."

We both laughed and released our intertwined holds on one another.

"Sorry," I offered.

He laughed a little and then turned serious. "Me too, but not for the same reasons you are." He rolled so he was lying beside me.

"What are *your* reasons?"

"I just want to be with you always, and in every way."

I propped myself up on my elbow to face him and made a promise. "You will get what you want." Confidently, I added, " I know it. We *will* make it happen. Everything that we want, and you will not lose track of a single minute."

He moved closer, so his head rested against my forearm. "I hope so," he said in a way that sounded less than optimistic.

I began running my fingers through his hair, and the gesture made me wonder why I had not done that sooner. I loved his hair. It was the darkest chocolate color with soft, inviting waves that I had never wrapped around my fingers before.

He was always the one cradling me and playing with my hair, yet here I was, twining the waves perfectly around my fingertips. It was a reversal that caught me by surprise. It was as if he was inviting me in to care for him and make him feel like everything was going to be okay.

I thought about why this shift took place right before my eyes, and the only conclusion I came to was that it was because we were in *my* element. He knew nothing about the bitter cold mountains or the angry ice flakes that were to come. The only thing he knew at that moment was that he trusted me during what, I was sure, was an uncomfortable time for him. And, instead of fear, he was showing need. A need to be with me more than anything else. A need that made me feel responsible that nothing bad happened.

A gentle smile flowed across my face. Even though it was a tall order, it was one that I wanted to fulfill. I kissed his forehead as he had kissed mine so many times, a kiss that spoke the silent words, "I'm here and I'm not going anywhere."

"I love you, Sophie." His arm wrapped around me and he buried his face in my chest.

I realized then, that not only was he mine to love forever, he was mine to care for forever. He needed me as much, if not more, than I needed him, and lying there together made me see that.

As perfect and indestructible as he was physically, he was vulnerable emotionally. And this was what I was there for. This is what he'd been missing for decades, someone to love him and care for him in a way that made him willing to give up everything for that person. In the way that I did.

Somehow, the fire was still racing through my veins, even though we had stopped kissing minutes ago. The burning was *still* there, the passion, the desire, the spark. It was lingering within me, and I felt so alive, so needed, and so wanted.

"I love you too," I whispered.

"Say it again."

"I love you too." I watched as the last wave curled away from my finger, and I leaned down and kissed his cheek tenderly.

"Again," he whispered, his eyes closed.

I kissed him again. "I could say it a thousand times, and it still wouldn't tell you how much."

"Me too," he said.

Chapter 17
THE SNOW GLOBE

M orning is not my favorite part of the day. I much preferred my sleep; however, with the wall of glass letting the morning light blaze in, I had no choice but to wake up. By myself. I felt all around and there was no one there. Still in the act of prying my eyes open, I sat up, piecing together my whereabouts. The loft was a bright white reflection of the falling snowflakes outside.

The chalet, Virginia, the snow.

"Holy crap!" I said in a raspy morning voice.

It was a beautiful sight, but I had no time to appreciate it. I threw back my covers and hurried to the bathroom to brush my teeth. A quick run-through of the hairbrush and I was done. I skipped down the steps in my flannel pajamas. Jackson and Rich were playing the board game again, and Dawn was lounging on the sofa.

I followed the sweet scent of cinnamon and bacon into the kitchen where Kerry and Wes were moving among the appliances in a professional manner. He still wore the gray sweatpants and black thermal henley that he had gone to bed in, and she was wearing Sponge Bob flannels. Both of them looked totally at ease, and once I was secure in knowing that Wes wasn't holed up in a corner, freezing, I cleared my throat. They both turned and smiled.

"Hey, sleepyhead," Kerry said. "You didn't tell me hottie here could cook."

"You better watch it," I warned. "Rich may not like you hitting on my guy."

She puffed air through her lips. "Oh, Rich doesn't care. I call him much more than that." Her smile was so devious, I didn't even want to know.

Next, my gaze settled on Wes, saying something along the lines of, "How could you let me sleep and just get up without waking me?"

And his spoke back to me, saying, "I'm a big boy, and you need your rest."

We smiled a mutual truce, and Kerry looked at us like she wanted to back away from the silent conversation.

"Um," she said, "I better get the eggs started."

I moved toward Wes, still a little perturbed that I was the only one left sleeping. He pulled my shirt until I was close enough for him to put his arms around me and give me a squeeze. I gave him a hug in return and allowed my senses to take over.

"What's that delicious smell?"

Speaking from the stove, Kerry answered, "Cinnabons. From the airport. We put them in the oven."

Yum, was all I thought.

"Did you see outside?" Kerry asked.

"How could I not? It's everywhere."

"Yeah, but it's still not sticking."

I hadn't noticed before coming downstairs. Looking out our windows, all you could see was millions of large white flakes falling to the ground.

"Really?" That meant that it wasn't cold enough for ice, though certainly still way too cold for Wes to function normally, but not cold enough to snow us in. Hopefully, we could still freely make it up and down the mountain.

Kerry interrupted my thoughts. "Yeah. And Dawn's bummed. But we can still probably get some good slope time in today."

"I don't know," I said, spinning myself away from Wes' arms. His maneuver was swifter than mine, as he allowed me to spin out, only to hug me from behind, his arm around my waist in a secure hold. He kissed my ear.

"Yeah, Kerry. I think we'll try it," he said. I turned around. "For a little while," he amended.

He was insane, completely, and I was sure he was going to make my job of playing the protector difficult.

"Whatcha doing?" Dawn said, hopping into the kitchen.

"We're talking about hitting the slopes today," Kerry answered.

"Awesome!" Her enthusiasm was a bit of a reminder of how fun it really could be if I could only let go of my terrible apprehension.

"Yeah, awesome," Wes added.

I wanted to elbow him in the stomach. "Would you stop messing with me?" I asked.

"What? I'm serious. I'm stoked."

A few more silent words flew between us and Kerry and Dawn cleared their throats in a duet.

"Good," Dawn said.

"Where's the sugar?" I asked, really needing a rush.

On cue, the oven beeped and Wes moved over to take out six round mounds of perfection. The buttercream icing was flowing down the sides of each bun. I instantly felt warm and fuzzy.

Wes smiled. "We ought to get these more often."

Rich joined us from the living room. "I'll take the bacon. Meat is for men. Sugar is for girls."

"I'll take some sugar," Jackson said, following him in. We all looked at him, trying to figure out what that was supposed to mean. Was he unafraid to show his feminine side, or simply mocking Rich? We decided he was mocking Rich.

"Did you beat him?" Kerry asked.

Jaskson smiled, but before he could answer, Rich cut him off. "I let him win."

We all started laughing. Jackson's chest was puffed out while Rich had a vertical crease plastered on his forehead.

Jackson patted his shoulder. "No worries, bro. We'll play again later."

"No, later we'll play something we can all play at the same time."

Kerry was so motherly all of a sudden. I couldn't figure out where it came from, and I wondered how often she and Rich came up here to play house together. Whatever the answer was, it was a nice to see her so happy.

"Okay, everyone," she continued. "Grab your plates. Feed yourself."

Breakfast was great. I had my huge, warm glob of baked dough, dripping with icing, and a glass of milk. Everyone else had eggs, toast, and bacon. Then, for dessert, they picked away at the cinnamon buns. I was a stuffed turkey after I made a happy plate with mine. That was all I needed.

Afterward, we debated about hitting the slopes. I knew I couldn't keep them away, so I just went along. Wes was eager to try it, and I had to trust that he would be fine. So we headed upstairs to pile on the layers.

We had spent many nights together, but never watched each other undress before. It was a tad awkward, so I went into the bathroom to change. When I came out, I caught him down to his boxers. I had seen them before when he was freezing to death and I had to strip him down to his underwear. I had also seen him in his swimming trunks before, but not like this.

In the other situations, I had done everything possible to keep my eyes off his physique, but this time, I stared. *OMG,* was all I thought, and then I felt my neck begin to twitch like Kerry's had at the airport.

"You okay?" he asked, sliding one leg into a pair of long johns.

"Um." I watched the muscles in his arms and chest flex as he pulled the pants up. "No, not really."

He laughed, but I was serious.

Without looking at me, he grabbed his long-sleeved henley and turned around so his back was toward me. I could tell he was still smiling. His effort to shield me from his hotness didn't work.

The muscles in his back were just as impressive as the ones in his front. Like the ripped guys at the fight club, Wes' back also formed a perfect V. And when he reached his arms up to pull his shirt over his head... Every. Single. Muscle. Flexed.

I decided the only way to end the drool was to close my eyes. I thought I'd died and gone to heaven when Wes saved me from Andy, and I was beginning to think it again. Everything was too perfect.

I wasn't sure what I had done to deserve such perfection, and then I remembered. That's right, as Amelia I had saved him from bleeding to death on a London street a hundred years ago. And who says being a good Samaritan doesn't pay off? Not me. It pays back and then some.

Three layers of clothing later, Wes was ready to add his warming gear. It was actually pretty neat, and once he had them on, I began wishing I'd taken him up on his offer and bought some for myself. It's one thing not to be a wimp about the cold when you're not actually in it, but it's another thing when Jack Frost actually shakes your hand. But I sucked it up and prepared myself in just a few layers and a nonheated down coat.

We drove down to where the road split, near the middle of the mountain, and headed over to the snow-covered slopes. Kerry and Rich had their own skis and went off to the lifts. The rest of us rented ours and headed off to the bunny slopes for some lessons. I thought Wes would stand out like a sore thumb, but he actually blended in perfectly. No one on the bunny slopes knew what they were doing, including Dawn and Jackson. All three of them looked like they were walking on glass, and everyone was bundled up like mummies.

I was having a great time watching them attempt to ski for the first time, and each of them looked so ridiculous that I wasn't even fixated on Wes' body temperature. It was the first time I'd seen him look uncoordinated, and it was hilarious. He was bundled up so much that I couldn't see one centimeter of his skin; and, therefore, I wasn't always prompted to wonder about his body temperature. He just looked like a warm, regular guy.

Surprisingly, Dawn and Jackson were the first ones to cave and ask to go back to the house. I hadn't factored in the fun-in-the-sun couple not being able to handle Jack Frost. They actually saved me from having to sneak Wes out of there when they turned out to be the shameless wimps.

I called Kerry on her cell to see how much longer they were going to be, and she told me that visibility was getting low on the slopes and they had decided to quit too. So after about forty-five minutes in the bitter cold, we were all headed back to the warm house and Wes' well-being was not what sparked the return. Today had been a success.

Back at the house, everyone took off their outer layers in the garage to keep from tracking tons of snow through the kitchen. When Wes started to take off his, I noticed him having a hard time unzipping himself with his gloves on. I offered to do it for him and he didn't object. That was the first sign that told me he was having difficulty. I quickly unzipped his outer layer and put my hands on his chest. The fleece coat beneath was warm, which helped calm my worry.

Dawn and Kerry were throwing snow chunks from their shoes at Jackson and Rich and none of them noticed Wes' weakness. They chased each other into the house, and I took advantage of the privacy.

"What's wrong?" I asked.

He put his hand up to his mouth to pull his ski mask down, but his fingers weren't cooperating. I pulled the hat off for him. His lips were turning blue and he was pale. Not pale like at the pier, but definitely pale.

"Wes! You promised."

"I'm fine. Let's just get inside."

"You are not fine," I hissed. "You can't even undress yourself. Why didn't you say something?" I yanked his heated gloves off and bent down to pull his boots off.

"Because I'm fine. My limbs are just a little numb."

"And your face too?" I snapped. "Ugh."

I wrapped his arm around me and walked him into the house. We looked as though we were just having a close moment, but my mission was to get him upstairs ASAP. He was still taking steps as if he was walking on glass, but this time I couldn't attribute it to being on the slopes.

Luckily, the rest of the crew had disappeared into their bedrooms, so no one noticed us. Despite the difficulty, I helped him up the steps one by one. Once we reached the upstairs, I tried to sit him on the bed but he held firm, standing.

"You need to sit."

He shook his head. "No, I need a warm shower."

"Right." I unfolded myself from his arm, slipped quickly into the bathroom, and started the water. When I came out, he was still standing in the same spot.

I knew he was suffering, yet he managed to appear as if he wasn't. I didn't even bother griping about it. I went over and guided him into the bathroom. The shower was running but his clothes were still on.

"I can take it from here," he offered.

I was tempted to leave him alone, because I knew he was trying to release me from the awkwardness, but like before, the necessity of the situation took over—or maybe it was my hundred-year-old nursing instincts. Whatever it was, I wasn't worried about boy-girl parts and who was seeing what. I just wanted him better.

"No, I'll help you."

I pulled his shirts over his head, one by one, until he was down to his bare chest. I quickly felt his chest with my good hand and the fingertips of my casted hand, and it wasn't so bad. It was cool, but not icy.

It wasn't until I moved his hands away when he tried to unbutton his own pants that I felt the chill. His hands were cool. I grabbed his wrists and felt all the way up his arms. They were freezing.

"I thought your coat was heated?"

"Just the torso part."

I shook my head and yanked his pants down. By that point, my hand was pretty much healed. The cast was set to come off the following week, so I didn't have to be gentle with it anymore, and now was no exception. I used my fingers to grip and tug at his pants legs. Once they were all the way down, he stiffly stepped out of the first layer and then I pulled the long johns off. That's when I felt his thighs. Freezing cold.

"Oh, my gosh," I mumbled half to him and to myself.

I pulled off his socks, being careful not to touch his feet, fearing if they felt chilly it would send me over the edge. All that was left was the boxers. I reached for them, but hesitated slightly.

He quickly picked up on my pause. "I really can take it from here," he said softly. He was doing his very best to contain a smile and the color in his face was returning.

"Fine," I said and turned around while he stripped down completely.

Once I heard him slide the shower glass open then closed, I turned back. His silhouette was visible through the foggy glass. He was standing completely still as the water spilled over him. After a few moments he began to move, dipping his shoulders into the water, one then the other, and turning around, giving each side of his body a chance to feel the warmth.

The bathroom wall had become my support as I leaned into it. More relaxed, but still concerned, I asked, "Why didn't you tell me?"

"Because I didn't know. I felt fine. Really. It wasn't until we started back that I noticed." He paused, and after a few seconds added, "And I thought I could make it inside without worrying you."

"That wasn't the agreement, Wes. Be honest with me, remember?"

I watched him tilt his head forward into the water. "I didn't feel bad, Sophie. Honestly."

"Well, that's it. We're staying inside the rest of the time." I crossed my arms firmly, whether he could see me or not.

He laughed, clearly beginning to feel better now. "That's fine with me. I just wanted to try it once, just to say I did it. And I have to say it was fun."

Visions of him and Jackson balancing themselves returned, and I couldn't help but laugh.

"See, you had fun too. Admit it."

"Fine. I did, but we're still not doing it again."

He slid the shower door open just enough to peek out. "You look cold too. Want to come in?"

"You are so full of it. You're just trying to distract me and it won't work."

He looked like I had accused him of the worst crime ever, but I wasn't falling for it.

"Besides," I added, "your clarity wouldn't be able to handle it."

And before he could bat those pretty browns at me, I left the bathroom, not even wondering if he was serious, but absolutely aware that he had accomplished his mission. He had made me forget how upset I was.

From the loft windows, I could see the snow picking up. Not necessarily in quantity, but in activity. There seemed to be the same amount of flakes falling, but now they were blowing in one direction. That meant cool air was coming in, and it now appeared to be more like a snowstorm and not just a snowfall.

I went ahead and turned the fireplace on and picked out some fresh clothes for myself. I needed a shower as well. It was after I'd picked out my own clothes that I realized Wes didn't have any clean clothes in the bathroom. I thought about picking out some for him, but that would feel too strange.

Just as that thought was bouncing around in my head, he came out with a towel around his waist. Without even looking at him, I scooped up my clothes and brushed past him. Although I tried to contain my smile, it didn't work. But I was able to contain the blush.

When I came out, he was lying across the bed in another pair of sweatpants and thermal shirt combination. He was on his stomach with his eyes closed, and I wondered if he needed some sort of recovery sleep. I gently sat down on the bed beside him, and one eye popped open. I guess not.

"Do you need sleep now?"

He smiled and closed his eye. "No, but I could use some food."

I looked at the clock on the wall, and it was 11:30. "Do you want me to fix you something?"

He opened his eyes again. "No, you've already done enough for me for one day."

"I don't mind."

He reached out his hand to me. Pulling me to lay beside him, he held onto me like a teddy bear. "I want to go with you, but I just want to rest a minute."

And so we did. I lay on my back with his face nestled into my collarbone.

His breath was warming my neck in a slow, calm pattern. It was comfortable and soothing, and we lay there until he softly asked me if I was ready to go.

When we came downstairs, it was quiet and no one was to be found. Both bedroom doors were closed so we assumed they must be napping. It reminded me of spending the morning at the beach and everyone being wiped out once they got back.

With the kitchen clear, Wes and I made ourselves sandwiches and chips. I noticed him make two big ones for himself, which was a bit odd. It wasn't until we sat down and began to eat that I realized he didn't just want to eat, he *needed* to eat. He wasn't shoving the sandwiches into his mouth or anything, but he was eating with serious concentration.

"You're worried about your metabolism, aren't you?"

He looked up without ceasing to chew. He swallowed slowly. "A little bit," he admitted.

"It's slows more when you're cold?"

He nodded and started on his second sandwich.

"Do you want another one?" I asked, leaning across the table, willing to give him mine.

He smiled. "No, this is plenty." He paused. "But I may have one of those Cinnabons too."

I hopped up before he finished the sentence. Two buns in the microwave, and forty-five seconds later I was back at the table.

"Two?" he asked.

"Yes, one for you and one for me." I pushed his across the table. "Now eat."

"You know," he said taking a bite. "This stuff will kill me before it makes me well."

My bottom lip dropped.

"It will," he assured me. "Do you have any idea how much sugar and fat is in one of these? Not good."

I pressed my lips together and tried to drag his plate back across the table, but he snatched it, stood up, and turned his back to me. "Nuh-uh, I want this."

"Wes, are you trying to make me insane?"

"No, just trying to get you to relax. If you can eat junk, so can I."

"Well, it's not working."

He turned around, still coveting his plate. "Well, maybe you should take a bite of yours then. A sugar rush will do you good."

He knew too well how to press my buttons until I realized I was being silly. "Fine." I smirked, biting into mine.

Just then, Kerry and Rich came out, looking well-rested and warm.

"Oh, yum, I want one of those too," she said, envying my snack.

She skipped the real food and made the sugar fest her main priority. I was still picking away at mine when she brought hers to the table. Wes had moved over to the counter and was conversing with Rich about the slopes. I watched him briefly and he appeared completely unfazed by his freezing episode.

I brought my attention back to Kerry as she unwrapped the outer layer of her bun and began digging into the center.

After two bites, she looked up and broke the silence. "It's sticking now."

"What?" I asked, although every nerve in my body knew what she was referring to.

Looking at me with a *Duh!* expression, she answered, "The snow."

Chapter 18
A NEW MEANING

B y evening, the snow had accumulated at least four inches and was showing no signs of stopping. We had all lounged around the house all day, sipping hot chocolate near the fire.

As dinnertime neared, we decided on spaghetti. I thought Kerry was going to take charge of that, but she surprised us all.

"We're not cooking."

Everyone looked at her.

"I think the guys should cook."

Jackson looked confused. Dawn looked like she swallowed a bug, and Rich looked just plain surprised. Then he looked around and was either offended by Dawn's expression or inspired by Wes' composure.

"All right," he said, standing up. "Fellas, let's show them how real men cook."

Wes was the first one to reach the stove.

"But none of you are Italian," Dawn said.

We all laughed.

Kerry looked at her. "Are you?"

"Actually, my mom is."

"Well then, do you want to cook?"

Dawn quickly shook her head. "No way."

"Then it's settled. Italian on the guys tonight."

"Man, and I'm hungry too." Dawn slouched in her chair, cupping her hot chocolate like it was all she had left in the world.

"Have you no faith in your guy?" Kerry asked.

"In the kitchen, no. He burned a Pop-Tart in the toaster oven the last time we were in a kitchen."

"I can hear you," Jackson sang from the kitchen.

"No worries," Rich said. "No burning anything to-night."

I watched as three-men-in-a-kitchen moved around, boiling water, browning meat, seasoning the sauce, and aiming to please their skeptical gals. I tuned out most of Dawn and Kerry's conversation. It was mesmerizing to watch Wes. He stood out from the three of them, even from the back. He was taller for one thing. All of them had nice physiques, but Wes's body just looked harder and more mature. Like he had reached his growth spurt years ago, and I suppose he had.

It was dark by the time dinner was ready, and Kerry had dimmed the lights and brought out her parents' wine glasses. We didn't have sparkling cider, which was a bummer, and none of us even liked the taste of real wine, so we made our own concoction. Dawn and Kerry mixed some regular cider with some Sprite. With our plates and glasses filled, we positioned ourselves by couples around the table with our man-made meal. Flames from the fireplace added the perfect glow as we enjoyed a tasty dinner.

Toning down the romantic atmosphere, Dawn gave her review. "Tastes okay. Tomorrow, we'll make it for dinner and see whose is better." We all looked at her, confused. "Well, Kerry and Sophie will. I'll watch."

"No way," Jackson said. "If I can do it then so can you."

She dropped her fork and sent him a cutting glare. "All you did was boil the water."

"*And* I put the pasta in."

We all chuckled.

"Well then, tomorrow I'll boil the water and put the pasta in and we'll see whose tastes better."

"Are we really arguing over who can boil water better?" I asked.

Kerry laughed. "Sounds like it. And that means we've been cooped up in this house for too long. Tomorrow we need to get out."

Dawn looked at her like she wasn't about to trek to the slopes again any time soon. Kerry must have decided that the Californians were in over their heads, even if it was only four inches of snow.

"We can build a snowman," she suggested brightly.

Dawn smiled immediately. Apparently that was within her comfort zone.

"So, guys, what do you think?" Kerry asked, looking around the table for our responses.

"I'm game," Jackson said.

I glanced at the window, and although it was pitch black out, I could hear the wind howling. I looked at Wes for his answer.

"Maybe," he answered.

Kerry wasn't expecting any maybe RSVPs and her frown showed it.

Wes tried to make his lack of commitment less offensive. "I have something to take care of before I get back to California on Monday."

I paused in my chewing, trying to decipher his words. I couldn't tell if he was wisely avoiding another scenario like this morning, or if he really had something to do.

Taking everyone's cue that we were all curious as to what might trump building Frosty, he continued. "I've been working on a speech I have to give, and I could use some downtime."

"What speech?" I asked, suddenly not caring if I had possibly outed a made-up excuse to stay inside. I was too worried that he might make another public statement in front of the media.

Wes looked at me. "Nothing, really. I'll practice on you tomorrow."

Dawn interrupted the odd tension. "I hate speeches. Hate them."

"Well, you might not want to take public speaking in college, then," Wes said.

The rest of the party nodded their heads, as if completely getting Wes' reason for the cop-out, but I knew better. He wasn't taking public speaking.

Everyone else went back to eating and talking across the table while my gaze stayed on Wes. Folding beneath my stare, he subtly shrugged one shoulder, letting me know that he had nothing else to give.

That was fine. We finished eating, and Wes made sure he stayed engaged in conversation with everyone else all evening. When I finally got him alone, he promised me that he was not making any more media speeches, but had a surprise for me and wanted to tell me about it tomorrow.

"Are you sure you're not up to anything risky?" I asked.

He blinked a long, slow blink, and sounding completely innocent, answered, "Yes, I'm sure."

We were out of Cinnabons by Sunday morning, so we had eggs, bacon, and toast again. The snow had continued through the night and everything in view from the window was covered in white. It was breathtaking, and because of how cold it looked outside, the warmth inside felt that much cozier. We all ate our breakfast together with the fire giving off extra warmth beside us.

"It looks nasty out there," Dawn commented.

Rich, who had taken charge as our weather guru, spoke up. "Yeah, the news said this morning that it's going to continue through Monday night. They're predicting a total of fourteen to sixteen inches."

"What does that mean for us?" Dawn asked.

"Well, it means we might not make it back down the mountain until Tuesday. If then."

"But what about our flights?"

Wes spoke up, soothing her. "Don't worry about those. I'll get us rebooked. We'll fly out when we can."

She didn't appear too relieved. "But my dad."

"Your dad knows you're with me," I offered. "He won't mind if you have to stay another day, as long as you get back safely."

She looked at Jackson then at the rest of us. "But Jackson is supposed to be camping for the weekend. What's his excuse? What happens when he doesn't come back on time? His parents will know something's up and call my house, and then my dad..." She was getting worked up now.

Jackson interrupted her. "Dawn, slow down. It'll be fine. I'll make up something. I'll tell my parents we got a flat or something and have to stay another night."

She didn't seem convinced. She looked at him pleadingly. "If my dad finds out I'm here with you, unsupervised, he will flip. *Flip!*"

Kerry was watching like it was a matinee. It was quite a show. None of us had seen Dawn so unraveled. She was always so fun and carefree, and never worried about getting into trouble. Until now.

"He'll never let me see you again."

She looked at Jackson with a fearful gaze that I recognized. It was one that spoke of love, hope, fear. It made me realize I wasn't the only one on the planet who cared about another person so much.

Jackson stood up, bent over the back of her chair, and wrapped his arms around her. Kissing her cheek, he said, "It'll be good. It will. He won't find out. Now come on." He pulled her up as she rolled her eyes and let out a frustrated sigh.

She looked at Rich. "Just call that weatherman and tell him to cut it out. We have plenty of snow already."

We all laughed quietly, and Jackson pulled her toward the bedroom in a way that I was sure would make her feel better.

"Well," Kerry said. "I'll clean up and then let's get out there. Before it gets too windy." She looked at Wes and me. "You sure you don't want to come? My mom keeps a whole box of snowman paraphernalia."

"I'm good," Wes said. "You guys go ahead."

"Suit yourself."

She and Rich cleared the plates and began mapping out their day while cleaning up.

Wes and I offered to help, but apparently throwing away paper plates didn't require too much assistance.

By 11:00, Wes and I had taken turns showering and putting on fresh sweatpants and long-sleeved tees. Everyone else was getting layered to go outside. Dawn came out of her room wearing what looked like ten shirts and three pair of pants. She could barely walk. I couldn't help but laugh.

Kerry and Rich had the fewest layers, which didn't surprise me. They were definitely more adapted to the cold. They did, however, put on snow pants and encouraged Dawn and Jackson to do the same. Always a good idea when playing in the snow. It sucks if you let your clothes get wet. All it takes is one fall and you can consider yourself a frozen goner. Snow wastes no time melting through clothing.

Wes and I actually got a kick out of watching Rich and Kerry bundle up like pros, in contrast to Jackson and Dawn fumbling around with their zippers.

"It helps if you put the gloves on last." I chuckled.

Dawn curled her lip at me. "Why don't you come, chicken?"

"Nope. Much rather be in here." She looked at me then at Wes and didn't bother arguing.

Once mummified, they headed out through the garage and into the storm.

"They're going to freeze," I said.

Wes laughed. "Better them than me."

"Ya think?"

We were still sitting on the sofa and our smiles met as we both realized we were alone and suddenly wanted to capitalize on it. Wes stood up and reached out his hand.

He slowly led me up the stairs, making my heart feel all fuzzy. By the time we reached the top, I knew that we were headed to a place we hadn't been before. It could have been the look in his eyes when he turned to me. Or it could've been his tense shoulders. Whatever his apprehension, I knew he was about to tell me something and the *speech* immediately came to mind.

"What are you going to do, Weston?" I asked, using his full name, afraid he was about to admit to something unexpected.

"Just give me a minute." He nodded gently and released my hand.

"Wes?"

"Just a minute."

"Just tell me what you're up to? Why are we up here? What are you keeping from me?"

He ignored my questions and started digging through his suitcase pockets. The whistle of the wind outside made me glance at the window. It was a white haze with snow-flakes blowing wildly in every direction.

Suddenly, I feared everything out there, everything I saw. Everything I believed Wes was planning to do once we got home. For once, I wished we could stay here forever. Locked in this chalet. In Virginia. Never leaving. Never going back into the storm. Never returning home to whatever he was about to do.

I started shaking my head, feeling as though the stress we had left back home had now caught up to us. It had plowed through the snow and blew into the house, stand-ing with us, reminding me of the unknown future.

I didn't like not knowing something, and there was no doubt that Wes had been keeping something to himself until now. Whatever it was he was about to tell me, he had chosen to wait until we were in Virginia. In a snowstorm. Trapped. Where I couldn't do anything about it.

"Wes, please tell me what's going on? Did something happen?"

Still ignoring me, he stood up and turned to face me. He was holding a box. A colorful box. Somehow, this box appeared festive, but Wes' expression told me otherwise. He was serious.

With hesitation, he walked over to me. The closer he got, the clearer the pattern on the box became. Snowmen, with hats and scarves, all over it. Confused, I arched my brows.

"Come here. Sit with me," he said.

He grabbed the blanket from the chaise and laid it out in front of the windows and fireplace. I sat down, Indian-style, with one knee touching against the glass. He sat across from me with one leg extended beside me and the other tucked in.

His eyes were warm, and although I was extremely curious about the box decorated in snowmen wrapping paper, I couldn't tear my eyes away from his.

"Is it Christmas?"

He laughed, seemingly a little more relaxed. "No," he answered softly.

"Then what? What's with the snowmen?"

After a long silence, he put the box on the blanket in the tiny valley between us. The snow beating against the glass made it seem as if we were outside, right in the midst of the snowfall.

"I knew we were coming here, so I wanted to stay with the theme."

I smiled a little, still waiting for an explanation. He reached up and moved my bangs behind my ear. "I want you to have this," he said, never looking down at the box. "But, before I give it to you, I want to tell you something."

My heart felt constricted, my pulse raced, my chest pounded. "Where are you going?" I asked, fearful that he was leaving me with a consolation prize.

He looked out the window and my gaze followed. "It doesn't look like I'm going anywhere," he joked.

I looked back at him. "Wes, be serious."

He moved the box, pulling me gently onto his lap. He leaned his back against the window and I felt his breath on my neck. It was slow, calm, and hesitant.

"Listen to your heart," he said. "It's going wild."

I moved his forearm away from my left rib cage, sure the ricocheting beat accentuated my nervousness. "Something's different. I don't know what it is."

He gave me a gentle squeeze before picking up the box. Still close enough for me to feel his breath on my ear, he began murmuring.

"I've been thinking about something you said to me a few weeks ago. About going away with me. At first I thought it was a crazy idea, and I still don't think it's possible right now, but I know one thing."

My breathing was steadying at the sound of the possibility and I leaned into him, seeking his comfort and hoping whatever he was planning included both of us.

"These past few weeks, you've opened my eyes to the idea of change. I'll never forget the past that has made us who we are, but now I want to be new, with you. I want Sophie and Weston to change the future. I want to take that detour around fate's path."

I felt myself smiling and tightened my elbows against his arms beneath mine.

"I've also felt what it's like to worry when you're away from me. When I have no control over your safety. When I can't be there to protect you.

"I've also felt your never-ending care for me. And when you're around me, I just want to let go and sink into it."

He paused again, and I felt the pulse of his breath on my ear. I absorbed it into my skin and into my veins. I closed my eyes until he told me to open them. Hovering a few inches from my chest was the box.

"And all of this has made me know one thing, Sophie. That I want you with me, always."

He put the box in my hand and I stared at the snow-men. They were laughing and having fun. Some were sipping hot chocolate and a few on the side were ice skating. I smiled and gently unwrapped the paper, being sure not to disrupt any of their smiles.

Inside were two smaller boxes, stacked on top of each other. I turned to look at Wes as if I needed a lesson on opening a present. He nudged me with his forearms, encouraging me to continue.

I removed the box on top and set the other one in front of me. Curiosity was killing me, but the moment was so tender, I didn't want to ruin it by flinging the top open. Slowly, I pulled it back to reveal a porcelain white horse standing on his hind legs.

Every bit of apprehension and tension escaped my chest in one long, built-up breath.

"A white horse." I turned to look at him. He was too close for me to see his eyes, so I pressed my face against his cheek. "A white horse," I repeated.

It meant everything. Symbolized all that I had hoped for. He was giving me his word that he would take me away. The two of us in a special place that was peaceful and ours alone.

I gripped it in my palm and pressed it against my chest, almost forgetting the remaining box. He had to pick it up to remind me there was something else. *What is it?* I wondered. *Folded plane tickets?*

Unable to contain myself, I turned the box upside down until the smaller one fell out. I picked it up and pulled the top off much faster than the first. A black velvet box remained. I opened it with much less hesitation.

Every ounce of tension that I had just exhaled quickly returned with one long inhale. My entire body stiffened as I stared at—a ring.

I turned my head, pulling far enough back to see his eyes. In the same moment, he lifted me, positioning me on his bent leg and more at eye level to him. My breath was labored and my eyes wide. He was watching me and studying my face for a reaction. I knew what I wanted, but the look I was giving him didn't mimic my feelings.

And instead of fumbling with a stupid question or comment, I wrapped my arms around his shoulders and pressed my face into his neck.

I felt him sigh and lean his lips into my ear. "I want you to be with me always. Every day. I want to take care of you and let you take care of me. I want it so badly." And with a binding whisper, he murmured, "I want you to *marry* me."

The tears I was holding back wasted no time traveling down my face, and although I held in the clichéd audible sniffle, I let them fall.

Not caring, I wiped them on my shirt sleeves and clearly and effortlessly answered, "Yes. Yes. And Yes."

He kissed me with a need that spoke of everything. He had made a decision about our life together that I hadn't expected, but knew in that instant that I wanted.

Once it registered completely, I turned my attention back to what was in the box. My hand was shaking. It was exquisite. I had never seen a ring like it. Staring at me was a large princess cut diamond with a golden hue to it.

"Is that...?"

"It's a yellow diamond," he said. "I thought it would go with the stones."

He pulled it out of its slit in the velvet and turned it around. Small brown stones encircled the entire ring.

"Axinite crystals," he whispered.

He had to have had it specially made for me and it couldn't have been more perfect. It looked classic but also new.

"Is this all *new*?" I asked.

He nodded, possibly unsure if I liked it.

Quickly, I shot down any doubt. "This is beautiful. It's perfect. I'm just surprised that you didn't go with something older. To represent us."

He shook his head. "I don't want this to represent the old us. This represents the new us. The Sophie-and-Weston us."

I stared at him almost like the first day I had seen him.

"So may I?" he asked.

I blinked. "May you what?"

His ridiculously delicious half smile returned. "Place it on your finger."

"Of course." I cleared my throat and watched as he slid the ring on my shaking finger, where I felt both the weight of *it* and everything it meant to me. At that very moment, nothing else mattered. Not that we were surrounded by a bitter storm. Not that I didn't want to go home. Not that I might die in a year or less. None of it mattered, because nothing could take away this moment. Nothing.

Chapter 19
TRAPPED

B y the time the rest of the crew came back inside, Wes and I were already downstairs. The television was on and we were cuddled up on the couch, watching for the most recent weather updates. Even as the weatherman carried on about the relentless, slow-moving storm, I couldn't bring myself to stop smiling the whole time. My grin turned to a laugh as soon as I saw everyone burst through the door with red cheeks and chattering teeth.

"Build a good snowman?" I asked.

Dawn and Jackson were too busy blowing into their fists to answer, so I looked at Kerry.

"Let's just say Mr. Snowman is not so tall. *And* he's a little lopsided."

"A little?" Rich said. "He's leaning over, about to nod off."

"Well, I think he's cute," Dawn said.

"I bet he is," I offered, hopping up. "I'll make some hot cider while you all warm up."

"Yum," Kerry said, as they quickly dispersed to their rooms for a dry change of clothes.

I heated the cider in a big pot on the stove and set out six mugs. The aroma of cinnamon and cloves filled the open space.

"That smells so good." Dawn was the first one in the kitchen. With her arms folded, she was rubbing her biceps.

"Not used to the cold, are you?"

"Heck, no. I don't see how people live here."

"Look outside." I pointed.

She turned to the live mural of snow-covered trees. "It's pretty, but I have to say, I like that view from the inside *way* better."

I laughed as I ladled her cider into a mug. She took it and held it under her lips, letting the hot steam travel beneath her chin and up around her face.

"Oh, gosh. This is so warm." She rolled her eyes, like it was making her high, and turned and made a beeline for the fireplace.

I ladled out some for Wes, which he took without as much greediness as Dawn. On my way back to the kitchen, Kerry and Rich burst through their bedroom door in a pillow fight. Well, not really. Kerry was the only one with a pillow.

"I'll get you!" she screamed.

I didn't even want to know what that was about. None of my business. But I did take it upon myself to warm everyone up. Kerry was the last to grab her mug and, as always, the first to notice something new.

"What's that?" she asked.

I curled my fingers into a fist. "What?"

"Don't what me? Is that what I think it is?" She grabbed my hand. "Holy crap. It *is*. He didn't." I stood still and innocently shrugged. She scrutinized my face. "He *did*. Let me see." She pulled my hand to within a few inches of her face, inspecting my ring. "Must have been some speech," she declared.

Then she turned and dragged me into the great room. "Have you guys seen this? Sophie and Wes are engaged." She held up my hand like I was the champion of the world. I pulled it back down.

Dawn jumped up, almost spilling her cider. "Shut up," she yelped.

She and Kerry began chattering a million miles an hour.

I glanced at Wes for rescue. He didn't budge. Then I took a quick peek at Rich and Jackson and saw shock, wonder, and mental calculation. Probably recapping our ages in their minds. Then they went over to Wes to give him a brotherly handshake with a look of, "What have you gotten us into?"

Yeah, we were on the young side, and we certainly wouldn't suggest that our decision was normal. But for us it was. We had so much at stake in our lives. So much to win and so much to lose, and not a whole lot of time guaranteed for it. But none of them knew any of that.

"Sophie? Hello?" Dawn snapped. "Are you freaking?"

Well, I didn't feel like I was freaking, but I did sort of have an urge to jump, so I shifted my weight to my toes and gave a little squeal. That's right, a squeal. And the girls capitalized on it, taking over with their own squeals, which overwhelmed mine.

"So, now that our news is out of the way, can I drink my cider?"

With a fierce stare, Kerry said, "You *will* tell me all about it."

I nodded, and the commitment was enough to have me escorted into the kitchen. I was sure I was the most excited, but by their behavior, no one would know it.

That afternoon we all lounged around on the sofa and watched a movie. Kerry's dad was a World War II buff, so he had a ton of those. We watched *Pearl Harbor* because it seemed like a compromise between the girls and the guys.

For dinner, the girls cooked, and although we wouldn't admit it, and the guys were too smart to say it, their spaghetti actually tasted a bit better but we called it a tie. After that, I wanted to go upstairs and spend the rest of the evening alone with Wes, but Kerry talked us into playing Taboo.

We changed into our pajamas first, and as soon as we had everything set up, Dawn's phone rang. Normally, no one would have noticed or cared, but the way she jumped to get it made us remember that she was still on edge about having her dad find out that Jackson was with her.

"It's Danny," she said. "Crap. He is *so* going to rat me out. I hate that guy."

"You do not. Just answer it," I told her.

She rolled her eyes. "Hello? Where are you? No, he's not with me. No, he's not. Damn that Jared. What do you guys care? I swear, Danny, if you say one word to Dad, I will stab you in your sleep."

Danny must've started talking because she huffed and became quiet. Then she started again. "Yeah, there's a storm, but we're waiting it out. As soon as the roads are clear we're coming back. I just need to buy some time. You guys can help cover for us. *Please.*"

Then a look of confusion crossed her face. "Yes, she's right here." She looked at me and reached out to hand me the phone. I hesitantly took it, wondering what Danny would have to say to me.

Dawn quickly whipped her head around toward Jackson. "Your brother told Danny you were here because he was following the weather in Virginia and was worried. That's just great." I tuned her out at, "If my dad finds out…"

"Hello?" I said.

"Hey, Sophie. Danny."

"I know. What's up?"

He paused for a minute and then spoke in a whisper. "I can't talk long."

"What? Are you at work?"

"Yes," he whispered.

"Your dad?"

"No."

My stomach twisted in disgust because that meant only one other person. "Chase?" I gritted my teeth.

"Yeah. Hang on. Okay, bro." He turned his attention back to me. "Okay, he's outside. Listen, I don't know what's going on, but I overheard some freaky stuff."

"Like what?" I wondered what kind of lies Chase was spitting out now.

"Well, I was in one of the aisles and Chase thought I was in the back. Anyway, these two men came in looking for him. They went into the aisle next to mine, and I heard them asking where you and Wes were."

"What kind of men? Those cops again?"

"No. They were dressed in suits, but I don't think they were cops."

"Well, why would they ask about me?"

"I don't know, but when Chase said you guys went to some place called Wintergreen, they got angry and asked why he was just now telling them."

I had specifically asked Danny not to talk about me to Chase after what he did at the party. I was quite irritated. "Wait a minute. How does Chase know where I am?"

He started to sound apologetic. "Because he was here when Jared came in to talk about the storm and Jackson getting back in time."

I rolled my eyes and sighed. At that point, Wes caught my eye, tuned in to the tone of the call, and stood up watching my every expression.

"So what else?" I asked.

"Nothing, he just told them that he had just found out himself, and they told him they were nearing the end of their patience with him. And then they left. I don't know, Sophie. He's been asking a lot questions about Wes and whether or not you know about his work and what not."

I didn't reply right away, because I was trying to figure out who it could've been and what business Wes and I were to them.

"Okay. Thanks, Danny. We'll be home soon. Probably Tuesday. Will you call us if anything new comes up?"

"Sure. Gotta run."

With the click, I handed the phone back to Dawn, who was still huffing about her own problem.

"What is it?" Wes asked.

We had acquired an audience, so I recapped as little as possible. "Just Chase. He's annoying Danny now and still asking questions about us. I don't know what his problem is."

Everyone continued with what they had been doing before the call. Except Dawn and Wes. Dawn was still worried that her cover might get blown, and Wes was relaxed just enough so everyone else didn't pick up on his tension. As we sat down, I whispered that I would tell him later, which was sufficient.

Kerry already had the game set up, so we couldn't really make our exit yet. To prevent ourselves from being tagged antisocial, I committed us to one game and talked up my fatigue. Dawn and Jackson went first. They barely got any points.

Jackson gave the clues and Dawn guessed. Jackson got buzzed so many times for saying a word on the card that Dawn gave up before their time was even up. The funny part about it was they were both laughing the whole time.

Kerry and Rich got a zillion right. She practically knew the word he was talking about before he spit out the first clue. It put pressure on me and Wes. I figured our best chance was for Wes to give me the clues. He was quick-witted like that.

Although we annihilated Dawn and Jackson's round, we fell short of Kerry and Rich's. Next, Dawn reached for the cards, determined to make a comeback. I was spotting her with the buzzer to make sure she didn't cheat.

Her first word was "Microwave."

She arched her back and said, "Square box."

Jackson guessed, "Soap?"

"No! Um...heat."

BUZZZ! "Heat's on the card."

"Damn it, this game sucks."

She threw the card like a Frisbee and we watched it fly and rotate like a helicopter until it hit the floor. I turned to look at the hourglass to see how much time she had. The sand was sifting quickly through. Frustrated, Dawn grabbed it and tilted it on its side. In the same instant, the lights went out.

The golden reflection of the fireplace lit up the space around us. Six of us looked around, as if to find the culprit who flipped the switch.

"Darn," Kerry said. "That always happens whenever it storms here."

Wes looked at me for confirmation, but all he got was a shrug instead.

Kerry got up. "I'll get the candles."

Dawn was completely still, but her gaze moved from left to right and all around. "This is kind of creepy *and* cool."

Rich followed Kerry and helped gather the candles, while Dawn glued herself to Jackson. Wes and I stayed put. Not because I didn't have an urge to move closer to him. I was just trying to make things seem normal.

251

"So how long does it stay like this?" Dawn asked, looking to me for an answer that I didn't have. I'd been to that mountain a few times in the snow, but nothing like this.

"I don't know. Never been here when it's gone out." Kerry answered from the kitchen. "Who knows? We're at the top of the mountain, so it could last a couple of hours or a day or two."

Dawn picked up her cider, swirling it under her nose for any remnants of warmth. "A day or two? That could be all the way until we leave. How will we keep warm?"

Jackson chimed in to calm her fears. "Dawn, it's just the lights. The heat is gas. It's working. See?"

"Oh. So we're good, then?" she replied, sounding relieved.

We all nodded, me more hopeful than she could ever realize.

Rich and Kerry came in with handfuls of candles, tall wide ones in glass holders. "We have more, but I think this is enough." Kerry's confidence further settled our anxiety.

"This is actually romantic," Dawn said.

For some reason that made me roll my eyes. Not being afraid of the dark was one thing, but feeling romantic about the inconvenience was another.

"Yeah, I suppose," I said making my way over to the window. It was too dark to see the snow, but not too dark to see some houses lit farther down the mountain. "That's strange. Come here, guys. Look, they have lights."

Kerry sucked her teeth. "That's not cool." Then she pressed her face against the cold glass. She looked to the left and then the right. "Well, I don't see any lights this far up."

She shrugged, accepting the misfortune of the location chosen by her parents. We all went back to the sofas and started planning.

It was Sunday evening and we were originally set to leave the next day. Our flight was scheduled out of Dulles International at 4:00. Our plan was to leave in the morning, but we knew that wasn't possible.

The snow was knee-deep and the roads weren't plowed yet. The good news was that the snow was supposed to stop during the night. That meant a cold and icy morning, but we hoped for a warmup in the afternoon to help melt some snow. By then, the main roads would be cleared. That left us being able to leave Tuesday.

Wes called in extra flight tickets, and then we all called our parents to tell them we might be snowed in for an extra day.

Mom wasted no time being Mom. "Did you do all of your homework before you left?"

"Yes."

"Well, if you stay past Tuesday, you'd better get online and start your work for the week. You're graduating in two months, and I don't want you to get behind."

I promised her I wouldn't, although deep down I knew it didn't matter. I could fail for the rest of the year, and it wouldn't pull my grades down enough to keep me from graduating. Plus my mom had already made me fill out an application for Berkeley last summer, so I was set.

Dawn called home next. Her call went about the same as mine. Mr. Healey was just concerned about her safety and schoolwork, and the call was pretty brief. Jackson passed on calling his folks just yet. His plan was to call tomorrow with an imaginary flat tire that would push him back a day.

With the folks and tickets taken care of, we went back to playing Taboo. We were on round three when a quick swoosh came from the fireplace. We all looked just in time to see the flame rise up into an orange-and-green flash and then dissipate.

My heart froze in one instant and my gaze traveled to Wes. If I ever wondered what he looked like in that steep turn with his flight instructor, I was pretty sure I was seeing it now. There was a hint of fear in his eyes.

"Kerry?" I said wearily.

"Um," was all she managed to say before going over to check the switch.

"It's not the switch, Kerry. The pilot is out." I whipped my head around to Rich, who was leaning over trying to get a visual under the faux logs.

"What does that mean?" I asked.

"Yeah, what does that mean?" Dawn repeated.

Wes, who had remained relatively silent and still during the light fiasco, stood up quickly and went into the kitchen.

"What?" I asked.

He kept walking. I followed close behind until he stopped short in front of the stove. He tried to light the burner and I heard a tic-tic-tic sound.

I peeked over his shoulder. "That's good, right?"

He shook his head. "Nothing's coming out."

His shoulders dropped, he turned his back to the stove, and his eyes said the same thing his voice said. "This is not good."

"What does that mean?" I whispered, although I already knew.

He just looked at me without commenting. His face was unchanged, although his eyes were different, something I wasn't used to. Confusion, concern, and questions filled them. I stepped closer to him until our bodies were almost touching.

"We don't know anything yet. It could come back on. Maybe they have a backup."

A faint smile of comfort tried to make its way across his face, but we both knew it was forced. We could not deny the fear that was welling up in both of us. The heat going out was more than an inconvenience. It was simply not an option.

I grabbed his hand and led him back into the great room. We sat down, leaning forward, elbows on our knees. "The stove's not working either. Do your parents have a backup for the gas?" I asked.

Kerry shook her head. "No. We've never had the heat go out."

Dawn and Jackson were looking like deer in headlights. "Are we going to die? Freeze to death?" she asked.

"No." Kerry answered quickly. "We just have to keep warm. I'll call Mom and Dad and see what they say."

She chose to leave the room and call them from the bedroom. Probably because she didn't want to show that she was worried as well. Silence took over while she was gone. Not a word was attempted until she returned.

"What did they say?" Dawn asked.

"They said they're going to call the gas company and see what's going on and call me back."

That sounded reasonable. Strange how none of us thought to do that ourselves. Somehow, knowing parents were taking charge of the situation made me feel better.

After about fifteen minutes, the phone rang. Kerry picked it up and took it back to the bedroom. It was at that point I noticed the room temperature had dropped. It wasn't a big difference, but it was enough to prompt me to scoot closer to Wes.

He placed his hand on my thigh, and I weaved my arm through his, leaning my head against his shoulder.

Kerry returned with a slow shake of her head. "They said they don't know what's going on. The gas company doesn't have reports of an outage."

My forehead creased. "That doesn't make sense."

"I know. She said to see if we can make it to the neighbors and ask them if their gas is working."

Dawn spoke up. "Can't you just call?"

"No. We've never had their phone number." She looked at Rich. "Want to see if we can get down there?"

He shook his head. "Not a chance. There's no way we're getting down that road without it being plowed."

Dawn was not afraid to show her increased concern. "So does that mean we're trapped?" She surveyed all of us until Kerry's voice prompted Dawn's gaze to lock onto her.

"It appears so," she said.

Chapter 20
THE DIVIDE

O nce it was clear that there was no solution, I made a quick excuse to get me and Wes upstairs. We didn't have the time nor the desire to mingle while we tried to think of ways to get him through this.

The bottom line was we needed a plan. At a minimum, it looked like we were going to be here until Tuesday morning. If the gas didn't come back on, that was almost forty-eight hours without heat. It was only a matter of time before the thirty-degree weather outside overran the temperature inside. The tension in my mind was taking over. My palms began to sweat.

"Wes, tell me what to do?" I urged, holding back the fear in my voice.

He pulled me close, wrapping me in his arms as if I was the vulnerable one. "I don't know, Sophie. We just wait." After a moment of comfort, he pulled away.

"What are you doing?" I asked.

"I'm getting out some underclothes. I'll need layers." He was calm, but his look of resolve told me that he was worried.

An urge forced me to run over to him, blocking his way. "I'm so sorry, Wes. I knew this was a bad idea. I knew better."

Still managing to be strong for my sake, he replied softly, "Sophie, calm down. I'm going to be fine. Nothing is going to happen to me. We just have to figure out how to get through this without bringing attention to me."

He leaned over and kissed me on my forehead before stepping around to get more clothes. He was right. He always told me the cold wouldn't kill him. Worse case, it would cause him to fall into a long, terrible sleep. He might be incapacitated and look like death, but he would pull through. All I needed to do was keep him as warm as possible until I could get him completely warm again, without anyone noticing something was wrong.

My optimism started to swell, so I went over and helped him find his long johns. He dropped his jeans and started stepping into a pair when my cell phone rang from below. I looked over the balcony to see it lighting up on the coffee table.

I hustled downstairs, leaving the candle behind with Wes. The screen guided me through the dark until I was standing right over it. It glowed, UNKNOWN NUMBER.

"Hello?"

A low, hoarse voice on the other end said, "Hello, Sophie."

I instinctively looked around, as if someone else was going to feed me information as to who was calling, but no one was there. They had all dispersed to their own rooms, and I was left in blackness.

"Who is this?" I asked.

"It's not necessary for you to know that right now."

"What? Is this a joke? Chase, is that you?"

"Oh, no. You're dealing with men now. And you need to listen carefully."

Something in me wanted to protest, or even hang up, but I didn't. My body stiffened, my mouth went on Mute, and my ears opened. Silence followed for a few seconds and still I wasn't able to speak. I stood there listening to my own breath until he asked me to put Wes on the phone.

"Who is this?"

"I already told you, that's not your concern. Go get Weston. Now. I know he's there."

I went completely quiet again, other than the sounds of my breath escaping my flared nostrils.

"No," I finally stated firmly. "Not until you tell me who's calling."

I heard a huff of breath on the other end. "Tell me something, Sophie. Do you like the cold?"

My lips tightened as I went to the window, fearing someone might be watching me from the trees. "Who is this?"

The man's voice was still low, but sharp, and seemed more casual now. "You answer my question first," he said.

"And that was?" I asked, scanning the darkness.

"Do you like the cold?"

"No," I hissed.

"Well, if you want the heat turned back on, then I suggest you put Weston on the phone."

My brain spun around inside my skull and flipped a few times before coming up with the conclusion that I shouldn't protest. Without responding, I turned toward the steps and felt my way upstairs.

Wes could tell by my eyes that something was wrong. He met me halfway across the room, reading my every expression.

"Someone wants to talk to you?" I whispered.

He took the phone without hesitation. "Hello?"

He listened for a few seconds then, with similar instincts, walked over to the window, scanning the landscape. I followed, staying close.

"Yes. No." He closed his eyes and lowered his head. He moved across the room and sank onto the foot of the bed. With his elbows on his knees, he held the phone in one hand and gripped his hair with the other.

I sat on the floor in front of him, trying to see his face.

"What do you want?" he asked quietly. Then, firmly, "I don't have it." After a long pause, he shook his head. "Why now? I'll be home Tuesday. That's good enough. You don't have to do this. No. That's not necessary. I'll do what you ask. You just do what you said *before* I leave." Without saying good-bye, he hit the End button and tossed the phone onto the bed.

I was on my knees now, making room for myself between his knees. He was clenching his teeth and I could see the tension bursting within. "Wes, who was that?"

"I don't know."

"Well, what do they want?" I asked quickly.

With a blank stare he paused and looked toward the floor. "They want me to go with them."

"What? When?"

"Tonight."

It didn't make sense. We were snowed in. No one was going anywhere. "How?"

"I don't know. They said they're coming and I have to leave with them."

"So tell them no. That's ridiculous."

"I don't have a choice, Sophie."

"Yes, you do. They can't make you."

"They can."

"How?"

"Because they're the ones who shut off everything. They're prepared to let us all freeze if I don't."

I grabbed his face and made him look at me. "Then we all freeze. You're not leaving with anyone."

His eyes were sad, defeated. "If I don't go now, they'll come in here and take me anyway. And they'll wait until we're vulnerable."

"I don't understand. What do they want?"

"They want information for a project they're working on."

"That makes no sense. They can set up an appointment back home."

Wes chuckled a little. "Sophie, people like this don't make appointments. They want something from me and they don't want anyone else to know they're getting it."

I shook my head, adding to the spinning sensation already present. "Wes, they can't just take you. You've worked too hard to let someone find out about you now."

He looked at me with more urgency. "That's why I have to go now. They don't know about me yet."

"You don't know that. Why else would they want you?"

He took my hands and placed them in his lap. "Our research. If they already know what I am, then they wouldn't have threatened me with letting *you* freeze in here."

I growled another very clear, "No."

"Listen to me and listen carefully. If I don't go with them now, they'll wait until we're all freezing, and if they see me like that, they'll know something isn't right. And then they *will* take me. So I have to go with them now, give them whatever information they want, and then I'll meet you back home."

I pushed his chest back to wake him from his dream. "They don't want to take you just so they can let you go. Don't be stupid."

He took my face in his hands. "Listen! They want something, and they know killing me or you isn't going to get it for them. If they think I have information they want, it's in our favor. It's all we have. We have to be sensible, Sophie. I'm useless in this cold. If I go, they'll take me out of here to someplace warmer and let you guys go home where you belong."

"I belong with you. I don't want you to go." I couldn't keep from crying. My tears collected where his hands still gripped my face.

He pulled me to his chest and rocked me gently. The more he rocked, the colder it became. I could feel it all around us, no matter how much I wished for warmth. No matter how much I wished we hadn't come.

"I was so stupid to bring you here. You can't even defend yourself."

He squeezed me, and I lifted my head so it fit in the nook between his collarbone and neck. His flesh was cool.

"Sophie, stop. Whoever these people are, they're serious enough to pull off something like this. If it didn't happen here, then it would happen somewhere else. This is not a new concern of mine. People have been looking for information for years."

"But how did they even know you were here?"

"I don't know."

I took in a huge, deep breath of cool air. My lungs felt the cold and every muscle in my body tensed. I jerked away as it hit me. "Oh, my gosh. Chase." I stood up, pacing.

Wes followed. "Chase doesn't have the means to—"

"Wait. I didn't get a chance to tell you. Danny told me that he overheard Chase talking to two men in suits and they were mad when they found out Chase waited so long to tell them where we were. It was him. I know it. Please, Wes. Something's not right. Please, don't leave. I can't just let you go with these people."

I felt like I was sinking into the floor. It was all so insane. How was I supposed to let Wes go with some strangers who wanted God knows what. It was too much. My legs went weak.

I felt him grip my arms, and we both settled onto the floor.

"I don't want to go either, but I can't let it get cold in here. I can't let them see me like that, and I can't let anything happen to you."

I felt my body turn to mush. Helpless, weakened, defeated. His voice was turning into distant echoes.

"We just have to trust that they only want to pick my brain."

I cringed at the thought of them doing anything else to him. What if they *did* know about him? What if they planned to do horrible things to him. I was so sick, so afraid, so angry. And all I could do was wait. I squeezed him tighter and blinked my eyes several times, trying to focus.

Within a half hour, I felt Wes perk up, listening attentively. He went over to the window, looking at the sky. I knew he heard something and within minutes I heard it too. It sounded like a thousand locusts, homing in on the house. Shortly after, the blackened sky was lit by a large white light that grew closer and brighter.

"It's a helicopter," Wes said, and then he dug his phone out of his pocket. With less than three taps on his screen, his phone was dialing out.

"Who are you calling?"

"Dr. Lyon," he whispered. Then, he covered his other ear, trying to block out the increasingly deafening sound. He walked away from the window as the line was ringing.

"Dr. Lyon, Wes here. There's something going on, and I need you to take precautions." He was adding to his layers as he spoke. "I'm in Virginia, and some men are forcing me into going with them. They want information about our research. I need you to lock down all labs and wait for my call. No. I know what I'm doing. Just do as I say, please."

Before there was sufficient time for Dr. Lyon to respond, Wes hung up the phone, turning his attention to me. His phone rang again, but he ignored it. "These guys are for real, Sophie."

I'm not sure if he thought telling me that would calm me, but it sent me into a frenzy. I grabbed his coat. "No. You can't go alone. I'm coming with you."

The helicopter landed right outside the front window on the unplowed road just beyond Kerry's driveway. Wes moved away from me and headed downstairs. At that point I heard Kerry's and Dawn's doors open and Wes turned to me.

Grabbing my shoulders tightly, he leaned right into my face. "Sophie, you can't make a scene in front of them. I promise you, I'll be okay."

"No."

"Stop it," he whispered in a near hiss. "This is serious. You have to help me get my stuff on, so I can make it to the helicopter. If they find out about my vulnerability, we're in real trouble. Please."

"But we can call the police? They can help us before it's too late?"

He shook his head quickly. "The police can't stop people who go to these extremes. And they'd never make it up the mountain in this weather. Besides, it would draw way too much attention to me. You have to trust me."

"It doesn't feel right."

"It'll be fine. Give me some time to settle this, and if you don't hear from me in forty-eight hours, *then* you can call the police. Now promise me you *will* go home, and stay safe. Don't go anywhere alone." He was nearly shaking me by my shoulders now. "Do you hear me, Sophie?"

I blinked away a few more tears and sucked in the rest. I must have nodded, because he pulled me by my hand and I reluctantly followed him down the stairs.

"What's going on, guys?" Kerry asked.

Wes took charge. "I'm sorry, Kerry, but something has happened at one of my labs, and I have to go right now. I'm sorry to leave so unexpectedly."

Dawn spoke up. "You're leaving us here, in the cold. What about us?"

He turned, losing patience, but still calm. "I looked into it. I was assured that the gas and electric would be on soon. They're fixing it right now."

She sighed then jumped up and down a few times. Her mood completely changed as the sound of the gas furnace reached us. I remained silent and went straight to the garage, afraid that my eyes or voice would give away my emotional state.

Inside the garage, I helped Wes into several layers, including his heated gear and snow boots. Our time together was cut short by the constant powered-down whine of the chopper engine and Wes' rushed effort to wrap up.

I looked at him and pleaded one more time. "Please. At least let me come with you."

His gentle smile returned. "I want you to," he admitted. "But I won't be able to slip through this if we're together. I'd be too worried about you and you'd be too worried about me. I have to concentrate on everything I do and say, and I can't unless I know you're home and safe."

I hated everything he was saying. I wanted to shove him away and pull him to me at the same time. I wanted him to fight to stay with me, to keep from leaving me. All the while, I knew those desires were unrealistic and selfish.

We couldn't put on a showdown with a helicopter. We'd be fools to refuse, and although I hated to admit it, he was right. He was better off going with them while he could still hide the one weakness that would give away his secret.

"Please, please be okay."

I felt his cool lips press against me, and he pulled me in for one last hug. "I wouldn't leave you now if I thought there was another way. And I wouldn't leave at all if I didn't think I'd come back to you. You just have to go home and wait for me."

Without another word, he reached up and pressed the garage door opener. An instant gush of cold air burst through, and he went out, stepping through the deep snow, toward the sound of our enemy. And, just like that, my joy, my comfort, my everything, disappeared into the windy, bitter, snowy terrain. Unable to bring myself to close the garage door behind him, I walked inside, feeling lifeless.

Chapter 21

HOME ALONE

D awn cornered me as soon as I got inside. "What the hell is that all about?"

It took everything I had not to break into sobs. I tried my best to explain, saying that someone had stolen something important and that Wes had to take care of it right away. Before she could respond, I went over to the window to get a view of the chopper. The spotlights were shining bright enough to see Wes trudging his way closer to it. Then he stopped, midway.

My heart froze when he looked back, almost as if he had changed his mind. *What's he waiting for? What's wrong with him?* I wanted him to hurry, or to turn back, anything but stand there.

Then the lights came on in the chalet and I watched him turn away, his last condition fulfilled. He approached the helicopter, appearing strong, and was met by two men wearing black jumpsuits.

By then, Rich and Jackson were also at the window. "Must be something important," Rich said.

I turned to him, afraid to speak, for fear of hysterical gibberish coming out.

Fortunately, Kerry was thinking the same thing I was. "What makes you say that?" she asked.

"Because that's a military chopper. No regular helo could land on this terrain."

My skin crawled at the revelation. I thought of the possibilities, of everything I remembered Andy telling me about secret government experiments. I thought about everything at once and how much I wanted to kick and punch the glass.

Anger escalated within as I watched the chopper leave with my Wes. I was so angry I had let him go, angry because I couldn't scream. The only thing that kept me from cracking in front of everyone was my trust in Wes' instincts. He had to have had no choice if it meant leaving me distraught and alone on this mountaintop.

Even with those thoughts, my rage didn't go away, because I knew one thing. Every ounce of happiness I felt leading up to this day had just been ripped out of me and was disappearing into the black night.

"I'm sorry, Sophie." The comfort in Kerry's voice began to make me believe she understood my situation, until she added, "This sucks." Then I knew she had no idea what had just occurred right under her nose.

It more than sucked. It was beyond words and the farther away the lights in the sky went, the sicker I felt. Without looking anyone in the face, I hid my tear-filled eyes and said as casually as I could, "I'm going upstairs. Excuse me, guys."

Leaving the lights off and the fireplace on, I curled into the chaise and wrapped myself in a blanket, like a baby, wondering how this could've possibly happened. I had considered so many possibilities before we arrived and what had just happened hadn't crossed my mind once, yet somehow I couldn't bring myself to be shocked.

Angry, upset, afraid? Sure. But shocked? No. It seemed like just a different means to shatter my happiness. Every day I had fought thoughts that fate had something bad in store for me. Even forced in happy visions of the future, all the while wishing something terrible wouldn't occur and take them away. But, no matter how much I had wished it, hoped it, no matter how much I reveled in our momentary bliss, I always secretly feared it wouldn't last.

Fate was cruel to let me experience perfection, only to have someone literally swoop in and take it away. My chest felt heavy and empty.

Then, adding even more weight, I traced my thumb along my new ring, wondering, *Why now?* When I knew the future was going to be me and Wes, together. Really together, where I lived with him, took care of him, and loved him. Most of all, I actually believed we had a future, yet here I was, alone in the dark.

I searched my mind again and again for anything hopeful and each time I came up empty. My first instinct was to cry inconsolably. Instead, something else took over. Building inside was a powerful urge to get back home and find who was responsible for this. The person who had taken away my life and my momentary elation—messed up my vacation.

Rich had said the helicopter was military, and when I thought military, I thought about Andy and what he told me about their unsuccessful experiments. Then I thought about Andy's grandson. Although Chase's picture didn't fit the one I had seen, he wore dog tags, and that was enough of a connection for me. Whoever Chase was, I was certain he was in on this, and I was going to find out why.

By the time Kerry came upstairs, I had rubbed my thumb nearly raw from constantly tracing the stones of my ring.

"Sophie, are you okay?" She made a spot for herself at the foot of the chaise and pulled my blanket's excess over her.

I thought about lying and then figured it was useless. "Not really."

"What happened? Did you have a fight?"

That's a bit extreme. How many couples fight to the point that one is angry enough to take off in a helicopter? "No." I half laughed.

"Then what?" she pressed.

"I can't really tell you."

"What does that mean?" Her face was intense.

"It means I just can't say."

She moved closer to me, nudging my knee. "Sophie, what's going on? You can tell me."

The look in her eyes didn't skip a beat from when we used to spend every day together as friends. Best friends. I weighed the appreciation I felt for her against the predicament I was in. No matter how much I wanted to tell her, or anyone else, I just couldn't.

Still, I didn't want to blatantly lie. Plus, I needed someone to help me feel better. So I decided to get as close to the truth as possible without revealing too much.

"I can only say that the people who came to get Wes want something from him, and I'm not sure he'll give it to them."

She leaned in farther, listening harder. "Like what?"

I took in a deep breath, still tracing my ring beneath the blanket. "Well, his family's research labs are getting close to a very big medical breakthrough. Possibly a cure for cancer or AIDS, and some people want to be the first to take credit. He's forced to live his life around that."

She tilted her head back, as if she understood. "I get it. Yikes." She paused. "So where did he go?"

I looked out the window. "I don't know."

"Well, why not. Didn't he say?"

I shook my head, now holding back tears. I didn't want to talk about it anymore and turned away from her. My gaze focused on the snowy terrain that I wished I'd never come to see.

"I don't think he knows."

"Shouldn't you call someone?"

I shook my head again. "No. He said he'll be fine. He'll meet me back home."

I didn't look at her, but sensed doubt in the air. But, like my mother, Kerry knew how far to press an issue with me, so I trusted her not to nag me further.

"Okay," she said, standing up. "Are you sure?"

"Yeah, I'm sure. And Kerry?" I called as she stepped away. "Please don't tell anyone. Wes knows what he's doing and a lot of this information is confidential."

She gave me a long sympathetic stare, and nodded gently before making her way downstairs.

The roads were plowed the next morning, so we decided to leave then. I packed our things and climbed into the Suburban, feeling alone.

The flight home was bad. Wes had chucked my meds at the cabin, so I was left to fly without him, without my meds, and with a stomach twisted with anxiety and loneliness.

Adding to the realization that he was gone was having to drive his Rover back to his house. Even Dawn and Jackson's carefree aura had dissipated. They both believed Wes had gone of his own accord, but the air still reeked "bummer" as they sensed me missing him.

Once we got to Wes', I transferred his bags along with mine to my Jeep because he felt closer to me that way. Jackson packed his things into his car and drove himself home. Once Dawn and I were on the road, I began thinking of ways to fix things. By the time we reached her house, I had built up enough nerve to ask for Chase's number. She looked at me, more than confused, so I clarified. "I need to ask him some questions. Something Danny said."

"Oh, sure." She scanned through her phone and wrote the number on a piece of paper. Once she went inside, I called my mom to tell her I was back and that I'd be home soon. Then, still sitting in Dawn's driveway, I dialed the scribbled number that was written in pink ink.

"Hello?"

I curled my lip at the sound of his voice. My nervousness was replaced by heightened irritation. "Chase, this is Sophie. We need to talk." A long pause quickly screamed guilty. "Now," I added.

"Where?"

I almost said the overlook because that was the natural place to talk. Then I remembered Wes' instruction to be careful. I had no intention of defying him now.

"Where are you?"

"I'm at work."

His response reminded me of how he had penetrated my life. "Is Mr. Healey there?" I asked through clenched jaws.

"No."

"Good. I'll come to you then."

Every mile I drove fueled more frustration. I had no idea what I was going to say, but one thing was for sure. He was going to give me some answers.

When I arrived, Danny was at the counter. His face lit up, as if he wanted to come around and give me a hug, but my expression must have prompted him to hold back. Instead, he gave me a confused smile.

"You're back. That's good. Does that mean Dawn's back too?"

"Yeah, she is." I didn't have time for small talk, so I cut to the Chase, literally. "Where is he?"

Technically, I could've been talking about Mr. Healey, but by my tone, he knew otherwise. His eyes got a bit wider.

"He's in the back." He pointed slowly, like I didn't know where to go.

"Thanks."

I went, expecting to see Chase sitting at the table with his legs propped up as always. Instead, he was standing, expecting me.

"Where is he?" I asked.

"I don't know what you're talking about." He had a smug look on his face, but a hint of guilt peeked through.

"You know *exactly* what I'm talking about."

He crossed his arms, shrugged his shoulders, and gave me nothing.

"I know you had something to do with it. I *know* you did. You hang around here, antagonizing me all the time, trying to provoke me and Wes, talking secretively to men in suits, working here. How convenient is that?"

Oh, my gosh. My eyes widened and my nostrils flared as I remembered Wes' words about Chase. It all made sense. The timing, the behavior, the grudge.

"Wait a minute. You're in on all of it. And you probably had something to do with Ms. Mary's death, so there would be a job opening here. And you played up to Danny. Didn't you?"

He pressed his lips together and stepped to the side to go around me, but I blocked the door.

"You're crazy." He attempted a laugh, but couldn't hide the worry in his eyes.

When he tried to move me out of the way, I swelled with courage. "You're sick. You're a lunatic. You're—"

"Get out of my way."

My courage peaked as he tried once again to get around me. I wanted to punch him in the face, but my cast was still on. Even though my hand was completely healed, I couldn't risk hurting it again for a punch that probably wouldn't have an effect anyway.

I wanted to hurt him any way I could, and at the moment he was piercing me with his arrogant stare. Eyes that faked a shine like Wes'. Eyes that spoke lies. Without thinking, I reached up with both hands and tried to scratch them out.

He stumbled back, raising his arms in defense. I backed him up until he fell onto the table, and even then I tried to gouge them out. I don't know what came over me. I just wanted him to feel pain and to know that someone was on to him.

"Stop it! You're crazy." His defensive tactics only fueled my anger.

"You're a liar," I countered, reaching over his protective forearms.

Then Danny came in and pulled me off him. I tried to wriggle free, but couldn't.

"What's going on?" Danny demanded.

Chase stood up and yanked his shirt straight. Walking past both of us, he huffed, "She's a lunatic."

Danny turned me around. "Sophie, what is it?"

I jerked myself free. "Wes isn't here. He's gone, and I *know* it's because of what Chase told those guys."

"Wait. What do you mean, gone?"

I had forgotten about the discretion I was supposed to hold on to for a few days. I tried to minimize it by backpedaling.

"It's just that some men wanted to talk to Wes, so they picked him up in Virginia. I don't know who they are or where he is. Wes said he'll be home. But we don't appreciate Chase snooping around his life."

"I don't get it. What would Chase be snooping *for*?"

I shook off the remaining hold he had on me. "Because Wes' labs have serums that can hopefully cure sickness, and some crazies are trying to get their hands on them to use as enhancers for drugs."

The confusion in his eyes registered a new look. A look of understanding.

I jumped on it. "What? What do you know?"

"Nothing."

"Yes, you do. What is it?"

He stepped back, as if to defend himself from an attempted gouging. "It's just that Chase tried to get me to use some stuff, but I wouldn't."

I looked at him, not believing him.

"It's not that I wouldn't. Use it, that is. It's just that I don't do needles."

My lips parted and fear took over at the possibility that Andy's attempt wasn't isolated after all. "Who's using them? How many people?"

"Not many. They said it's too expensive to get a lot of."

"Who is 'they'?" I stepped closer, desperate for information.

"Just Chase and Tim," he added when a questioning look appeared on my face. "Someone Chase hangs with."

I studied Danny for a minute, and something in me believed that he was clueless. Had maybe even been used. I pushed my way past him as gently as I could. "I gotta go."

My fists clenched my steering wheel the entire way home. By the time I arrived, my tan knuckles were white where the skin had been stretched so long. My mom must've been looking out of the window, because she opened the door as soon as I pulled into the driveway. My mind was still whirling with information, or the lack thereof.

She picked up on my mood quickly and offered to take my bags, as if I were too weak to carry them myself.

"No, thanks. I got it." My voice was soft, but still lacked genuine ease.

"Is everything okay?" She was completely in tune to my mood, but she attributed it to my visit with Kerry. "Did you have a fight with Kerry?"

I was actually glad she asked that because it prompted a natural laugh. "No, Mom. I'm okay. I just miss Wes."

She rolled her eyes, but sighed in relief. "Good gracious, Sophie. You have it bad. It's only been a few days. You can call him and have him come over for a visit."

We were in the house by then and I wanted to go straight upstairs, so I turned to give her a kiss on the cheek. "Thanks, but he's away right now."

With that mediocre explanation for my obvious distress, I dragged my bags up to my room and lay on my bed. Within a few minutes, I released the built-up frustration and fear in the form of tears. Again.

Chapter 22
THE ALLY

I woke up Tuesday bright and early because of my mother. She came in, nudging my legs. "Come on, Sophie. You have to get up. Your appointment to get your cast off is today."

I blocked the light coming in from the window with my hand. Once I was awake enough to realize it was a new day, I jumped up to find my cell phone. No calls. I tossed it on the bed, feeling my throat tighten. Thirty-six hours and counting.

"You're really missing him, aren't you?"

"You have no idea."

I recovered my toiletry bag from my suitcase and headed to the bathroom. My mom wanted to drive me to the doctor, but I insisted on going alone. There were so many emotions flowing through me, making me afraid I wouldn't be able to hold it together with her asking trivial questions about my trip.

Plus, the doctor's office was actually inside the hospital, and that couldn't be more safe, so I ventured out by myself. Of course, the hospital did nothing but remind me of Wes. All the white jackets sent reminders of Wes' labs, which made me miss him and fear for his life even more than before.

Getting my cast off was a blur, until my hand was completely free. Then I held it, and massaged it, bending it in all directions. It was a huge relief to have full use of my hand again. It made me feel free and new and in charge of myself in a way that I wasn't expecting. A way that made me refuse to sit and wait for Wes to call. I began calculating how much more time.

He said to give him forty-eight hours to handle the situation. Well, time was running out. I decided to give him until that afternoon to call me, and if he didn't, I would contact the police. No one would be spared, especially not Chase. I didn't care if I was jumping to conclusions or not. The police were going to hear everything. Except, of course, about Wes' transformation.

I stepped out of the elevator on the first floor and saw Danny leaving the hospital. My initial reaction was worry.

I jogged after him. "Hey, Danny. Is everything okay? Where's Dawn?"

"Oh, she's good."

I searched his eyes, wondering what was going on, but afraid to ask.

"It's Chase," he answered flatly. I jerked my head back slightly, not getting it. "He had a car accident last night. Drove right off the road. Almost died. It's pretty bad, Sophie."

"Oh. Sorry to hear that."

"What are you doing here?"

"Um…I just had my cast removed."

He looked down. "Hey, look at that. You sure did."

"Yeah, well, I gotta go find a bathroom before I start home." I was searching for the signs and hoping Danny would buy into it, when what I really had to find was more information. Once he was gone, I made my way over to the information desk.

"May I have Chase Chambers' room number, please?"

They told me where he was, and I reluctantly headed back up the elevator, not having a clue why or what I was hoping to find. His room was all the way at the end of the hall, and the walk there seemed to take forever. I paced outside his door a few times before finding the nerve to knock.

After a few soft taps, no one came to the door. Hesitantly, I pushed it open, expecting to see family members lurking in the corners, but no one was there. Not even a card, or flowers, or any sign that a loved one had been by. Only an unrecognizable Chase.

The room felt cold and eerie. My gaze traveled to his pillow, taking in that his head was wrapped from the top of his skull to beneath his chin, and that tubes were up his nose.

My body was stiff, but not from rage or even fear. I felt horrible for him. My Amelia instincts wanted to touch him and check him over, but my Sophie body wouldn't move. Instead, I just stood there, watching him.

I eventually made my way over to him, just to see if I could glean any unspoken answers from his motionless body. The closer I got, the more the hairs on my neck stood upright. I froze and stared at him, assessing any possible threat. He was completely still, until I saw his index finger twitch.

I quickly looked behind me, tempted to leave, but didn't. My gaze locked on his finger, wondering if I had imagined it. There was definitely movement, and eventually his thumb and pointer finger touched. The motion entranced me as I watched how they moved in a circular motion. It soon became clear to me that he was trying to signal for a pen and paper.

Stepping closer to him, I rummaged through my handbag for the items. I still had the scrap with his number written on it. I flipped it over and slid it beneath his hand, and the pen between his fingers.

His grip was weak, and he had not opened his eyes. I was glad about that because I was afraid he would change his intentions if he knew it was me. After a few seemingly endless moments, the pen still had not moved.

I wondered if I had misunderstood his movements and considered slipping out undetected. I weighed the outcomes and decided my curiosity was too intense. Not caring if he knew it was me, I softly let him know someone was there and to go ahead and write what he needed to write.

I expected him, at the sound of my voice, to tighten his grip on the pen or show some sign of discomfort, but he didn't. Instead, his hand began laboriously forming letters. Although very uneven and slanted, the formation of each letter was clear. Slowly, the letters turned into words. I twisted and squinted to see—until the shock hit me.

NO ACCIDENT.

I leaned close to his ear. "Chase, are you saying some-one did this to you?" I waited and there was no response. My heart raced. "Chase, squeeze my hand if the answer is yes." I placed my hand in his, despite the odd sensation of hairs now standing up on my arm.

With a weak but very sure squeeze, he confirmed my suspicion.

My heart thumped and every muscle in my body turned to steel. Suddenly, I was beginning to realize something huge was going on.

I steadied the pen in his hand, asking the obvious question. "Chase, do you know who did this?"

His hand was shaking now but moved across the paper until the letters read, *TIM*.

Tim? I had heard the name before. Once from Danny, and somewhere else I couldn't place. My mind was racing too much to figure it out. I had to get out of there. "Chase, I'll give this to the right people. You'll be okay." I patted his arm, because it seemed like the right thing to do. The feeling seeping through my veins was uncertainty. Not knowing what to do or who to go to for help.

I closed the door behind me and leaned against the wall. The paper was still crumpled in my hand. I was sure of a few things. I knew with every bone in my body that Chase had something to do with Wes' kidnapping; I just didn't know how much. He was involved with a substance that sounded very similar to what Andy had described. He also wore dog tags, which linked him to the military.

What I didn't understand was why someone would try to kill him by running him off the road. What sort of threat was he? That was unknown, but what *was* known is that it was someone named Tim. I ran through it all in my head, trying to figure out what to do.

Where had I heard that name before? Then it hit me. I hadn't heard it before. I had *read* it on Andy's Facebook page. His grandson's name was *Timothy*.

It couldn't be. *Yes, it absolutely can.* Suddenly, panic began to build and I needed to get out of there. I almost ran past the nurse's station then made a split-second decision to go back.

They could tell I was upset. Concern showed on their faces. "Can we help you?"

"Um. I was visiting Chase Chambers, and he wrote this." I showed them the paper. "His crash was not an accident. This person tried to kill him. You may want to call the police." I set the note on the counter and turned away.

"Excuse me. What's your name?"

I kept walking, moving toward the elevator. Whatever was going on here was not something I could handle just yet. I needed to go somewhere to think and sort through it all.

I entered the elevator alone, turning over in my mind what I had learned. Chase knew Andy's grandson. Chase was using a serum. I wondered what Chase knew, what Tim knew. The questions burned inside me, because I didn't know how much Andy had revealed about me and Wes to anyone else. And if he did reveal all of it, and Tim and Chase knew, then whoever had Wes had to know too.

I began to feel sick, right there in the elevator. I steadied my breathing, searching for calming thoughts. I ran down what Wes had told me. He was so certain his secret was still safe, but it didn't feel so safe now. I needed air.

I closed my eyes, cursing fate and wondering why this was happening. Why on earth would Wes find me again only to be taken away himself? What was the point? We were so worried about me living past nineteen and all along it was him we needed to worry about.

Oh, my gosh. I realized everything right then, and began to hate myself for not having figured it out sooner. It's *never* been about me. It's always been about him. Keeping *him* alive and safe. Tears welled up in my eyes, as I realized how selfish I truly was. This was always going to happen. Fate knew that these people would be after him, that his secret and even his own life was going to be threatened and, damn it, he had his guard down because of me. Because of us.

I cringed at our stupidity and then wanted to kick the walls of the elevator. "What was it all for?" I shouted. "Why bring us together only to…"

I banged my head against the wall behind me, knowing now. We were brought together, so I could save him *again*. I wasn't on this earth to meet the boy of my dreams and fall in love. My purpose was to make sure Wes would be okay. *And then what happens?* Tears spilled over, because I knew.

I die.

No. I shook my head, wiping away the unwanted tears and feeling of defeat. Life could not be that cruel. I refused to believe it possible.

The elevator door opened just as I sucked up my hysterics and accepted my purpose. What the future held for me was not important right now. Nothing mattered other than getting Wes back, and the only thing I knew was that I would have to figure out how.

Feeling alone and overwhelmingly lost, I stepped into the lobby in a mad dash for the exit. On my way, I felt a hand touch my elbow.

"Ms. Slone?"

I jerked my arm away, feeling another threat home in on me.

"Ms. Slone, please. I just need to speak with you."

I looked up without breaking stride and saw a familiar face, the one from Wes' lab. The man who spoke at the press conference.

"My name is Dr. Lyon. I work at The California—"

"I know where you work." I stopped walking. Optimism resurfaced as I remembered the phone call Wes had made to him. Maybe he knew something or had heard something.

I stepped close enough so a whisper would suffice. "Have you heard something?"

"No."

My knees started to buckle with fatigue. "Dr. Lyon, I don't know what's happening. I don't know what to do."

He placed his hand under my elbow again, supportively. "That's why I'm here."

He gestured toward the passageway beyond the elevators. "Would you like to get some coffee?"

I just looked at him, trying to figure out what language he was speaking when what I wanted to hear was a language filled with answers.

Sensing my reluctance, he added, "We can talk there."

I looked around and no one seemed to be paying attention to us so I, at least, felt the threat level begin to drop.

"All right."

We walked without talking. Every so often, I glanced at him in hopes of discovering details about him that I would find trustworthy. His age had radiated wisdom and authority on the television, but in person, he appeared a bit more fragile. Although he kept up with my pace easily, his white hair and wrinkled skin made my age estimate for him go well into the seventies.

Still, he was authoritative.

We reached the café and both ordered coffee. I was preparing to pay, but he insisted, which made me feel a sense of protection, as if he was a father figure, or grandfather figure. With our coffees in hand, we found a relatively quiet corner, but I took the liberty to survey the room for anyone else who might have followed me. Paranoia was setting in, big time. I kept scanning for threats then scanning again just to see what people were doing and eating.

Eventually, I realized I was just buying time before I had to speak to Dr. Lyon.

Not being sure of why he wanted to see me, or what he knew about Wes, made me covet our secrets, even though I desperately needed someone to trust. I took a deep breath and let my gaze settle on him.

He was carefully sipping his coffee, which prompted me to focus on my own. I inhaled the sweet caramel scent that was wafting through the opening in the lid. Feeling much more at ease, I brought the cup up to my mouth. His eyes narrowed as he looked at my left hand, which reminded me of my bittersweet gift. The one I hadn't even allowed my mother to see yet.

"Is that from Weston?" he asked, not sounding too surprised.

Setting down the cup, I put my hands under the table and cleared my throat. "Yes."

He took another sip and smiled softly. "I'm sure you're eagerly awaiting his return."

I nodded, reaching for my coffee—with my right hand this time. As if he finally had enough of beating around the bush, Dr. Lyon leaned forward, shifting his coffee to the side.

"Ms. Slone, I'm speaking with you today because, like you, I need to make sure Weston returns unharmed."

"Where is he?" I asked.

"That's what we need to find out from you."

"What information could I have that would help you?"

"Anything you can tell me about the night he was taken would help me tremendously."

I felt like an interview was about to follow, for which I was not prepared. The major reason being that I didn't know what Wes would or would not want me to say.

Without sounding too disrespectful toward an elder, I softly replied, "I'm not sure I can trust you." And to give me a good out from the conversation, I added, "Wes told me he didn't trust anyone."

He smiled gently again and answered, "That's good. He's not supposed to."

"Then how can I trust you?"

He took another slow sip of his coffee. "Because Dr. Thomas did."

My breath caught in my throat at the mention of Wes' uncle, the same doctor who had started all of this. *What trust would Dr. Thomas have put into this man?* At that point, I realized this conversation had gone deeper than Wes currently being missing. For Dr. Lyon to drop that name on me was a message of some sort. He was letting me know that he had ties to a very important part of Wes' past, but it also felt like he was feeling me out to see how much I knew.

However, I wasn't willing to be sucked into telling this man anything. I couldn't be sure if he wanted Wes back, or the information Wes held. I decided I wasn't going to dance around his motivations. I couldn't. I didn't have the time.

"Dr. Lyon, I just want Wes to return."

"No more than I."

I was pretty sure that huge assumption was false, but before I could come up with a reply, he continued speaking.

"Listen, I don't know what Weston has told you, but I'm here to protect him. That's my main priority, and I trust my people to help me do that."

"Your people?"

"Yes, Ms. Slone, just as there are people willing to take Weston for the wrong reasons, there are people willing to protect him for the right ones."

"Wes never told me anything about people protecting him."

"That's because Weston doesn't know. The things Dr. Thomas asked me to do for Weston were asked in confidence."

We were walking a fine line, unsure how much each of us knew. One thing for sure, I wasn't willing to give away that I knew anything about Wes, other than what was in relation to his current life.

Sounding completely clueless, yet intrigued, I asked, "What was it that Dr. Thomas told you?"

Either not willing to give away too much, or calling my bluff, he carefully danced around the question, still managing to keep my full attention. "Dr. Thomas told me enough about his research to know that I need to bring Weston back before the people who have him figure out exactly who it is they hold."

From then on, I felt pretty sure that Dr. Lyon was aware of Wes' transformation. Except, Wes would've told me if there was someone else who knew about him, which meant that Wes didn't know that Dr. Lyon knew.

But that didn't mean what Dr. Lyon was saying couldn't be true. I kept my gaze on him, and he, too, never released me from his stare. I still wasn't willing to give away my own privies surrounding Wes's life, so I gave him nothing. We seemed to be in an information stare-off.

It did make sense that Dr. Thomas would've trusted someone to care for Wes after he died. He couldn't expect Wes to do it alone, but I wasn't sure. I needed more.

"So you knew Wes' father then?"

The leading question actually prompted a small laugh from him and to cover it up, he took another sip.

"We can talk about unimportant things or we can talk about bringing Weston back."

It seemed clear that he wasn't going to give me any more information, so I thought I'd try one final test.

"Wes told me I could call the police if I didn't hear from him in forty-eight hours. I was going to call them this afternoon."

If he had evil intentions, I figured he'd either get up and disappear or come up with a million reasons why I shouldn't call. After a minute of thinking and appearing unfazed by the near threat, he answered.

"If Weston told you to do that, then you should. But it will be for your own safety, Ms. Slone. Not his. The police will not be able find him, but bringing attention to the matter may keep you safer."

"Me?"

"Yes. If they are not satisfied with what Weston has to offer them, they'll use other methods of persuasion."

I leaned forward, unconcerned with my own well-being. "Tell me what you think would keep Wes the safest?"

"Us bringing him home swiftly."

I no longer cared about whether or not I trusted Dr. Lyon. I decided that he was my best chance at finding Wes.

I scooted closer to the edge of my seat, locking my worried gaze on him. "How can you bring him back?"

As if we formed some sort of pact, he leaned in closer, his expression less worried and more intent. "I need you to tell me what you saw when he was picked up."

"Well, they came in a helicopter," I said flatly. "My friend said it was military."

He sighed and pressed his lips together. "As I suspected."

"So the government has Wes? Are you serious?"

"Not the common government, no. The people who have him are sliding in under the government's radar, but are assuredly using its resources to fund their operation. We've been following their activities for years. They want to find a serum to make their performance drug work better. Once they find it, they'll give it to the U.S. military—and then sell it for millions to other countries. If you think war is inhumane now, just wait."

I leaned back in my seat. "This is horrible."

"No, this is good. Because that means they're looking for information. Not Wes. He's just an avenue, which means we have time to get him before it's too late."

My optimism returned once again, as I found myself needing Dr. Lyon to be our solution.

"I know who might be able to lead you to him."

Dr. Lyon's eyes widened with surprise and pleasure.

"His name is Tim. I think he's working with whoever took Wes. My...friend," I winced at using the word, but kept talking, "was working with them too, but for some reason, they just tried to kill him. I think he knows something." I was talking fast, and I could tell the doctor was listening attentively to keep up.

"Do you know where we can find this Tim?"

"No, but I can find out." I'd already made Tim's connection to Andy, but I knew nothing else. I reached into my purse and grabbed my cell, hoping Danny was at work.

He picked up on the third ring. "Healey's Used Books."

"Danny, this is Sophie."

"Hey, Soph."

"Hey, I have a question. Who is that guy Tim you were talking about?"

"Tim is one of Chase's friends."

Not anymore, I thought. "Yeah, I know that. But who is he? Where does he live?"

"Don't know."

"Well, where do you guys hang out?"

"Only at the fight club."

"He goes to the fight club?" I hated the visual that returned in my head, along with the panic I had felt when I was actually there.

"He doesn't just go there. He runs it. He's the leader. Why?"

"Oh, my gosh." My chest tightened. "Thank you." I hung up without answering, waiting for my brain to catch up with my senses.

I couldn't believe it. I had been two feet from the guy. I had seen his sick pleasure at watching someone else get beat to a pulp. Watched how the crowd marveled in his presence, his arrogance.

Had he planned the whole thing? To use Chase and Danny to get close to us? My stomach twisted.

"Ms. Slone?"

Hearing my name snapped me out of my thoughts. I looked at Dr. Lyon, more than willing to provide what I knew.

"I know where you can find him."

I wrote down everything. About the location of the club, how I believed him to be Andy's grandson. I also told him what Andy said about the government experiments and their soldiers. He took in everything, never allowing an ounce of surprise to cross his face. When I was finished, he nodded and passed me his card.

"This is most helpful. I have no doubts that we will have Weston back before the week is up. These people gain nothing from harming him, as long as they just want information. They can't hold him longer than a few days, otherwise people will start asking questions. We just need to make contact as soon as we can. Before they dig too deep."

I nodded.

He stood and was about the leave when I asked one more question, not that it seemed relevant. I just wanted to know, and maybe something in me wanted to hang on to another reason to trust him.

"Didn't Dr. Thomas help you with your hemophilia?" He looked taken aback by my knowledge of that, so I added, "I asked Wes about you after the press conference."

"Ah." He smiled slightly. "Yes." We were both standing now, and he gently patted my shoulder. "He did, and that's why I'm here today. He gave me a good quality of life. So, you see, Ms. Slone, I owe him my life. And I will get *his* Weston back."

Leaving me speechless, with a thousand thoughts and emotions flowing through me, he walked away, with the line finally being crossed.

I stood there, aware for the first time that I wasn't alone in wanting Wes home. Even though, somewhere, I believed Wes knew what he was doing, it certainly helped that someone else was in our corner. It also helped to know there was a plan to get him back.

A familiar feeling that I had let slip away was returning, and I held on to it—hope—clinging to it with every ounce of my soul. And I took it with me as I walked out of the hospital, heavily contemplating whether or not it was enough.

Then I decided it was, simply because it had to be.

ACKNOWLEDGMENTS

I 'll begin with a huge thank you, again, to my husband and children. You show me what unconditional love really is! My passion for reading and writing is all-consuming, and you certainly didn't ask for the roller coaster of emotions that go along with it, so I appreciate you guys more than anything!

Next, many thanks to people who gave me insight. Freddie for a peek into Midway! My test readers, Troy and Danny. Also, a huge thank you to Sharon K. Garner and Kimberly Martin, who craft my work with their mad skills. Sharon, I am so thankful for the care you put into this book. You always know what I'm really trying to say, and your edits have taught me to be a better writer. Kimberly, without the pretty bow you put on everything, none of what I do would matter, so thank you!

I must also give a HUMONGOUS thank you to some people who really wowed me with their enthusiasm for *The Pace Series*. To the fans who amaze me and also put a match under my rear to keep bringing you stories! To Michelle, from Windowpane-memoirs.com, thank you for being the first reviewer to not only take a leap and purchase *The Pace*, but also for posting its very first review online. I'll always remember how that made me feel! To Ka-Yam, who is the first international fan and who blew me away with your well wishes from Germany. Thank you for giving me that first moment when I realized Sophie and Weston would be traveling overseas. To Reggie from Theundercoverbooklover.blogspot.com. What can I say? *The Pace* as the Best Book of 2009... It made me speechless. And to Valerie at valeriekwrites.blogspot.com, for thinking enough of *The Pace* to nominate it for the 2009 Cybil's Award. I can now relate when someone says, "It truly is an honor just to be nominated!"

And to the many, many more reviewers/bloggers who first featured *The Pace*. There are too many to name here, but I want you to know that I appreciate what you do immensely. You guys motivate me, inspire me, and also teach me about my own writing, so thank you for your comments and support!

Not to be forgotten is my mother, who wears many hats, one of which is fantastic content editor. You make me write better stories, so thank you for that! To Curtis Paul for your support. And to the talented Jennifer Murgia who took the newbie author ride with me. Thanks for being a great friend and awesome motivator too!

And finally, only because I want to end on it. Thank you to God for making every single thing in my life possible and for guiding me whenever I need it, which is always!

Visit
www.thepaceseries.com
for information regarding

THE IRON QUILL
(The Pace Series Book 3)

Breinigsville, PA USA
10 August 2010
243394BV00001B/26/P

9 780982 500514